# The Here and Now

## LL MEYER

Cover by: Murphy Rae at Indie Solutions,
www.murphyrae.net
Cover art by: Annie Spratt,
https://unsplash.com/@anniespratt
Formatting by: Elaine York at Allusion Graphics,
www.allusiongraphics.com

Contact: lisalynn_meyer@outlook.com

# The
# Here
# and
# Now

# Other Books

Not So Far Away (A Worlds Collide Duet, #1)
The Here and Now (A Worlds Collide Duet, #2)

His Lucky Penny (The Penny Books, #1)
Pennies for Wishes (The Penny Books, #2)
Find a Penny (The Penny Books, #3)
Pennies from Heaven (The Penny Books, #4)

Written as Lisa Lynn Meyer
A Touch of Silence

For my beloved daughter, Mariana, who lives
her life with one foot in English and the other in Spanish.
*Te amo muchísimo, Chulis.*


Special thanks to Leila for all her moral support
and superior proof-reading skills.

# Chapter One

## Ellie

The thing about life is it's unpredictable.

I'd know. I've experienced my fair share of its whims. The unexpected ups and downs – whether defined as curveballs or twists of fate or just dumb luck – have brought me untold joy and pain over the years.

This past year, especially, has been one of the most difficult of my life; soaring highs and plunging lows have made for a topsy-turvy existence to which I'm still adapting. I wouldn't have it any other way, though, because the tumult brought Scott McCarthy into my life. To say that he saved me from myself would probably be over-dramatic, but I acknowledge the moment he found me on that sidewalk as a pivotal one. That our paths crossed again ten months later when he came flying over the counter at my work while being chased by the cops is something I'll be eternally grateful for. I got the chance to repay his kindness and it laid the foundation for a friendship that became so much more.

The *more* that followed took us by surprise . . . and we've stumbled along the way, but I'd say we're now equally dedicated to each other. Which makes this email I'm reading all the more difficult to bear. Because, while living through my own highs and lows is one thing, it's quite another to watch the man I love struggle with a particularly painful twist of fate of his own.

*Dear Ms. Summers,*

*I understand your reluctance to champion my quest to engage with my new-found grandson; however, since you are my only link to him, I'm afraid I must resort to desperate measures. May I appeal to your sense of pity for an old man who would very much like to get to know the boy – now a man – of whose existence I was not aware of until just weeks ago?*

*Please, ask him to consider getting in touch with me. Sincerely, Richard McCarthy.*

I assume Richard McCarthy got my email address from my CV which was sent out to a number of people who attended his charity gala two weeks ago, the one at which Scott came face-to-face with not only his grandfather, but also his father and two half-brothers for the first time.

Since then, Scott has put a lot of effort into pretending that he's put the whole episode behind him. After the initial shock, he'd stubbornly dug his heels in, saying he already had a family, one that'd always been there for him and his loyalty to them was unswerving.

When I showed him the first email from his grandfather, he'd wavered slightly . . . until it became apparent that it was only his grandfather – and not his father – who was trying to get in touch with him. At that point, something inside of him solidified and his stubbornness became an unyielding, unassailable wall. I guess *feeling* rejected by a father who never knew you existed is very different from *being* rejected by a father who shows no interest in you. On the surface, it's very clear cut and simple for Scott. Underneath, I'm not so sure.

Since he won't want to read this email when I tell him about it, I hit the delete button. Two seconds later my phone vibrates with an incoming message.

**Scott: U home safe yet?**

A warm, fuzzy feeling sparks in my chest.

**Ellie: Yes, just got in the door.**

Normally on Friday nights, we go out. Dinner and a movie, that kind of thing. Instead, I worked the late shift at the café tonight, so I could . . .

**Scott: U still sure about tmrw?**

Yeah, that. *Tomorrow.* Scott has finally invited me to meet his girls.

**Ellie: Yes! I'm so excited.**

Excited and outrageously nervous. Maybe it's absurd to be put on edge by three little girls, but the thought of them not liking me is terrifying. I can imagine our relationship surviving anyone's disapproval but theirs.

I go over everything I know. Rosa, age 6, is his biological daughter. She has a sweet and tranquil disposition. I've considered a mercenary approach that involves focusing most of my attention and energy on her since technically she should be the most important to Scott. But even if it didn't offend my sensibilities so much, I doubt Scott works that way.

Then there's his niece, Daniela, age 7. Actually they're cousins since she's the daughter of Scott's uncle who was killed in a drive-by shooting when Daniela was a baby. Supposedly, of the three girls, she's the ringleader, the one with the most dominant personality. Scott's always chuckling about something she said or did; he calls her his little gangster-in-the-making.

Lastly, there's his youngest sister, Carmen, age 8. She's a bit of an enigma. Scott says she's very quiet and responsible, the one who can be counted on to make good decisions.

My phone vibrates again.

**Scott: We'll be there to pick you up between ten and eleven.**

**Ellie: Ok, I'll be ready.**

After a moment of hesitation, I type out another message.

**Ellie: I love you. Sleep well.**

**Scott: I love you too, Opal. Dream of me.**

A smile blooms across my face and I can't resist sending one more.

**Ellie: Oh, I'm sure I will...hopefully something along the lines of what we did last night.**

This sets off an hour or so of intermittent sexts and playfully dirty jokes while I tidy up my apartment and get ready for bed . . . and I couldn't be happier. Hopefully fate isn't planning any more surprises for either of us because, right now, our joint curve ball is hovering in a sweet spot that I could definitely get used to.

The knock on my apartment door the next morning sends the butterflies in my belly into a riot. While I managed to get a reasonable amount of sleep last night, I woke early and the morning's wait has dragged by like molasses. Chucking all pretense of decorum, I rush to the door and get a glimpse of Scott and the tops of three dark heads through the peephole.

"Hi," I say breathlessly as I pull the door open. My gaze starts with Scott and then lowers to take in the girls who are lined up in front of him. The awkward pause dissolves when I smile and stick out my hand to the first girl on the left. "Hi, I'm Ellie. You must be . . . Carmen?"

She just stares up at me until Scott nudges her gently from behind. "Uh, yes, I'm Carmen," she says softly, cautiously reaching for my hand. We shake.

"*Tío, está bien bonita,*" says the girl in the middle. *She's beautiful.*

I laugh. "*Y tú . . . eres Daniela, ¿verdad?*" All three of them gasp as I shake Daniela's hand. *You're Daniela, right?*

"*Papá,*" Rosa squeaks, turning wide eyes on Scott. "*Habla raro.*"

Again, I laugh, completely charmed. Loosely translated she thinks my Spanish sounds funny. I realize I should tone down my accent. *"Perdón,"* I apologize with a much more Latin American pronunciation. *"Se me olvidó que mi acento suena chistoso. ¿Está mejor así?"* Is it better like this?

They all nod, giggling up at me. I extend my hand to Rosa and introduce myself, sticking to Spanish.

Scott clears his throat, jerking my attention up. "Is it okay if we use your bathroom?" he asks in English, his lips pressing together with mild irritation. *Oh shit, should I not be speaking Spanish with them?*

"Oh, of course," I step back and after they all remove their shoes, I lead the girls through to the bathroom.

"One at a time," Scott calls from the living room. "And don't forget to wash your hands."

I hover in the hall for a moment, unsure if I'm supposed to wait with them. "Just holler if you need something, okay?" I ultimately tell them.

Scott's leaning his hip against the patio door, looking out, but he turns as I enter the room. Hastening forward, I whisper, "Did I do okay?"

He scoffs, reaching for my hip to pull me close. "No, you didn't." My stomach swoops with dread, but then he laughs. "You didn't even say hello to me."

I give him a half-hearted whack to the bicep. "That's not funny."

"It's not, I know. It's awful." His nose nuzzles along my neck where I feel his smile against my skin.

The soft titters floating from down the hall and the sound of the toilet flushing tell me we don't have much time left, but when I try to pull away, Scott refuses to let me go. Deciding to follow his lead, I relax into his reassuring presence. "So, um, no Spanish then?"

"What? Why not?"

Lifting my head from his shoulder, I try to decipher his confused expression. "You seemed annoyed and you answered me in English."

"Oh, no. It's not that. I don't like that the little punks are pulling the bathroom trick so they can come in and snoop around."

I blink. "That's a thing?"

He snorts. "Oh, it's a thing all right. They know they've got me because I can't say no."

"That's genius."

"Diabolical genius, maybe," he says with humor, making me think he's actually proud of them. His eyes lift to the hall. "Rosa, did you see what's on the fridge?"

His firm grip on my hip keeps my impulse to spring away from him like a cat from water mostly in check. All I manage is to jerk stiffly while he acts like he stands with his arm wrapped around a woman in front of his daughter every day of the week. When Rosa turns to the fridge, he whispers into my ear. "Relax, Opal. If we act guilty, they'll pick up on it."

Taking a deep breath to steady myself, I nod, unable to remember the last time I felt so out of my depth.

"Hey, our cards!" Rosa exclaims as Carmen joins her. "You kept them?"

"Of course I kept them," I say. "They're so pretty."

After Carmen makes a cursory inspection to confirm that yes, the cards are prominently displayed, she makes her way over to us. "Ellie?" she asks shyly.

"Yeah?"

"Is it true your real name is Elsa?"

I smile. "It is. Like Elsa from Frozen, right?"

Her face lights up. "Yes, have you seen it?"

"Uh, yeah," I say, like the idea that I haven't is outrageous. "A bunch of times with my nieces. I know all the words to the songs."

Daniela shows up. "You can sing?"

"Oh, I wouldn't go that far," I say with Scott chuckling in my ear. "But I make up for my lack of talent with enthusiasm. You should hear me in the car."

"We love to sing," Rosa says and the girls all nod their heads in agreement.

"Great, then I'm sure your dad won't mind if we belt out some tunes in his truck." Scott's grunt has me repressing a laugh as I turn to say, "Right? I'm sure you know all the words too."

"Unfortunately," he grumbles, then straightens up off the patio door, setting me beside him. "Okay, let's feel them," he says, holding out his hands.

Mystified, I watch the three girls take turns gripping his hands. When he gets to Daniela, he raises his eyebrows at her.

"Fine." She runs back to the bathroom where I hear the water run.

"With soap," he calls.

Unexpected emotion rises to form a knot at the base of my throat, doing its best to cut off my air supply. I mean, I knew Scott was a parent, but actually seeing him in action is . . . surreal. In the best possible way. He's not just a dad. He's a *dad*.

"Should we go?" he asks.

"Sure," I choke out.

He shoots me a mildly concerned, sideways glance, but otherwise remains quiet.

As we're leaving, he hangs back as I lock the door. "What's wrong?"

Watching the girls turn the corner down the hall, I steal a quick kiss. "Absolutely nothing is wrong," I whisper. "You're so good with them."

Pleased by my comment, he helps himself to another kiss before taking my hand. "Come on, Opal. Let's go to the park."

After the girls are settled into their booster seats in the truck, we head up to Coyote Point. I practically purr with contentment when Scott reaches over and threads his fingers through mine. The giggles this elicits from the backseat has a faint blush of embarrassment blooming on my cheeks, but Scott just shakes his head gently and chuckles to himself.

Soon I hear, "Ellie?"

I turn in my seat. "Yeah?"

"Can we sing now?" Daniela asks.

"Um," I waffle, looking to Scott for guidance.

"Don't look at me," he says.

Does he think I've made a promise I can't keep? *Ha!* I made sure to download the soundtrack last night. I pull out my phone and connect it to the stereo. "Should we start with *Let It Go?*"

I get a chorus of, "Yeah!"

Scott has a mostly pained look on his face for the duration, but the girls and I have a great time. After two renditions of both *Let It Go* and *Do You Wanna Build a Snowman?* I take pity on him.

"You guys want to watch something really cool?" I ask, stopping the music and pulling up YouTube on my phone. I hit play on the video and hand my phone back to Rosa who's sitting in the middle.

Scott lifts his chin in question.

"It's Jimmy Fallon doing *Let It Go*."

The alarm on his face has me reassuring him. "It's completely kid-friendly. I promise. I thought you could use a break from all the howling."

"You weren't *that* bad," he says, throwing me what I don't think he realizes is a panty-melting grin.

The Coyote Point playground with its castle and dragon theme has the girls excited and Scott needs to call them back to remind them of the 'rules' before they take off running. As he watches them go, I watch him. Yes, he's still the Scott I know, the one who needs a haircut again, the one whose sense of humor matches mine, and the one who I love with a fierce protectiveness, but now he's also the one who speaks to his kids with patience and calm confidence. If I was in love with him before, now I'm –

He turns to me, about to say something, but stops when he sees my face. "What?" The dark brown of his eyes glows in the sunshine.

"Uh . . . I'm just trying to wrap my head around the idea of . . ." I gesture vaguely to the play area.

"The idea of *me* being responsible for human beings?" he says on a laugh, then turns back to the playground. "Carmen! We're over here." He points to a bench a few feet away.

Once we're seated, I ask him, "Why do you say it like it's ridiculous?"

His lips tilt, giving his expression an ironic bent. "Because it *is* ridiculous. This adulting thing . . ." He shakes his head ruefully.

"You're good at this adulting thing."

"Not by choice."

"I doubt many people do it by choice," I tell him, wondering why he doesn't feel his efforts to be a good parent are worthy of praise. "Personally, I find it incredibly attractive."

That clams him up, but he seems to be searching his mind for some kind of rebuttal. I put a stop to that by changing the subject – kind of. "Speaking of adulting, my graduation ceremony is in a couple of weeks."

"Oh, yeah? You going to invite me?"

I flip my sunglasses up onto the top of my head to gauge his reaction more closely. "Of course I'm going to invite you," I say with a sureness that slips with my next words. "You're going to come, right?"

"I'd like to see you keep me away."

I bite my lip. "Even if my parents will be there. I mean, you won't have to sit with them or anything, but I can't guarantee my mom will . . . behave herself."

After the way my mother treated him at the charity gala, I wouldn't blame him for wanting to avoid her at all costs, but he just gives my hand a reassuring squeeze. "Don't worry. I can take care of myself. Besides, I'd put up with almost anything for you."

Relieved, I tease him. "Oh, really?"

"Really," he confirms, leaning in to plant a kiss on the corner of my mouth before he turns his attention back to the slides, searching for the girls to make sure they're all right. "You think I could bring them?"

"The girls? You think they'd want to go?"

He shrugs. "It's a big deal, right? Maybe they'll get

inspired or something."

"Yeah, maybe. Either that or they'll die of boredom."

"That's pretty unlikely," he says, his tone bordering on sardonic. "You won their ever-lasting devotion with that stunt you pulled in the truck."

My mouth falls open and I feel my cheeks heat for the second time today. "That was not a stunt . . . that was . . . that was an attempt to cultivate a foundation from which to grow a healthy relationship with very small humans."

"Uh huh. Spout all the high-sounding bull you want, but that, Elsabeth Summers, was a stunt. I'll give you credit, though. It was a pretty successful one."

I'm loathe to concede the point, but I hear the hope in my next words. "You think?"

He laughs. "You're awesome, you know that?"

"What? Two seconds ago you accused me of trying to manipulate your children."

"No one's manipulating anyone," he says with easy, good humor. "I'm happy that it means so much to you that you're willing to stoop so low."

Our eyes clash, his amused, mine mildly incensed. "If there weren't small children in the area, I'd give you the finger, Mr. McCarthy."

Smirking, he pulls me closer. "Don't get all kinky on me now, Opal."

Our soft laughter is interrupted by, "Tío?"

Looking up, we find Daniela standing not two feet away. "Can I leave my sweater here? It's too hot."

"Yeah, of course you can," he tells her, playing it cool. "Actually let me get a picture of you, okay?" He stretches out his tall frame to retrieve his cell from his jeans pocket and snaps a pic of her. "Tell your sisters I need one of them too," he calls as she's running away.

"Okay!" she yells over her shoulder.

I can't stop the smile on my face at how adorable she is. "Why the picture?" I ask.

"Oh," he says absently, scanning the playground. "So I have a picture of what they're wearing in case something happens."

*In case something happens? Like what?* Then my stomach flips over. Something like abduction. Yikes. I have a lot to learn about taking care of kids.

# Chapter Two

## Scott

She's so good with them.

It's like a fifty ton weight has been lifted from my chest. I don't think I grasped how much I had riding on Ellie and the girls getting along. I have no idea what I would have done if these two huge pieces of my life hadn't fit together. Thankfully I'll never have to find out.

After an hour at the playground, we follow the San Francisco Bay Trail along the water, carefully avoiding the joggers and the cyclists. At one point, the girls run on ahead while Ellie and I walk hand-in-hand. With the sun shining and the breeze coming in off the water, things are . . . perfect. An idea that slowly begins to rile my pessimistic side. Because nothing this good can last. It's got to be some kind of illusion.

But before I can fall too far down that rabbit hole, we come to the bench where Ellie and I have spent so much time together and I'm reminded that things between us haven't always been ideal. In fact, I should probably chill out and enjoy the moment because *nothing* about our situation is going to make for easy sailing. We're going to have to work for every second of our happiness.

As if she's reading my mind, Ellie gives me one of her bright smiles and I can't help but respond to it. Taking my own advice, I relax and marvel at how well everything is going. Not long into the afternoon, the girls are so comfortable with Ellie that they start quizzing her on random topics at random intervals whenever there's a lull in the conversation.

"Ellie, do you have any sisters?"

"Ellie, what's your favorite color?"

"Ellie, did your mom teach you Spanish?"

"Ellie, do you like ponies?"

I love that she takes it all in stride and responds to their questions like they matter, with more than one word answers. And even better, she's careful to ask for their opinions on the same topics, making sure that all three girls are given equal opportunity to respond.

Then there's the logistical aspect. For lunch later at McDonald's, one of my biggest issues as a single dad is resolved when Ellie goes with them to the restroom. Plus, with the adult-to-kid ratio on a more even keel, everything is easier. Instead of having to wait forever outside the restrooms for the girls to come out, I can stand in line to order, and then Ellie carries the second tray of food and helps them fill their cups with juice. It's so much less stressful not having to do everything on my own.

"So, who's this Anne Marie I keep hearing about?" Ellie asks as she slides herself around to my side of the booth after the kids have finished eating and taken off for the indoor playground.

I watch her take one of my fries and pop it in her mouth. "Yeah, the famous Anne Marie," I say absently, more interested in the way she licks the salt from her lips. "She's Daniela's best friend slash arch nemesis."

"And Anne Marie's mother?"

Something in her tone draws my eyes up to hers. "Her mother?"

*"Anne Marie says her mom thinks my Tío is the most handsome dad,"* she mimics in a high-pitched voice.

"What?" I get out on a choked exhale. "Daniela said that?"

"Uh, yeah. Do I need to stamp a *back off bitches* label on your ass?"

"Are you jealous?" I ask, unable to stop self-satisfaction from spreading across my face. "Anne Marie's mom is like thirty-five."

She narrows her eyes. "Even worse."

Chuckling, I lean into her. "I've already got my cougar, Opal. No need to bring out the claws." I plant a kiss on her mouth. "Though they're pretty hot." I shiver, remembering how she sometimes digs her nails into my ass when I'm inside of her.

She rests her forehead on mine. "You're thinking what I'm thinking, aren't you?"

I groan. "Only if you're thinking of all the ways I'm going to make you come later."

"Okay," she breathes. "We need to change the direction of this conversation." She tries to pull away, but I follow her, and give her another, mostly chaste kiss. After an entire afternoon of not having guilt-free access to her mouth, I can't seem to resist.

The rumbling sound of a drink being finished off through a straw interrupts our moment. Pulling away, I find my daughter staring at us, mischief written all over her.

Trying to keep a serious face, I ask in my most neutral tone, "Can I help you with something, Rosa?"

"Nope," she says cheekily. "Just needed a drink of my juice."

"Sounds like it's pretty much gone." She gives it another pull and I feel a grin forming. "Go play, *chismosa*."

Calling her *nosy* doesn't dim her delight the least. "Okay!" I follow her progress and find the other two girls also watching us from the top of the jungle gym, grins firmly in place. Rubbing my palms down my face, I turn back to Ellie.

"She's just curious," she says.

"Yeah, let's go with that." I grab my Coke and shake it gently. There's nothing but ice left.

"Their Spanish is pretty good."

"You think?" I ask, lowering the cup back to the table. We've been slipping in and out of Spanish all day. "I feel like we use the same sentences over and over. As soon as anything is difficult to say, we switch to English."

She nods. "That's normal since at school and work you have to think and solve problems in English. You just need more input that comes from Spanish sources."

"You mean other than telenovelas?"

Laughing, she takes the last French fry off my tray. "Yeah, probably. But they can't hurt, right? I used to watch them with Amelia when I was little too. So educational."

Arriving home in the late afternoon, I have every intention of dropping the girls off and then logging some alone-time with Ellie on the pretext of having to drive her home. Unfortunately, life rarely goes to plan.

As I'm helping the girls climb out of the truck, my grandmother is dropped off by a neighbor fresh from her

Saturday afternoon knitting circle. Her face comes alive with interest when she sees Ellie. She even breaks out her English for the occasion.

"*Ellie habla Español, Abuela,*" Carmen informs her.

My grandmother gives me a suspiciously accusing look, one that morphs into delight when it's turned on Ellie. "*¿De verdad, mija?*"

¿Mija? I'm the one delighted now if a little perplexed. It seems Ellie merits being called *dear* or *sweetheart* on principle, and my grandmother is quickly rewarded as Ellie turns on her natural charm that's only amplified by her slightly lispy Spanish accent.

Before I know it, Ellie has graciously accepted a dinner invitation and is being led into the house, arm linked with my grandmother's, her head bent to make up for their wildly differing heights so she can hear what's being said.

"*¿Ya vienes?*" Carmen asks, reaching for my hand. *Are you coming?* Everyone has already gone in the house and she's peering up at me with concern.

"Yeah, let's go."

Inside, I'm hit with a twinge of nervousness. I've never been to Ellie's parents' place, but I know it has to be better this. Glancing around the small, cluttered living room that's immediately inside the front door, I can't find it in me to be embarrassed though. Yeah, the furniture with its floral pattern is dated and kind of dumpy, but this is home. And seeing Ellie's sneakers lined up near the door with everyone else's only makes it feel more so.

Following their voices to the kitchen, I find that Ellie has been installed in my spot at the table, a glass of *horchata* in front of her. Rosa and Daniela are singing Ellie's praises, telling our grandmother how she made our day so much more interesting than it usually is. If it weren't so true, I think I'd be offended.

"Where's *he* going to sit?" Carmen interrupts sternly after assessing the seating arrangement. My little sister is always going to bat for me.

"It's fine," I tell her. "I can sit over here."

The chatter immediately starts up again with refrains of *Ellie did this*, or *Ellie said that*.

A few minutes into the narrative, I send her a questioning look to make sure she's okay. She tells me she's fine by way of a broad smile that I can't help but return. I'm sinking into the pleasure of the moment when I catch sight of my grandmother's slightly surprised, slightly triumphant expression at the exchange. My exasperation only appears to make her happier.

A quarter of an hour later, Desiree and Mari come in together and I have to repress the very real urge to jump up and physically run interference between Ellie and my oldest sister. Not that I could stop Desiree from making her signature cutting comments if she wanted to unleash them. Luckily, Desi is nothing but polite and curious . . . or is it intrigued? Everyone is. Soon Ellie is being bombarded by question after question. I'd intervene on her behalf if I thought she needed it, but she handles the questions, even the more probing ones, with ease, her Spanish flowing effortlessly. Plus, I learn a few things, like she prefers ponies to Barbies, sweet to salty, she drives a Jetta that she got for her sixteenth birthday, and she has two nieces and no nephews.

When my grandmother stands up and announces that it's time to get dinner started, Ellie offers her assistance, but she's told in no uncertain terms that guests don't help. Daniela invites/begs Ellie to see their bedroom, and the other two immediately join the chorus.

Ellie looks to me for . . . permission, I guess. I shrug subtly, telling her it's up to her if she wants to take that on. I'm assuming she knows she'll be stuck in there for a while. In return, she directs a little grin my way as the girls tug her out of the room.

Desiree's snort of derision yanks my attention from the now empty doorway. *"No mames,* Scotty." She's gaping at me, my grandmother and Mari also staring, with similar looks of disbelief on their faces. *"No mames,"* Desiree repeats, just in case I didn't catch what loosely translates to *Are you fucking kidding me?* the first time.

"What?" I ask tetchily, feeling the smile I didn't know was on my face falling away.

"Did you see that?" Mari says, horrified. "They're already having conversations with their eyes. I think I'm going to gag."

"We're going to need an enormous bucket," Desiree adds.

I'm about to tell my rotten sisters where to go, when my grandmother starts gushing. "Oh, mijo, she is wonderful! An absolute dream!"

My irritation dulls considerably in the face of her approval. "You like her?"

"I love her. The girls love her. And so do you, obviously. I am very pleased."

I shoot my sisters a smug look.

Mari makes heaving noises as my grandmother turns to retrieve dinner ingredients from the fridge, coming back out with an onion for each of my sisters.

"Abuela!" they chime in synchronized outrage, then Desiree grouses, "That's Scotty's job."

"Not today it's not. You know I don't appreciate that vulgar language in my house."

"That was her," Mari cries, jabbing a finger at Desiree. "What did I do?"

"You made fun of your brother."

"Yeah," I tell her with a smirk. "You made fun of me. Shame on you, Mari."

"And you," my grandmother says, "are not off the hook. We're having *mole de olla*, so get the big pot out for me, please."

I repress a groan. That pot is way in the back of the bottom cupboard and I have to haul everything out to get at it.

"And why did you tell me that she is not Latina, mijo?"

Pulling my head out of the cupboard with the pot in tow, I look up at her from where I'm crouched on the floor. "She's not actually Latina."

"But her Spanish is better than all of yours," she accuses. "How can that be?"

I set the pot on the stove and she waves me to the sink where there are vegetables that need washing. "She's a Spanish major in college."

"With that accent?" Mari says skeptically.

"She lived in Spain for a while."

"*¿En Barcelona?*" Desiree says, affecting a ridiculously strong lisping Spanish accent that has Mari in fits of giggles.

My sisters then proceed to make a game of concocting a 'story' to explain how Ellie's Spanish got so good just to continue with their severely exaggerated lisping. I swear I try not to laugh, but it's impossible not to succumb. Honestly, I don't think Ellie would mind and they're not being too mean about it. Even my grandmother can't resist a few chuckles before she puts a stop to it.

"Fine. Spoil our fun," Desiree says, her face animated with playful impudence. "We still need to discuss the real issue here anyway."

From my place at the sink, I throw her a hard look. "What's that?"

"The fact that you guys are going to have gigantic babies together."

There's a bit of a pause before the raucous laughter starts. I give them the stink eye, but soon I'm sucked in by the fun.

It's been a good half hour by the time I successfully slink from the kitchen, hoping the younger residents of the house have gone easier on Ellie than the older ones have gone on me.

Making my way down the hall, I avoid the spot on the floor that creaks so I can hover outside the girls' bedroom door to shamelessly eavesdrop. I deduce that the topic of conversation revolves around My Little Pony hairstyles.

I stick my head in the door and all four of them beam up at me from where they're sitting on the floor in a circle with every Pony and accessory they own spread out among them. "What are you guys doing?"

"We're playing ponies," Carmen supplies with what, for her, is an unusual amount of excitement.

"We're going to have a pony parade after we get them all dressed up," Rosa announces.

"It was Ellie's idea," Daniela adds, almost on top of her cousin's words.

I sit between Ellie and Rosa who are nearest the door. "That's nice of her to play with you," I say, leaning in to kiss Ellie's cheek.

"It reminds me of being little," she says.

"Watch this, Tío. Ellie taught us." Daniela turns to Carmen. *"Piedra, papel, o tijeras."*

"I won!" crows Carmen. "Paper beats rock."

"Again."

They go again and all I'm thinking is *how do my kids not know about rock, paper, scissors?*

"They needed to decide whose pony would lead the parade," Ellie explains.

"Is there nothing you can't do?"

Raising a brow, she goes back to running a tiny plastic comb through the pony's pink mane. "I can make a list if you like . . . and it includes cooking." She lowers her voice. "I should be helping. I don't want them to think that I'm a spoiled rich kid who's too good for that kind of thing."

"Well, aren't you?" I say with a straight face. The way her eyes practically bug out of her head makes me laugh.

"That's not funny, Scott," she whisper-hisses. "What if . . . what if. . ?"

"Don't worry. They love you, just like I do."

Ellie is relaxing against me when giggles come at us from every direction and she stiffens back into an upright position. "Rosa," she exclaims. "Don't you have a pony for your dad to beautify?"

That only increases the level of giggling.

"Here's Rainbow Dash, Papá." She passes me a blue pony and a comb, and I barely refrain from glowering at her. She knows how much I hate this stuff. "What?" my daughter asks innocently. "It was Ellie's idea."

"Come on, Papá," Ellie adds glibly. "I bet you've got mad pony-hair skills."

I don't, but the girls are always trying to rope me into this stuff, and their hopeful expressions smother the protests that I can taste on my tongue.

We spend close to an hour with the girls, during which Ellie has an unending supply of patience with them, making sure to spread her attention equally among them. Not going to lie, it has me daydreaming of her turning the evil step-mother routine upside down and inside out even if it is way too early for that kind of thing.

When my grandmother calls us for dinner, I send the girls to wash their hands, leaving me alone with Ellie for the first time today. My lips are on hers the second the girls are out of the room. A minute later I murmur, "Do you know how many times I've wanted to do that today?"

"Probably only half as many as I have," she breathes, meeting my lips again.

It takes a minute or two but we finally make it to the kitchen where everyone around the table looks up. "Ellie, you can sit here," Carmen exclaims, patting the empty chair beside her.

"Nope, she's going to sit here beside me," I counter, surprising myself. "Daniela, go sit over there, please."

"I don't want to sit in Mamá Lilia's spot," she whines.

"It's fine," Ellie says, starting to go around the other side of the table, but I stop her.

"Daniela." I raise my eyebrows at her, until she gives a little huff and does as she's told. "Thank you." It's possible that not having Ellie to myself all day has begun to chafe at my nerves a bit.

Once the bowls of soup have been redistributed and Ellie is next to me where she belongs, my grandmother says grace, then as soon as we pick up our spoons, she asks Ellie about school. Rolling a tortilla along my palm into a cylinder to dip it in my dinner, I listen with half an ear to the name of the class she's taking, something about crossing the border and perspectives through fiction. My awareness sharpens though when I hear Ellie pose a question to my grandmother. She frames it in the most respectful way possible but it still jams my heart into my throat.

"*Le puedo preguntar, ¿cómo termino aquí en California, Señora?*"

"*May I ask how you came to be here in California, Señora?*"

It takes a second but even the girls pick up on the rising tension around the table. I watch my grandmother regard Ellie cautiously and I'm on the verge of interjecting with who knows what, when she answers.

"You may."

Except my grandmother doesn't add more, only bends her head back over her bowl to blow calmly on her dinner. Desiree shoots me a look that includes an arched eyebrow, telling me if I don't smooth this over, she will.

"I grew up in a small village near Acapulco."

My mouth falls slack with surprise, along with Desiree's and Mari's. My grandmother never talks about her past.

"My prospects there were . . . limited," she goes on. "I was eighteen when my mother died and she took my only reason for remaining in the village with her. My cousin, Jaime and I decided to strike out on our own."

*Jaime? Abuela has a cousin named Jaime?*

"What did your family think of the decision?" Ellie asks, while the rest of us swing our heads back and forth between them in frank astonishment.

"I didn't have much family to speak of. My mother had migrated north from Guatemala in her twenties and then married my father who had only one brother."

Audible gasps sound around the table, including mine.

"My great grandmother was from Guatemala?" Desiree squeaks. "Why don't I know this?"

"You never asked," my grandmother says with a casual wave of her hand. "Anyway, that is ancient history. I was telling you about when I left home." She gathers her thoughts, then continues. "Jaime and I heard that there was work to be had in the *maquiladoras* along the border with the United States."

"Papá?" Rosa whispers from beside me. "What's a *maquiladora*?"

"It's a factory, I think," I whisper back.

"What year was this?" Ellie asks, while my siblings and I listen all agog.

"1965."

"So very early in the program."

*Program? Which program?*

My grandmother nods, giving Ellie a pleased look, like she enjoys speaking with someone who knows shit. "Yes, the American factories were just beginning to pop up. It was not a . . . safe environment. Neither the living nor the working conditions, particularly for an unmarried woman."

"So you decided to cross the border," Ellie states.

"Yes, just so. I'm not sure my eighteen-year-old self quite understood the implications of starting a new life in a new country. But there was nothing for me to go back to, and I could not stay where I was."

"Did you pay a *coyote* to take you across?" Ellie asks.

"Coyote?" Daniela asks, struggling to follow the conversation. "Like a wolf?"

"No, it's like a nickname." Mari tells her in English. "A *coyote* is a person who takes people across the border illegally."

"But what's illegally?" Daniela then asks, making me wince. I'm sure this is part of the reason why my grandmother never talks about anything before she got married here in California.

"It means," Abuela explains evenly, "that I wasn't allowed to come to the United States, but I did it anyway."

"Like Rocio's dad?" Daniela asks with alarm and I frown, wondering who Rocio is.

"Yes, *mi amor*. Like Rocio's dad."

"But Abuela, Rocio's dad was sent away," Daniela says, her concern growing. "Are they going to send you away too?"

"No, don't worry. I'm not going anywhere. Not now."

The conversation ends up on a tangent about Rocio, who turns out to be a girl at school, and her dad, who was deported back to Honduras, and how his situation is different from Abuela's. Which is to say it's not; the only difference is the era in which they crossed the border and that my grandmother found a way to legalize her status and Rocio's dad didn't.

When Daniela is satisfied, I turn the talk back to what I really want to know. "So, *did* you pay a *coyote*, Abuela?"

"No. Not exactly. A group of us paid a *patero* to take us across the Río Bravo into Texas."

Mari is shocked. "You swam the Rio Grande?!"

"I did not, in fact, swim," my grandmother says without humor, probably because people lose their lives every year doing just that. "A *patero* is a boatman."

"But how did you know where to go when you got to the other side of the river?" Desiree asks, sounding almost stricken.

"One of the young women in our group had heard from a friend of a friend of a kind of safe house. We followed her blindly." She shakes her head. "I don't know what we were thinking. But there's something about youth that makes risk acceptable. In short, I was a fool."

"But you made it?" I ask, pretty much astounded, listening to this story for the first time in my life.

She did make it, and as we all listen, I can barely imagine my seventy-two year old grandmother as an eighteen year old girl traipsing across the country with her cousin, lying low, working illegally and living in paranoia of being deported for more than ten years before she met and then married my grandfather. It just seems so far-fetched. My sweet, loving grandmother, the illegal alien.

But it makes me realize how easy it is for Chicano kids like me and my sisters, especially because we're second generation, to forget that life wasn't always so simple for those who came before us.

# Chapter Three

## Ellie

Was I being nosy? Yes. But it's not like I was going to hound Scott's grandmother to share her experiences if she was reluctant. I admit that the appalled expression on Scott's face when I asked the question made my chest tighten with dread. I thought, for a second, that I'd seriously screwed up. But then she started talking and everyone around the table hung on her every word. Even cousin Jaime, who died in a car crash in 1974, was news. Apparently, family history isn't something they ever discuss . . . which holds a certain logic. I imagine that, however common, there's a stigma attached to being an illegal resident, not to mention the habit of secrecy when your very existence is a crime. That can't be easy to shake no matter how many years have passed.

It's late by the time everyone's curiosity is sated. Scott sends the girls, who are drooping off to sleep in their seats, to get their pajamas on and I'm admonished for trying to help clear the table. The matriarch assures me her grandchildren, including Scott, can handle it. I watch with more than a little interest as Scott and his sisters get the leftovers put away, load the dishwasher, and scrub the enormous pot like they've done it a million times, all while chatting and gently teasing each other. It's almost intimate, and it fills me with what I think is envy. I don't have this kind of relationship with my family.

Feeling content and full, I almost miss how the casual atmosphere in the kitchen changes.

"What do you mean she can't do it?" Scott says, aghast. "She's cancelling now?"

"Yes," his grandmother says with her usual composure. "And I can't cancel this appointment with the doctor. So one of you will have to do it."

"Well, it's not going to be me," Mari says firmly. "I have the review for my chemistry final on Monday."

"I just missed a day at work a couple weeks ago," Scott says, and they all turn to Desiree.

"No, come on, you guys. These are my last couple weeks as a high school senior."

The looks this excuse elicits from her family members tells me it falls somewhere between dismal and pathetic, possibly even risible.

"Fine," she says, drawing the word out into two syllables. "But the little punks will have to entertain themselves."

"What's going on?" I ask, uninvited, butting into their business before I can stop myself.

Scott groans. "There's a teacher conference on Monday and someone has to watch the girls."

"Oh," I say, smiling. "Monday's my day off, I could do it."

"Yes," Desiree says with triumph, switching to English. "Ellie can do it. I knew I liked her."

"What?" Scott says, annoyed with his sister. "No. She's not doing it."

"I don't mind."

"Yeah, she doesn't mind, Scotty."

They all turn to take in my eagerness. "I don't mind at all. We'd have so much fun." I can tell everyone except Desiree is dubious, and with a nauseating flash I realize that I've overstepped. "But it was just an idea," I backpedal, worried that I've put Scott in an uncomfortable situation. Maybe he doesn't want me looking after his kids.

But he counters with a tentative, "Are you sure? I won't make a habit of it or anything."

My head tilts. "Make a habit of what?"

"Asking you to watch the girls. I know they're my responsibility."

Okay, so if I'm reading the situation right, we both think we're stepping on the other's toes. "If you're okay with it, I'd love to help out."

The grin pulling at his lips eases the last of my trepidation. "They can be a handful, you know that right?"

"I have no doubt."

Scott is forced to spend the short ride from his place to mine listening to me happily go on about how excited the girls and I are to be spending the day together on Monday. By the time he's parallel parking his truck on the street near my building, I only half-jokingly ask him if he's going to drop me off and run.

Once he turns the engine off, he crooks his finger at me, wanting me closer. "Opal?"

I lean in, all playful innocence in the light from the street lamps. "Yeah?"

"I love you."

"Oh yeah?"

He wraps a hand around the back of my neck and pulls me closer. "Yeah." The word touches my lips before he actually kisses me sweetly. "Come on. Let's go inside." The suggestion woven into that statement only serves to boost my soaring mood higher.

Meeting me around the front of the truck, he takes hold of my hand. "Everything went so well today," I say, enthusiasm dripping from every syllable. "Except maybe it was touch and go there for a minute with your sister."

He grins at me, his spirits as bright as my own. "Desi's always like that. I wasn't too worried though. I'm pretty sure if push came to shove, you could take her."

"Pretty sure?" I choke out. "Shouldn't you have given me a heads up?"

"Nah. I've discovered no one on the planet is immune to your charm, not even my crazy-ass sister."

Scott unlocks the front door of the building with the key I gave him last week and stands back to let me pass.

"I have a confession to make," I say, giving him a bit of a grimace over my shoulder. "Ever since you took me out for that first dinner and a movie, I've been so nervous about meeting your family."

"What? Why?"

"Because it's always been obvious how much your family means to you. I was worried that I'd mess it up somehow."

Pausing in the hall outside my apartment door, he turns me to face him. "You were never going to mess anything up."

When I make to object, he places a finger over my mouth. "Are we done talking about my family?" He reaches around me and inserts the key in the lock. "Because I think there are better ways we could be spending our time together."

Walking backwards into my apartment, I pull him along, my giggles spilling out into the dark entryway. It takes a second to register that something is wrong, but a sudden, horrible feeling assaults me from both sides. First from Scott, whose gaze snaps up over my shoulder, and then from behind me, where I hear the rustling of movement. I don't get the chance to scream, I don't even get a chance to breathe before Scott has me behind him.

"Who the fuck are you?" Scott grits out harshly, his fury-filled voice cutting the air like the sharpest of blades. With my heart in my throat, I scramble to hit the light switch and catch sight of a man getting to his feet from where he's been sitting on the sofa.

"Gunnar! Are you insane?!"

The fact that I know the man standing in my living room doesn't appease Scott. From beside me, I feel raw violence pouring off of him. "What the hell are you doing here?" I demand of my ex-boyfriend with my hands pressed over my racing heart.

"Pipes, we need to talk."

*Is he serious?* "Then you call me like a normal person, Gunnar."

"You know you've blocked my number," he says pleasantly, casually, as if being in my apartment, waiting for me, is the most normal thing in the world. "And you've cancelled all your social media."

"So you break into my place?" I ask, adrenaline giving way to anger as I take in his lean, dark-haired and very familiar figure.

"Like I said, we need to talk."

"No." I shake my head. "We don't." I step forward but Scott catches my arm, keeping me next to him.

"Get. Out," Scott orders in a low, very steady, very threatening tone.

Gunnar flashes Scott a look of skeptical disdain before dismissing him completely. "This, Piper," Gunnar says, gesturing vaguely at Scott. "I don't like it. I've given you more than enough time to work out your problems, a year to the day to be exact. It's time you were back where you belong."

My surprise that he knows the exact date that I broke things off with him barely registers in the face of his sheer gall. "Where I belong?" I echo. "Is this a joke? How many times do I have to tell you that we're not getting back together? Not now, not ever."

"Enough!"

I jump at the volume of Gunnar's voice.

"Last warning," Scott says coldly. "Either get out or I put you out."

Gunnar flattens his lips into a thin line, clearly not appreciating Scott's presence. I've always known he was arrogant, but here, standing in my living room in his designer jeans and Gucci jacquard blazer, I see him for what he really is. Entitled. He never loved Piper, but he feels entitled to her. "You think this guy is going to buy you Louboutins?" he asks. "Or take you to Prague for the weekend?"

Scott takes two menacing paces forward and Gunnar hastily moves a half-step to the left, shocked, I'm sure, by the possibility of Scott lowering himself to physical violence.

"Wait!" I say urgently. "Before you throw him out, I need him to understand." Scott turns to me, the question in his eyes barely recognizable beneath the fury.

"I need him to understand that he and I are over. That this isn't some kind of ploy to string him along." I look to

Gunnar now. "I never needed those things from you. I took them because they were all you offered."

"Don't be –"

"Gunnar! Stop. You need to listen to me. Really listen. I don't want to see you ever again. I want you to hand over the keys and I want you to leave – for good. Please, don't call me. Please, don't show up here. Please, don't drop by my work."

"No, I –"

"This isn't a negotiation, asshole. She wants you gone from her life. Full stop. And so do I."

Gunnar's expression holds something akin to incomprehension, underpinned possibly with . . . pleading, something I've never seen from him. And I feel nothing for him. It might be a terrible thing to think, but it's the truth. "Please go."

"Is that what you really want?" he asks like he can't quite believe I'm not choosing him.

"Yes, it's what I want."

Gunnar's eyes travel from me to Scott and back again before he reaches into his pants pocket and pulls out two keys on a simple ring. Giving Scott a wide berth, he makes his way around the coffee table to place the keys on the kitchen island. "You know where to find me if you change your mind."

"I won't," I tell him dully before he takes his leave.

The sound of the door closing rouses Scott into action as he follows Gunnar's path and twists the deadbolt angrily, swearing under his breath. I drift forward and sink down onto the edge of the couch, wrapping my arms around myself.

"You okay?" he asks, passing me by to go into the bathroom and then the bedroom. When I hear him open my closet, I realize he's checking for more intruders. I don't call him out on the absurdity of his actions because I have to admit that finding someone inside my home like this has left me shaken. Scott reappears and throws back the curtains covering the patio door and proceeds to check the lock he installed all those weeks ago. When he's satisfied, he doesn't come to sit with me. He paces on the other side of the coffee table.

"That asshole has some nerve," he says bitterly. "I can't believe he had the balls to come in here like that." He doesn't give me a chance to say anything. "Has he done that before?"

"N–"

"Why, *exactly*, did he still have a key?"

There's an accusation in that question and I don't appreciate it.

"Or better yet, why didn't you tell me he still had a key?"

"Are you finished?" My tone gets his attention but doesn't soften his attitude.

"Fuck no, I'm not finished." He grips his hair with one hand as he continues to pace. "Your goddamn ex-boyfriend was hiding out in your apartment in the dark. I mean, what the fuck?"

Okay, I get it. Scott's pissed. But I'm rattled and he isn't helping the situation. My arms tighten around my middle in an attempt to stop the slight tremors that have started up.

"What if I hadn't been with you?" Scott challenges, pausing mid-step to give me a glare. Apparently he needs an answer to this one.

"Nothing would have happened," I say truthfully. "He's not violent."

"Are you kidding me right now?"

Sucking in a deep breath to fortify myself, I get to my feet to stand in front of him. "I know you're upset," I say softly. "So am I. Look." I hold out a shaky hand and he immediately takes it and pulls it to his lips.

"Shit, I'm sorry," he says, placing the hand over his heart and then encircling me with his arms. "I'm the one being the asshole now." He buries his nose in my neck and I hear him swallow hard. "I just . . ."

Lifting my arms from between us, I pull him closer, scratching my nails gently along the short hair at the back of his neck. "I know," I soothe. "Let's forget about it, okay?"

He pulls back to glower at me, and I can't stop a tired grin from pulling at my lips. Even if his protectiveness is a bit over the top, it's still welcome. No one's ever cared about my well-being like he does.

"Jesus, woman. Don't tell me to forget about it. You have no idea how tempted I am to follow him out and beat his ass."

That gives me pause. "But you won't, right?"

With a heavy exhale laced with disgust, he shakes his head.

"Because," I go on, "I need you here, with me. Not out wasting your time on a man like that." His frame still feels stiff in my arms, and I can see that he's going to need some persuasion to move past this. Pushing up on my toes, I kiss the side of his mouth. "Didn't we have other plans?"

His little grunt of agreement couldn't be more grudging, but his expression softens slightly. I kiss the underside of his jaw, loving the scratchy feel of his five o'clock shadow as I trail my lips down his neck, sucking gently as I go. The shiver that travels through his body has me smiling against his collar bone.

Nuzzling at my ear, he says, "You distracting me, Opal?"

"Yes. Is it working?"

Without warning, his hands slide lower and pull me up by my thighs, forcing me to wrap my legs around his waist as I suck in a surprised breath. He carries me into the bedroom and then after a moment of hesitation, he places me on my feet. Gently, he disentangles my arms from around his neck so he can start with the pacing again. "No, it's *not* working."

I pull my T-shirt over my head, and reach back for the clasp on my bra. His steps slow to watch as I pull it off and reach for the button of my jeans. I smile at the exasperated sigh he lets loose when my jeans and panties come off in one fell swoop. Coming to a standstill, he takes me in from head to toe before stepping up to me. One of his big hands wraps gently around my throat and the other skims down over a hardening nipple.

The hand around my throat tightens. "You're mine," he states, sparking an unexpected thrill. "I don't give a fuck what that asshole can buy you or where he can take you, you're mine."

Given the chance, I would have responded by spilling every ounce of the devotion I have in my heart for him. But he takes my lips in a rough and insistent kiss instead, as if he's daring me to argue with the claim he's staking. My knees become unsteady when his tongue slides against mine, every stroke pulling me more firmly under his spell.

I'm expecting him to move things along but he just continues to consume my mouth, gradually setting every inch of me on fire. When his hands finally start to wander, I melt further as his thumb finds my nipple, softly pressing it against his forefinger before trailing away. He shuffles closer, maneuvering one of his jean-clad thighs between my own and reaching around to grip my ass with both hands. The pressure he brings to bear on my clit sends pleasure rippling through me. With a deep groan, I start bucking against his thigh, chasing the highest of highs.

"That's it. Ride me. Just like that." His hands pull me more tightly against his flexing thigh and I luxuriate in another wave.

A hand slides up my back to fist the hair at the nape of my neck so he can guide my lips back to his greedy mouth. I'm completely lost in my body's response to him, happy to grind away on him . . . until I'm not. Because I'm not going to come this way and the realization has me squirming and pleading with him.

"Scott," I whimper. "Come on." I push at his shoulders, desperately wanting him to at least undress.

His thigh flexes again and I moan loudly, tremors reaching all the way to my toes. "Come on what, Opal? Huh?"

God, he loves to taunt me when I'm like this. I know he gets off on controlling when and how often I come. The closer he takes me to finishing without letting me fall over the edge, the better he likes it. But the adrenaline of the night has made me jittery and I'm not willing to play his games tonight.

"Quit messing around, Scott," I pant. "I want you inside me."

"Is that right?"

Color me surprised when he relents almost immediately by sitting me on the edge of the bed and then pushing me to lie back. He follows me down, hovering over me, his eyes flinty with possession before attaching his mouth to my neck, nipping and licking and sucking his way down to my breasts. Latching on to a nipple, just the tip, exactly how I love it, he plays first with one side and then the other. All the while, I writhe and arch my back by pushing my heels down into the mattress. When my core bumps his clothed torso, I've had enough.

"Scott," I whine. "Get your clothes off already."

Finally. I watch him strip off his T-shirt, followed by his jeans, exposing all that beautiful skin and that incredible cock of his. My mouth waters at the sight of it bobbing, thick and hard.

I start wriggling my way farther up onto the mattress to make room for him, but he stills me with a hand to my thigh. I blink at him questioningly as he sinks to his knees on the floor and spreads my thighs wide to stare down hungrily at my pussy. My mind blanks . . . well at least until the first touch of his tongue, then I almost come out of my skin.

"Unhhhhh, fuck," I cry, every muscle in my body bunching and straining, preparing to escape what I'm strung too tight to handle right now. But his hands clamp down on my thighs, telling me I'm not going anywhere, telling me I'm going to endure every second of him eating me out until he's done with me.

"D-d-damn it," I stutter as he forces my hips back to the bed while his lips and tongue devour me. "Scott," I plead, railing in the back of my mind against this. He knows that, as a rule, I don't find this relaxing. To me, it's a bit like touching a hot stove or plunging into an ice bath. Any way you slice it, it's too intense, especially when I'm already on edge.

"Enou–,"

He silences me by slowly pushing two of his fingers into me. The deliciously relentless back and forth slide pulls me apart, piece by piece, along with his lips suckling at my clit, until eventually he succeeds in flipping that universal primordial switch that floods me with a crescendo of ecstasy.

I'm still coming, still in the throes of the high when he drags his mouth up my body to swallow my gasps, letting me taste myself.

"There you go," he whispers into my lips, still holding his fingers impossibly deep inside of me, "squeeze me tight." He sucks on my tongue as his thumb brushes my overly-sensitive clit, setting off an incredible aftershock.

I ride it out, completely overwhelmed and barely lucid enough to register when he pulls away to get a condom.

An arm pushes under my shoulder and his fingers spread into the hair at the nape of my neck. Hauling me up the mattress, he settles himself between my thighs. His cradling of the base of my skull feels wonderful as does the way he runs the head of his dick through the slipperiness of my pussy. Anticipation vibrates down my spine when he nestles the head in exactly the right spot and then pulls my knee up along his hip.

"Open those pretty little eyes of yours, Opal," he says, jostling my neck gently to get my attention. "Look at me. Want to watch you take me." My eyes flutter open. "That's it." He pushes forward. The feel of him inexorably spearing into me has my mouth falling slack and my eyelids becoming heavy once again. "Uh, uh, uh," he admonishes. "Open." He increases the forward pressure when his ingress slows as it meets some resistance and I squirm. "None of that. We both know this beautiful pussy can take it all."

His dirty words send a hard shot of added lust careening through me.

"You were made for me."

He's deep now, at that point where pleasure and discomfort always meet for that brief erotic moment before my body acquiesces to his.

"That's my girl," he moans, his forehead touching mine. "All of it." The rough curls of his pubic hair press into my clit when he's fully seated. We pant and nuzzle at each other. "Like heaven," he whispers, kissing the side of my mouth. "You good?"

I feel my head nod within the cradle of his fingers.

"Mmmmm," he hums. "Love your pussy twitching and jerking to adjust for me. So fucking hot."

Damn, that mouth of his. His possessive, domineering streak in bed when the right combination of buttons is pushed has been a most welcome surprise in our relationship.

With the incredible sensation of him filling me, I breathe him in, drawing my nails down his back until I have the firm globes of his ass cupped in my palms. He starts to move and I'm done for.

.

# Chapter Four

## Scott

If there's anything better in life than fucking Ellie, I've yet to find it. Nothing even comes close in my opinion. The heat of her pussy snug around my dick on every stroke is like nothing else and it almost has me forgetting that her douchebag of an ex broke into her place and announced he wanted her back.

On my next stroke, I grind against her clit. "I won't give you up," I rasp. She mewls, her chin lifting. The way her swollen flesh tries to hold me inside of her as I withdraw is almost as good as shoving back in. "I refuse. You're not going anywhere." My demanding tone has her pussy clenching. "Fuck," I grunt, both exhilarated and dismayed to feel the echo of that clench in my balls.

"You couldn't," – she pants, I thrust – "get rid of me," – again – "if you tried."

"I hope not." Another thrust. "Now come."

Even if I know she doesn't actually come on-demand, the illusion is a total trip for me – and her. It's all just a question of timing. Her tells are subtle, but once I learned them, they became more obvious than a billboard drenched in neon lights; bared throat, arched back, tightening core, and those fingernails of hers digging into my ass. On their own, sure they signal arousal, but put them all together with her uneven breaths and her restless squirming and I've got my girl right on the threshold.

"Don't make me tell you again," I rasp harshly . . . or maybe it's desperately, because she's not the only one about to slide sideways into the bliss. My balls are so tight, so close to letting go that I'm light-headed with the anticipation.

"Oh, fffuuuuuuck." One second her pussy's clamping down hard, telling me she's gone over and the next my eyes roll back as my own orgasm lets loose, swamping me with euphoria.

When I come back to myself, my first thought is decidedly sappy. But with her laid out beneath me, my dick still lodged deep inside of her, my nose in her hair, breathing in the scent of her, I can't help myself. I want to stay here, like this, with her nails grazing along my spine forever. But I can't. The condom needs to be dealt with.

Groaning, I withdraw myself from her and then get to my feet, looking for the trashcan.

"When are we getting rid of those?"

I frown. "The rubbers? Uh, never."

The dreaminess in her eyes tells me she thinks I'm joking. I'm not. I've already got three kids to look after and imagining another is like facing a firing squad. I'll be wrapping my dick up tight for the rest of my life.

Settling back on the bed, I open my arms and she burrows into their circle. Quiet settles around us, but my mind circles back to the horrible sensation of finding a man lying in wait for my woman. I should have torn him limb from limb. Or at least made him bleed a little. He deserved worse for violating the sanctity of her home like he did.

"I don't remember the last time I had such a good day," Ellie says on a contented sigh.

"Mmm."

"The girls were okay with me, don't you think?"

I mumble something noncommittal and she props herself up on an elbow to study me. "I'm going to go out on a limb and say you're not even listening to me."

Blowing out an annoyed breath, I wrap a palm behind her neck, trying to pull her back down to my chest, but she resists. "I'm listening to you. And you're right. The girls loved you, my abuela loved you, I think even Desiree loved you. Today couldn't have gone any better . . . until the end."

Her mouth twists with a repressed smile. *What the hell?*

"You mean how you gave me not one blinding orgasm, but two? Yeah, that was terrible."

"Opal," I grouse. "You not taking that guy's appearance seriously isn't helping me right now."

"I told you he's harmless."

Renewed anger flares inside my chest, sharp and painful, but before I can argue further, she says, "And I like that you're offended on my behalf, but –"

"Offended?! He broke in, El. I can't let that go."

"Yes, you can. Because I'm asking you to. I know Gunnar. I know how he thinks and he has the message now. He's not going to reduce himself to begging, believe me."

That, right there, is bullshit. Ellie doesn't realize how much she affects people. She's like the sun with every living thing straining to be in her presence, to garner her attention. That douche knows what he's lost, and now it's a question of whether he'll accept it. If El says he will, chances are good . . . but there are no guarantees.

A jabbing finger to my ribs pulls me from my thoughts. "Oww. What was that for?"

She sits up and glares down at me. "Get out of your head, Scott. You're ruining my after-glow."

"What?" I give a short huff of amusement. "Your after-glow?"

"Yeah, you know, that glazed, post-sex stupor during which you pet my hair and tell me how beautiful I am and how much you love me. You're not doing it right." She puts on an indignant expression, crossing her arms over her chest. "Plus, when I fish for compliments about how well such an important day went, you're supposed to supply them."

"Is that so?"

"Yes, it's exactly so."

Chuckling softly, I pull her down and settle her back on my chest, kissing the top of her head. "Fine. You were an incredible success today. And you're so very beautiful and I love you more than you can possibly imagine. And . . . and since when do I pet your hair?"

"Okay, I may have made that part up," she admits. "But I refuse to let anyone bring us down. We passed a huge milestone today, don't you think?"

"Yeah, we did," I agree.

"The girls are wonderful, Scott. They're polite and articulate and so full of joy. And you have so much patience with them. They love you so much."

Despite knowing that she's deliberately distracting me, some of the tension in my shoulders lets go. "Well, I love them so much too."

"I know you do. And I can't believe that you're actually going to let me babysit them."

The wonder in her voice has me shaking my head. "You're doing me a favor, El."

"Pffft. That you trust me with them is a huge compliment."

"I don't see why. They loved you today, and in my experience, kids are pretty good judges of character."

She snuggles herself closer. "So I have an appointment to get my hair trimmed on Monday," she says. "Do you think I need to cancel it or would it be okay if I took them with me? It shouldn't take very long. They can read the magazines."

I shrug against the sheets. "I don't see why not. Just remind me to leave their booster seats."

I feel her smile against my skin. "Okay. I was also thinking of taking them swimming at my mom and dad's. You said they take swimming lessons, right? Would that be okay, too?"

"Uh . . . at your mom and dad's?" She must hear the reluctance in my voice. Who can blame me though? After meeting her mother a few weeks ago, I'm not eager to expose the girls to the woman.

"Don't worry. My parents are still in Palm Springs. Amelia will be there though. Maybe she can help me feed them lunch," she muses. "She must know what kids like to eat."

My sweet Ellie. I love that she cares so much that things go well. "Sure, I bet they'd like that. So car seats and bathing suits. We'll be here bright and early on Monday morning."

After that, I mostly listen to Ellie who chatters on about this and that. Bit by bit, though, my thoughts slink back towards her ex's appearance tonight. The fact that in a few minutes I'll have to leave her here in the apartment by herself is killing me. Every single molecule in my body rebels against even the slightest possibility of her not being safe, of me not being here to protect her. But for the life of me, I can't think of a single solution, either short or long term. I mean, what am I going to do, move her into my grandmother's house so she can sleep on a foam mattress with me in the middle of the living room? And it's not like I can pack up the girls and set up shop somewhere else . . . right? My grandmother is as much a part of their lives as I am, I can't just uproot them from everything they know. Besides, I can barely keep one household afloat, let alone two.

Now there's a dose of reality I could do without.

---

I don't get to see Ellie on Sunday; she's working and then doing the homework she would have done on Monday, and I've got church and Sunday night dinner to which Father Martín is invited this week. I do hear about her constantly though. My grandmother has nicknamed her *la güera*, which translates affectionately into *the white girl*, Desiree and Mari tease me constantly about being in love, and the girls go on and on about how nice and pretty and perfect Ellie is. Not that I mind. Listening to my family endorse the woman I love is not a hardship.

By the time Monday morning comes, the girls are bouncing with excitement. Despite the early hour, I don't have to push them to get ready. They're all waiting by the front door, backpacks slung across their shoulders, sweaters and sneakers on, big smiles plastered on their faces ten minutes before our scheduled departure time. Apparently, miracles do happen.

I text Ellie and get her to meet us next to her car so we can transfer the booster seats. When we pull up in her building's parking lot, she's leaning against the hood of her silver Jetta in the sunshine and I'm hit with a nice shot of well-being at the sight of her. Even if I'm practically an afterthought to her enthusiastic greetings for the girls, I relish the feel of her lips on mine.

"Morning," she whispers against my mouth.

"Morning." I give myself about a five second window to savor her with our foreheads pressed together before I pull away. "Do you have your keys? I'll pull the car forward to get the boosters in."

She hands them over and then gives her full attention to the girls. I unlock the car and get in. Looking around, I can't help but shake my head at the mess, and it's got a gym-sock smell to it that kicks my mild OCD into overdrive. Ignoring the urge to take the day off work to scrub her car down from top to bottom, I start it up. For a car that's ten years old, it doesn't have very many miles on it, but when the check engine light doesn't disappear, I frown.

I pull forward and get out.

"How long's the check engine light been on?" I ask her as I start pulling the seats from my truck.

Her shoulder ticks up. "A while."

Irritation wiggles in my gut at her blasé attitude. "Don't you think you should get that checked out?"

She laughs as she re-twists the elastic at the end of Daniela's braid. "I can barely afford to put gas in it," she says as if that explains everything. And I suppose she has a point even if it has me gritting my teeth.

With the seats in place, I re-park Ellie's car and notice what the glowing yellow icon on the dash distracted me from the first time around; she's got less than an eighth of a tank of gas.

I hug the girls goodbye, give them the standard warning to behave themselves and then turn to Ellie. "Call if you need anything, okay?" I say, pulling out my wallet and handing her forty bucks. "And fill up the car."

Cue the stubborn mule glint in her eyes. "I'm not taking your money, Scott."

If she thinks she's the only one who can play hardball, she's mistaken. "I'm not going to risk you running out of gas with the girls in the car. Take the money."

Shit, now she's horrified. I didn't mean to freak her out, but I can't have her driving all over the city on fumes. Still, she hesitates, so I push the money into the front pocket of her jeans.

"Carmen, can you remind Ellie to get gas later, please?"

Ellie squints, telling me I'll probably pay for that later. Don't care. Keeping all four of them safe is more important. If she doesn't like that, she can kiss my Latino ass.

"Fine," she huffs. "But I'll pay you back."

"Fine," I huff back, leaning in to kiss her good bye. "Have a good day."

Her icy demeanor melts slightly. "You too. But don't think we're not going to talk about this."

"I look forward to it." Squeezing her hand, I'm about to leave when I remember the girls have homework that still needs doing. "Can I ask a favor? They're supposed to work on some school-wide project. Can you help them out with that a little? Please?"

There we go, icy demeanor gone. "Of course," she says, "I'd love to help. Right, girls?"

"Right!" they all chirp back.

"Okay, I'll pick them up around five/five fifteen."

Driving away, I briefly watch them in the rear-view mirror, the girls following Ellie back inside like little ducks all in a row. Oddly enough, instead of dread at leaving them with her for the first time, I feel almost nothing but confidence.

My usual Monday morning meeting with my boss, Dean, goes smoothly. And then when I arrive on-site, I find my right hand guy, Thomas, has everything in hand. It goes a long way to helping me through the morning. Yes, I may glance at my phone a few times to make sure I haven't missed any calls, but I'm chill.

I stay on-site to eat my lunch and fill out the paperwork for payroll hours. When I'm finished, I finally give in to the urge to check on them.

**Scott: Everything going ok?**

It takes about 7 minutes, 45 seconds to get a reply. Not that I'm keeping track or anything.

**Opal: All good. We're about to leave the public library. Heading over to my parents to have lunch and go swimming now.**

*The library?*

**Scott: Ok. Have fun. Love u**

**Opal: love you too**

I'm idly wondering if Ellie would ever admit to things not being as peachy as she makes them sound when the guys start wandering back in from their lunch break. Doing a mental headcount, I come up two short. I almost groan aloud when I realize who's missing; Jorgie, that lazy ass, and his new pal and my long-time pain in the ass, Harrison.

"Hey, boss, you smell that?"

I'm about to deny smelling anything when I get a good whiff of the unmistakable odor of pot. My heart plummets. *He wouldn't, would he?* Jorgie can't be that stupid. No one's that stupid.

I follow a bunch of the guys up to the second level of this massive house we're working on. In the far corner, on what will be the master bedroom's balcony, Jorgie's lack of all sense becomes official. For almost a minute, half the crew and I watch the two of them pass a joint back and forth before they even notice us.

From his perch on a stack of two-by-fours, Jorgie smiles. "What's going on, guys?" he asks affably, like he doesn't have a care in the world. Well, right now, he probably doesn't.

Pushing out a heavy sigh, I hang my head, hating what has to come next. Somehow, I say it calmly and firmly. "I'm going to need you to clear off the site immediately."

"Relax, Scotty," Jorgie intones, blowing out smoke and then trying to pass the joint back to Harrison. But Harrison seems to have a better grasp on the severity of the situation because he refuses to take it.

"The final decision rests with the head office," I go on tightly, "but the policy is clear. No intoxicants on the job. Period."

"What?" Jorgie sputters, laughing now. "This shit is legally available at the shop on the corner, Scotty."

He and I both know he didn't get it legally on the corner, but that's beside the point. Plus, his use of my nickname is beginning to eat away at my self-control. "Get your things together and go."

Harrison finally finds his voice. "You can't do that, *Scotty*."

"Dude," Thomas says scornfully. "We all saw it. You're so done."

"Okay," I say, rubbing my hand across my jaw, ignoring the wobble in my stomach. "Show's over. Let's get back to work."

The guys and I file back downstairs. A few minutes later, Jorgie and Harrison follow, but do they leave quietly? No. They argue until I have to threaten to call the cops to have them removed, making me feel even more like shit. No matter what Jorgie's done, I don't think I'd actually be able to go through with it. I already feel like a traitor of the worst kind.

Once they're gone, I call Dean and fill him in on the situation. I feel moderately better when he tells me I've done the right thing and that I should get the guys who witnessed everything to write statements.

By the time the statements are written, there's not much time left on the clock so I send everyone home early. I take a few minutes to pull myself together before I text Ellie.

**Scott: Hey. I'm done early. Where are you guys?**

**Opal: We're still at my parents place. Come over!**

She texts me an address.

**Opal: We're in the backyard. Come around the left side of the house.**

What a day. Unfortunately, I can't say it improves any when I google the address and find out it's a mansion right in the heart of Palo Alto. Then, a half hour later, I'm hit head-on with the mind-boggling reality that was Ellie's life growing up. From the outside alone, I can tell we're talking *millions* of dollars for a house like this. There's a massive fountain in the middle of the circle drive for fuck's sake. All it does is further tighten the knot that's been lodged in my chest for the last few hours.

Spotting Ellie's car over on the left, I park next to it and make my way around the side of the house. I hear them before the manicured foliage gives way to reveal my girls – all of them – splashing and laughing in a giant swimming pool that's set against one of the most idyllic settings I've ever seen . . . and for inexplicable reasons, the sight seriously aggravates me.

# Chapter Five

## Ellie

We've had the best day. Okay, maybe not *the best*, because there were a few hiccups, but overall, I'd say it was a resounding success.

In the morning we worked on their homework, a school-wide brainstorm of ideas to reduce the average person's carbon footprint. I thought it was a great project and the girls fed off my enthusiasm. We came up with a ton of possibilities.

Then we hit the salon where my mother has me on her account so I can 'look my best' at all times. I've gotten to know the women who work there pretty well over the years, so while I was getting my hair cut, the girls got to choose a color for their nails and it would be billed to my mother as one manicure. Everyone thought it was a fabulous idea until we were finishing up and another customer chastised me for poisoning small children with toxic chemicals. Ironic, really, after spending the morning discussing a healthier planet. The damage was already done though. I lived, I learned.

The public library was next on our list of stops. I wanted them to pick a book in Spanish that I could read aloud to them to improve their vocabulary. This proved more challenging than I was expecting. A squabble broke out when they couldn't come to a consensus, so I allowed them to each choose a book, which then turned into three or four books each. At that point it was already one o'clock and it dawned on me that they must have low blood sugar since we hadn't eaten lunch yet. More living, more learning.

Luckily Amelia had lunch ready for us when we arrived at my parents' place. That was a few hours ago and since then we've been having a blast in the pool.

"¡Papá!"

Rosa sees him first, and it starts a mad rush through the water to reach the ladder to be the first to get to him.

"Don't run! It's slippery," I yell as one-by-one they speed walk to greet him.

When I catch up, the girls are gushing about our day and showing him their shiny nails. From a distance, he sparked the usual internal swooning in me, but up close, I realize something isn't quite right. His pleasant expression is forced and his arms are folded over his chest defensively.

Thinking the tension is due to my lack of babysitting skills, I smile brightly and reassure him, "We survived *and* we're all in one piece." Leaning over the girls, I push up on my toes to kiss him on the lips, but I get the corner of his mouth instead. A flicker of disquiet hits me, but it's squashed when Rosa makes her big announcement.

"Papá, you have to see what Ellie taught me! Watch, okay?"

"Me too, Tío," Daniela adds.

"Me three," Carmen says, following her sisters back to the pool.

"Rosa's been working up the nerve all day," I whisper to Scott as we watch her make her way to the diving board at the deep end. "She just finally took the plunge," I say, giggling at my pun, "in the last half hour since she knew you were on your way."

"Are you watching?" Rosa yells, perched on the end of the diving board.

"I'm watching."

She jumps and Scott's entire body stiffens beside me when she hits the water with a splash. He moves closer to the pool. "Don't worry," I tell him. "She's got this." We watch her surface and swim awkwardly to the ladder. "Awesome, right?" I whisper.

"Yeah, awesome," he says flatly, sounding far from impressed. I turn to face him, real concern bubbling inside of me now. His jaw clenches before he yells, "Great job, *Calabacita!*"

"Watch me, too, Tío!"

He watches Daniela jump as Rosa approaches us. "Did you see me?" she asks breathlessly.

"I did. Pretty amazing. Why don't you got get changed? We're going now."

"Awwwwww. Can't we stay a little longer?"

Carmen splashes down as Daniela arrives. "We're going?" she asks, appalled.

"Yep," Scott confirms. "Go get your stuff together."

"But I don't want to go," Daniela whines.

"They can swim for as long as they want," I say, trying to be helpful, but it earns me a dark look. "Or not."

Daniela mimics his posture by folding her arms over her chest. "Well, I'm not going. I'm staying with Ellie."

"Can I stay with Ellie, too?" Carmen asks with excitement, not having heard the rest of the conversation.

"No," Scott says firmly. "You can get your sisters ready to go. We're leaving in ten minutes."

Carmen looks crestfallen, like a scolded puppy. Rosa only watches with big eyes, but Daniela is on the verge of mutiny.

"Um, maybe," I start, but Scott turns another dagger-filled glare on me, making my mouth snap shut.

"Carmen, take them to get changed," he orders. "I'll meet you guys out front."

Even though Daniela protests, Carmen takes her by the arm and begins hauling her away toward the pool house. Rosa follows glumly in their wake.

"What's up with you?" I ask, trying to keep my tone civil.

"Nothing. Do you have the keys to your car, so I can get the booster seats?"

He avoids making eye-contact, which gives me pause. This is new territory for us, so instead of laying into him for taking his mood out on the girls, I hold my tongue. "Yeah, sure. I'll grab them."

Returning, I make an attempt at a peace offering as I hand over the key. "I was thinking we could go get some dinner together."

He shakes his head. "Nah, we need to get home. The girls have school tomorrow."

I frown. It's quarter after four in the afternoon. "Listen," I say, "if this is about the nail polish, I'm really sorry. Next ti–"

"I thought you didn't have money for gas?"

*Huh?* I stare at him blankly, unsure what he's trying to say. But he's quick to clear up my confusion.

"Why would you get their nails done when you don't have money for gas?"

"Oh . . . no. My mom lets me use her account at the salon," I explain, but now that his words have settled in my gut, I don't like them. What exactly is he accusing me of? Immaturity? Irresponsibility? Stupidity?

"So your mother paid for it?" His expression morphs from incredulous to outraged. "My kids are not charity cases."

Not going to lie, I'm stunned speechless.

"Can you just send them out when they're done?" he says, his angry tone telling me how disgusted he is with the situation.

*What the hell?*

I turn on my heel and march toward the pool house with as much dignity as possible while wearing a bikini.

"Hey, girls," I call out from outside the door. "How are you doing?"

"Ellie, we can't get my shirt on," Rosa calls.

Hesitantly, I open the door and find the three of them in varying stages of undress, Carmen trying to help wrestle Rosa into her T-shirt with one of the sleeves balled up. "Here, let me help."

In sharp contrast to earlier, their dispositions are decidedly somber, which only serves to further twist my exasperation with their father deeper into my belly.

"Ellie?" Daniela asks quietly after we've said goodbye to Amelia in the kitchen. "How come he's mad?"

Considering the pros and cons of avoiding the question or even of pretending Scott's fine, I end up going with the truth. Just because they're young doesn't mean they're gullible. "I'm not sure. But he's not upset with you guys, so don't worry." Which is true. And if he's not upset with them, he must be upset with me.

We come to the front of the house. I ignore him as I say goodbye to the girls, giving each one a solid hug. When they're settled in the back seat, he turns to me, about to say something, but I cut him off, holding out my hand. "You have my keys?"

"Yeah, uh . . ."

"Thanks."

Keys in hand, I turn to go, not interested in anything he has to say right now.

"El," he calls, but I don't stop. "I'll call you later?"

"Sure," I throw over my shoulder. *I might even answer.*

I make my way back into the house and find Amelia sitting in the breakfast nook with a cup of coffee and a crossword puzzle.

"Thanks for helping me out today," I say, slumping down into the chair across from her.

She regards me carefully. "He didn't want to come in and say hello?"

Shaking my head, I give her my best guess. "He must have had a rough day . . . or something."

Her tactful hum carries unspoken words. "I think I might disapprove of the way his arrival sucked the life out of you and the girls if I weren't so impressed with the girls themselves."

I can't hold back a scoff. "That's got to be their grandmother's influence." Amelia's wry amusement at my comment does nothing but irritate me further. "He was a total —" I want to say *he was a total dick*, but Amelia wouldn't like that so I go with, "He was a total jerk to me."

"No one said this was going to be easy."

"He didn't even say thank you."

"Yes, well, being someone's significant other is often a thankless job."

My pique grows because I was prepared to have to defend him to her. "You're the last person I would expect to make excuses for him."

"I'm not making excuses. I'm making allowances. There's a difference. But I expect you'll need to make plain to him that such behaviour is not only uncalled for, it's destructive."

I lower my head onto my arms on the table, feeling defeated.

"If the two of you are going to make a relationship work, there will have to be a period of adjustment. Some growing pains, so to speak. And you'll each have to decide if it's worth the pain."

I feel the prickling of imminent tears. "What if he decides I'm not worth it?" I say into the tabletop.

She tsks. "What if he does? If that's the case, you're better off without him. Your self-worth is not negotiable, Ellie. My best advice is to begin how you mean to move forward. Let him explain, but make it clear that bullying won't be tolerated."

Lifting my head, I try to stem my tears as Amelia's expression softens.

"But also understand that he can't help but be wary of your influence over his children. He may even be jealous for a time."

"What?!" Indignation rears its ugly head. "Jealous of what?"

"Come now," Amelia says, giving me a pointed look. "Surely you can put yourself in his shoes and see that he's not accustomed to sharing them with you. Or the opposite, sharing you with them."

"But that's crazy."

"True. But love rarely goes hand in hand with logic, does it?"

My only response is a noisy exhale.

"Like I said, it won't be easy. But you're the strongest woman I know, *mi amor*. You need to show him that that strength means you'll be there for him, but that you won't let him walk over you."

"That doesn't sound easy either."

"No, but that's life, as you well know."

"Yeah," I sigh, my ire wilting. "As I well know. Thanks for the advice."

"You're most welcome. Now help me put away the lounge chairs, so we can lock up the house."

---

After spending the day with the girls and their exuberance, the quiet of my empty apartment is oppressive. The only thing I can find the energy for when I get home is flopping down on the sofa and wrapping myself up in a throw blanket.

Despite my best efforts going over well with the girls, they were lost on the one person whose opinion mattered the most. Thinking maybe I missed a call or a text somewhere over the course of the day, I pull my phone out from my back pocket. There's nothing, of course. I was so careful. But after re-reading Scott's last texts about being done with work early, I realize he must have been really worried that I was making a mess of things . . . which is entirely reasonable. That doesn't explain, though, why he lashed out at me without asking a single question. I'd been ready for his questions too. I'd been going over my 'report' in my head all day. I didn't feed them candy, I checked their library books for inappropriate content, I made sure they ate their lunch, I watched them in the pool like a hawk. And I'd been so careful with what I said and how I acted around the girls – all damn day.

Except, I screwed up with the nail polish, didn't I?

He hadn't seemed overly concerned about that, but he had been angry. With me and my decision making process. That produces a flash of indignation. None of what he'd accused me of had been founded. It's almost as if he'd been looking for something to be angry about; he'd been mad before he found out the bill for the manicures would go to my mother. Ugh. I should be outraged and offended by his behavior. The moral high ground is mine, I'm in the right . . . so why doesn't that make me feel any better?

As the evening wears on and he doesn't call or text me, my mood shifts further and further into melancholy. The simple fact is I put my all into the girls today, but it wasn't good enough. When my phone finally buzzes on the coffee table beside me, I almost don't bother reaching for it.

**Scott: I owe you an apology.**

The words re-ignite my resentment and my thumbs stab out a hasty reply.

**Ellie: Yeah, you do.**

But then, when he doesn't send anything more, regret triggers an invasion of nausea in my empty stomach. This sense of helplessness is awful. How can I know he was wrong today, but still want him to forgive me? How weak and pathetic.

The sound of his key in the door a few minutes later doesn't ease my turmoil.

Since the apartment is dark, he heads straight for my room, then nearly freezes mid-stride when he finds me on couch. Neither of us says anything as he comes to sit next to my hip and brushes my hair back from my face with a gentle hand. The moment our gazes meet, tears rush to form in my eyes.

"I'm sorry," he whispers, his Adam's apple bobbing in his throat. "I screwed up again."

The admission only serves to add a shuddering breath to my waterworks.

"Oh, El. Come here." He pulls me up and settles me on his lap, tucking my head under his chin. "I'm so sorry I hurt you . . . again."

All I can do is clutch at his shirt, trying to pull him closer while I sniffle. God, where is the woman who should be tearing a strip off of him right now? Who should be setting the ground rules for our relationship so this type of thing doesn't happen again? I need to pull myself together.

"I didn't mean to come down on you like that," he says softly. "It's like my whole shitty day snowballed into an avalanche and I let it flatten everything."

He let it flatten me, he means.

Fortifying myself with a deep breath, I sit up to face him. The light from the street leaves his face half-bathed in shadow, but there's so much remorse in his expression that it knocks back the desire to make my points. "So it wasn't me?" I ask pitifully.

"No! Of course not."

"You didn't even ask me how it went today," I accuse, wiping at my cheeks.

"I know." He hesitates, then asks me earnestly, "How did it go today?"

I make a sad tittering sound. "It was great . . . except for the nail polish. I'm so sorry about that."

"It wasn't the nail polish," he says, wincing. "It was your mother and –"

I hold up my hand. "That I can understand. But what was with the crack about the gas money?" I ask him, still truly perplexed. "Do you think I'm careless with money? Did you not get the fifty dollars I left with the secretary that you loaned me?"

"No," he mutters, hanging his head. "No, I don't think you're careless with money, El. And yes, of course I got the money."

"So . . . why?"

Following the path of a tear with his index finger, he says, "Nothing today had anything to do with money. It was just . . . a convenient way to . . ."

He doesn't want to finish, so I do it for him. "A convenient way to take a shot at me?"

Exhaling heavily, he reluctantly agrees. "Yeah." He leans in to rest his forehead to mine briefly. "God, I really messed up. Can you forgive me?"

His words trigger a memory and instead of answering his question, I consider a different idea. "Do you remember a few weeks ago when I told you that I loved you?"

He goes rigid and I realize he thinks I'm bringing it up to rake him over the coals. I quickly continue. "I had an emotional melt-down? An irrational, baseless melt-down?" I take hold of his hand and trace his palm, feeling a bit mortified with the memory. "Do you remember?"

"Yeah, of course I remember," he says, closing his hand around mine and then looking up into my face with concern.

"You didn't hold it against me."

His head cocks in question, uncertain where I'm going with this.

"You were kind and understanding," I tell him. "And I truly appreciated that, so I'm going to do the same."

A line forms between his brows. "Opal, I . . ."

"Sorry, I'm being cryptic. What I'm trying to say is that I'm sure there'll always be times when we let our emotions get the better of us."

He grunts softly with what I think is disapproval, perhaps not liking the insinuation that he gets emotional.

"Hear me out," I say, squeezing his hand. "When we get overwhelmed, I get weepy and you get mad."

He's about to object, but I continue. "I'm not saying that's a bad thing, but I am saying that we need to learn how to deal with the crying and the anger without hurting each other." Our eyes lock and I watch him consider the efficacy of my statement before I go on. "Because I'm not the enemy, Scott. I'm the person you're supposed to lean on when life sucks."

He grimaces. "Leaning is one thing, El, but I don't want to crush you with all my bullshit."

Getting to my feet, I push him back further onto the couch and straddle his thighs. "Well, your bullshit is now our bullshit." He shakes his head like the idea is crazy, but I place my finger over his lips to stop him from contradicting me. "I'm tougher than I look, Scott. I would hold up the world for you."

He takes hold of my wrist and pulls my hand away from his face. "I know you would, sweetness, but I love you, and I don't want you drowning right alongside me."

"But that's what love is, it's –"

"Love is drowning?" he interrupts, the sarcasm dripping.

I feel a grin tug at my lips. "I'm a great swimmer."

His feeble laugh withers. "You say that because you don't know how strong the current was today."

"Then enlighten me."

His shoulders slump and he lowers his head to my shoulder. "I don't want you to think I'm making excuses for how I behaved."

Stroking the back of his neck, I say gently, "Telling me what happened isn't making excuses, it's basic communication."

It takes him a while, but eventually he lifts his head. "I had to fire Jorgie for getting high on the job."

My heart falls. "Oh, Scott, I'm sorry."

"Did he go quietly? No. He made a big production, calling me out as a traitor to my roots in front of my entire crew." He runs a hand down his face in defeat before he continues. "Then, I went to pick up my kids at the mansion where my girlfriend grew up, which completely wigged me out and made me feel inadequate in ways I don't want to examine. Then, I find out that my kid, who I've been working so hard with on her swimming, had jumped into the deep end for the first time by herself when I wasn't there."

"Scott, I –"

"Hang on. Then, as you know, I treated my girlfriend like shit, which made my kids give me the silent treatment. But they made sure to inform my grandmother how much of an ass I'd been, and listening to them re-tell it from their perspective hit me so hard I felt like I was going to crumble right there in front of them, which made me want to run. But the only place I wanted to go was back to you." He lifts his hands to cradle my jaw, swiping away the last of my tears with his thumbs. "Except I wasn't sure you'd forgive me."

"Of course I forgive you. But you can see how you created half of those problems for yourself, right?" His lips push together into a decidedly unhappy line, so I consider letting everything go after the whopper of a day he's had, but then I remember Amelia's words about moving forward how you mean to go on. To soften my words, I kiss his lips gently first. "You leaning on me, I can take. But you attacking me with no explanation, isn't okay."

"I didn't *mean* to attack you."

"I know. But if we're going to share our lives together, I want to be your anchor, not your whipping post."

"Jesus, woman, you're killing me here."

"I'm sorry. That's not my intention. I just want us to be on the same side of the divide, you know?"

"I do know, and you're right. About all of it."

"Oh, yeah?"

"Yeah."

"A girl could get used to hearing that."

The corners of his mouth tip up. "Are we good then?" he asks, his expression hopeful. "If I promise not to put on a repeat performance?"

"Please," I say, leaning in to kiss his lips. "You know perfectly well that I'm going to cry again at some point and you're going to get mad."

He surprises me by nodding. "Yeah, okay. But I promise to be more careful. I love you so much."

I kiss him again. "I could *definitely* get used to hearing that."

"I love you so much," he repeats, making me giggle. "Am I allowed to drag you into the bedroom, caveman style, and make this whole thing up to you now?"

"I don't know. Depends on what *caveman style* involves. There won't be any dragging me around by my hair, which, by the way, you have yet to notice that I got cut."

He studies my hair. "It looks the same."

I push at his shoulder in mock outrage. "I'll have you know I got at least a quarter of an inch taken off."

"Well, maybe it'll be more noticeable when you aren't wearing any clothes." He pushes forward to the edge of the couch and then stands with me wrapped around his waist, carrying me to the bedroom.

"Scott, I'm too heavy for you to be hauling around like this."

He maneuvers us through my bedroom door. "Sorry, but it's a necessary component of my caveman style." He settles us on the bed and lets his weight push me into the mattress.

"Any more components I should know about?" I ask cheekily. "Maybe some ropes?"

He laughs. "You'd like that, wouldn't you? Such a dirty girl, my Opal."

Any reply I may have had is cut off by his mouth on mine.

# Chapter Six

## Scott

After the upheaval of that Monday afternoon, the next couple of weeks are peaceful in comparison. I don't hear from Jorgie, but I'm good with that – for now. Honestly, his level of self-involvement is staggering; he endangered my crew, embarrassed me with my boss, *and* threw the job I got for him in my face. But believe me, I know Jorgie's not the only one who has some growing up to do. His actions may have spurred me on, but it was me who tore a hole in the fabric of my relationship with Ellie. So far, the stitches are holding . . . I'd even go so far as to say they've bound us more firmly together. It's a funny thing love, how it ransacks your soul, looking for those emotions that normally just simmer and brings them to a full boil. One would think I'd go out of my way to avoid the intensity. But no. When it comes to Ellie, I irrationally embrace it wholeheartedly.

It's with these thoughts rolling around in my head that the girls and I cross the Stanford campus on foot to the stadium for Ellie's graduation. On her advice, we parked closer to where we'll end the day than where we'll start. I don't mind. It's a nice walk. In their best dresses, under a sunny June sky, the girls skip ahead on the sidewalk, chattering away with excitement and I couldn't be more pleased with my decision to bring them.

Once we're in the actual stadium, the girls are even more excited, especially with the pomp and circumstance of the initial stages of the ceremony. But as the weather gets warmer and the speeches become more tedious, their patience wanes. This isn't unexpected though and I distract them with the game of quietly speculating where in the sea of black gowns Ellie is sitting. Then we move on to what they're going to study in college, like it's a given that they'll be going. I figure it can't hurt to put the idea in their heads now while they're so young. They've asked Ellie about it a few times and they always listen carefully to every piece of information she gives them. I'm not sure if it's the subject they're enthralled with or Ellie herself, but I'm not going to complain either way. Predictably, Carmen and Rosa want to be kindergarten teachers, but Daniela informs me she's going to be an actor. I love how she seems to mull it over when I say that would make her a drama major.

By the time we file out of the stadium, their energy is flagging. After the trek back to where the diploma ceremony for the Political Science graduates will be held, I sit them down in our chairs and open Carmen's little backpack to hand out granola bars in the hopes of forestalling any outbursts brought on by being tired and hungry.

Closer to the stage, I spy Ellie's parents and then in the section for the graduates, I see Ellie herself, standing and waving at us. We all wave back and the way I can feel my smile to the very depths of my heart almost embarrasses me.

Thankfully this ceremony isn't quite as long as the commencement. When it ends, I watch Ellie briefly touch base with her parents before she makes her way over to us. She throws her arms around me and we squeeze each other tight.

"I did it," she whispers excitedly in my ear.

I bury my nose in her neck, soaking her up. "Congratulations, sweetness."

When she pulls away, I'm surprised to see her eyes are bright with emotion, so I pull her back against my chest and hold her close for another moment. "I'm so happy for you," I tell her as she nods her forehead against my collar bone.

"Ellie?" I hear.

We look down at the three animated faces tipped up at us.

"Oh, you guys," Ellie gushes. "You look so pretty."

Their smiles get impossibly wider.

"Did you hear us clap for you when they called your name?" Daniela asks. "We clapped as loud as we could."

Ellie leans over to pull Daniela in for a hug. "I did hear you. I loved it. It was like having my very own cheering section." She doles out hugs for Rosa and then Carmen too. "Were you guys terribly bored?"

"No, we were good," Rosa announces.

"They *were* good," I confirm, liking Rosa's diplomatic answer.

"In that case we should go get some lunch." She looks to me. "Maybe your dad will take us to Chipotle since it's my favorite."

"I think that can be arranged."

"Ellie!" a voice calls and we all turn to watch a woman in heels and a classy black dress approach.

"Soph? What's wrong?"

"Nothing's wrong," she says sweetly.

Ellie doesn't answer the woman with words, just facial expressions that they trade back and forth for long moments.

If I'm not mistaken, they're annoyed with each other. It's actually a fairly entertaining display and I'm on the verge of laughing when Rosa tugs on my sleeve.

"Who's that?" she whispers in Spanish.

"I think," I say in English, "that this is Ellie's sister, Sophie."

Ellie turns to me and I catch the tail end of an eye roll. "Yes, this is my very nosy sister, Sophie. Sophie, this is Daniela, Rosa, Carmen . . . and Scott."

Sophie greets the girls warmly. "It's very nice to meet you, ladies." Then she gives me a cool once-over.

*Uh oh.* I smile hesitantly. "Nice to meet you." It comes out almost sounding like a question.

When she doesn't respond, Ellie says, "Knock it off, Soph." Turning to me, she explains apologetically, "My sister seems to think I need a bodyguard."

Not sure if I'd buy this girl as a bodyguard. With her long, honey-blond hair and bright blue eyes, she has a decidedly innocent air about her. But anyone who wants to protect Ellie is okay in my books.

"You don't have to worry about El," I say lightly, trying to be charming. "She calls me out every time I deserve it."

Sophie's reserved manner lets up slightly. "Good to know. Though I'd prefer she didn't need to call you out at all." For good measure, she follows up the reprimand with a piercing look.

Okay, so two things are clear to me here. One, Ellie tells her sister a lot about our relationship, and two, I really like this woman. "Yeah, that makes two of us. I'm working on it."

Her attitude warms further . . . and right there, in front of me is Ellie's smile on another woman. Definitely sisters. Though she's not as tall or willowy.

"Are you coming to lunch with us?" Daniela asks Sophie. "We're hungry."

I cringe at Daniela's directness, but Sophie seems to find it charming. "I'm not, no. I'm sure I'll see you another time though." Then to us, she says, "You two I'll see later for dinner, right?" Strangely, it sounds more like a warning than a reminder, but then again, I know how much Ellie is dreading going to this thing tonight at her parents' house.

My girl's face becomes tight with tension, so I slip my hand into hers in a show of silent support. She's hinted at cancelling a few times, but so far I've kept her convinced that we should go. Maybe I'm projecting my need for my family onto Ellie, but I want her to have a relationship with her parents and siblings.

"Yeah," Ellie says, resigned. "We'll be there."

I watch with amusement as Ellie's index finger moves toward the doorbell for the second time, then jerks back again as if repelled by an invisible force field.

"Have I already apologized in advance?" she whines.

"You have," I tell her. She's worried about her mother's attitude, but I'm more interested in the fact that she would ring the doorbell at her own house. I guess it's been a while since she's lived here . . . but still. "I'll be fine, Opal . . . unless, of course, you don't want to go in because you're embarrassed by me."

She fixes me with a hard stare and I feel my lips curve into a grin. It's possible I'm baiting her.

"I'm not even going to dignify that with a response," she replies haughtily.

"Then stop worrying." For her sake, on the surface, I'm the embodiment of laid-back, teasing nonchalance. "I've got your back, you've got mine. Piece of cake." But inside I'm not quite so sure of myself.

My little speech inspires her to square her shoulders and deliberately press the doorbell. "You're right."

"I know."

Her mild exasperation is interrupted when one side of the double doors is opened by a woman in a maid's uniform. My attention doesn't remain with her for long though because Sophie comes scurrying toward us, her heels clicking on the marble floor.

"Why are you so late?" she accuses, pulling her sister into a hug. "Hi, Scott."

"Hey."

"Who's here?" Ellie demands, pulling away without a word of greeting.

"Dad and Matty, of course, and Chris and Evan got here a few minutes ago."

"Wives?"

"No," Sophie says, her mouth holding onto the O shape, her eyes widening, like that's significant.

"So no kids?" Ellie squeaks.

Sophie shakes her head.

"Where's Mom?"

"She went upstairs when Chris and Evan arrived."

"Okay, so we go in now."

I snort. "Why does it sound like you guys are planning some kind of tactical mission?"

Ellie pushes out a withering noise before she informs me, "Because we are. The good news is that it's brothers only. The bad news is that it's brothers only."

"What? That makes no sense."

"With no wives or nieces," Sophie explains, "there'll be fewer chances for a big family spat. But also fewer chances for distractions, which means you'll be more of a target."

I feel my eyebrows tick up. "A target for what?"

"Don't worry," Ellie says seriously. "Soph is going to run interference, aren't you?"

Sophie's gaze lands on me as if she's taking my measure. "Fine. Since my sister really likes you. I'm warning you, though, if you continue to make her cry, you'll seriously regret it." Turning on her heel, she leaves us standing there.

"I thought you said she was a people-pleaser," I say incredulously.

"Ignore her. We've got bigger problems." She slips her hand around my elbow and starts us walking.

I stop her from following her sister into a room off the main hall. "Hey," I say. "We're going to be fine, no matter what. Okay?"

Some of the stiffness drains from her posture. "Yeah, okay. I need to calm down."

Nodding, I lean in to kiss her cheek. In her heels, we're almost eye-to-eye and her proximity sends an unexpected dose of attraction arrowing down to where I least need it considering the circumstances. "Let's do this," I murmur, "before I haul you into the nearest coat closet."

Her face lights up. "Can I take a rain check?"

"There's the woman of the hour!"

Ellie's father comes out and all thoughts of clandestine trysts are obliterated.

"Hi, Dad."

"Sweetheart, you look wonderful." He kisses Ellie's cheek and she relaxes a bit more, which in turn, eases the abrupt uptick in my nerves. "Scott, nice to see you again." He extends his hand and I shake it.

"Thanks, you too."

"Come on then. Ellie's brothers are eager to meet her new beau."

We follow her dad into what I assume is the living room. But *living room* doesn't quite cut it because it's enormous, with a high ceiling and giant windows that are covered by vertical blinds. Everything about the décor screams money in a minimalist kind of way, including the uncomfortable-looking black leather furniture that's arranged around the room and contrasts sharply, yet tastefully, with the much lighter walls and flooring.

Her siblings stand as we approach. Her three brothers are all tall and dark-haired like Ellie and their father, and they greet me politely with handshakes. Although some of my irritation with the high ball glasses in their hands lessens when they appear legitimately happy to see their sister, I don't get why they're drinking in front of her.

Almost straightaway they begin teasing Ellie about how it's taken her eight years to finish her undergrad, so I'm able to sit back and observe. Chris and Evan, her two older half-brothers, are obviously close; they're both lawyers and they work with their father. The middle child, Matt, who's almost a physical carbon copy of the father, gets ribbed for being the only one of them who doesn't have a college degree now. He takes it in stride with a casualness that I recognize as the same unyielding self-esteem that surrounds Ellie. In fact, the four eldest Summers children ooze charm and confidence. Which leaves the youngest, Sophie, as the odd man out. Truthfully, she sticks out like a sore thumb. Not only is she the only blonde, but she's also a lot shorter. And her people-pleasing tendencies become much more apparent as the conversation continues. She expertly referees it all, nudging it away from potential sore spots, while encouraging neutral topics wherever possible.

"Where's Amelia?" Ellie asks after a while.

"She went to check on the caterers before you got here," Sophie says, then, noticing the hostility on Ellie's face, quickly adds, "But don't worry, she's not working. I'm sure she'll be back any minute."

Ellie gets to her feet. "Well, we're going to make sure," she announces, pulling me up. "She's supposed to be a guest tonight."

In the foyer, she blows out a loud breath.

"You okay?"

"Yeah. I just always feel so awkward around them."

"That was awkward? You seemed fine to me."

"Good," she says absently. "Yeah, good. Usually if the conversation stays light, it's fine. I was worried if we stayed much longer, my brothers would start in on the politics, and I'd lose my head. Again."

"Your family talks politics?"

She finds my skepticism quaint. "Oh, yeah. Big time. And suffice it to say, we have differing viewpoints. I'm not only the black sheep of the family, I'm the bleeding-heart liberal. Basically, they all think I'm an idiot."

"I'm sure that's not true."

The tight grin she throws my way tells me she appreciates the support even if I'm as far off the mark as I can get. "Come on, I'll show you my old room."

We go up the left side of the double staircase and I can't help but be intimidated. This place is insane with its shining marble floors, giant chandelier, actual artwork on the walls, and not a speck of dust anywhere. "I thought we were going to the kitchen."

"I changed my mind." With an expression that strikes me as almost scheming, she leads me down a wide hallway with closed doors on either side. Opening the third door on the left, she steps into the most generic bedroom I've ever seen. "This was your room?" I ask doubtfully.

"Yeah. It doesn't look anything like it did when I lived here though. As soon as I went to live in the dorms, it was decontaminated." She walks in and turns a slow circle as if picturing it how it once was. "At one point, I painted the walls black."

Shoving my hands into the pockets of my dress pants, I lean against the door frame to watch her. "Your parents went along with that?"

She scoffs, wandering farther into the room, which is at least the size of my grandmother's living room. "It's not like I asked for permission."

Grimacing, I follow her, trying and failing to imagine a scenario in which my girls would do something like that. "You really were a nightmare teenager, weren't you?"

She nods. "I really was. I went through every rebellious phase imaginable." At the window, she trails her hand along the heavy beige drapes. "During my emo/goth phase, these were black too."

"To go with the walls?"

"Exactly. That phase got cut short when my mom threatened to send me back to private school. Then for a while I hung out with the stoners, but they were so mellow that I got bored."

My bark of laughter draws her smile.

"I was also an All-American girl slash cheerleader."

Shit, is it wrong that my dick swells slightly? "That doesn't sound very rebellious."

She tilts her head in begrudging agreement. "I guess not. Neither was my nerd phase." Amused by the memory, she tells me she wore fake horn-rimmed glasses, though she admits she kept her plaid skirts uber-short and paired them with combat boots. Yeah, this is doing nothing to discourage my growing arousal.

On the other side of the room, she pushes open another door. "You had your own bathroom?" I say, my disbelief bordering on accusation. "That's . . . not right." I come up behind her to find double sinks and a huge glass shower. "You don't know torture until you've had to share one bathroom with three sisters."

She hops up on the counter and lets her eyes slide down my body. They come to rest on my rapidly tightening groin. She licks her lips before she's kind enough to mention the increasing state of affairs in my dress pants. "What's going on there, Scott?"

Drifting forward, I lean back against the wall across from the sink, not bothering to deny anything. What would be the point? The material of these pants does little to mask the problem. "That's your doing. Filling my head with thoughts of you in short skirts."

Her lip curls slightly with disgust. "Don't tell me, you have a cheerleader fetish?"

I shrug. "I'm not opposed to cheerleaders, but I think it was the combat boots and the glasses that did it for me."

"Really?" She draws out the word, and then licks her lips again, the little minx. "Can I tell you a secret?" I blink as she very deliberately starts to spread her legs. "Scott?"

"Huh?"

The hem of the dress only allows her to open her knees so far. "The secret," she prompts. "Do you want to hear it?"

"Yeah, uh, sure." She lowers her hands and starts to inch the dress up. My mouth goes dry. This shit is definitely inappropriate in her parents' house . . . especially with images of her as a teenager filing through my dirty mind.

"You're not paying attention," she pouts, and I wrench my gaze up to hers. "Would it help to know my secret has to do with you and getting myself off?"

*Getting . . . say what now?* The naked hunger in her expression lodges my unease deeper in my gut, but my dick responds to it with keen enthusiasm. *What is she doing?*

The tops of her thighs are now visible, but still she continues to raise the hem, slowly rocking her hips back and forth to free more of the material from beneath her. And then my mind blanks when she's exposed enough that it becomes obvious she's not wearing any panties. I get one hell of an eyeful of plump, pink pussy, spread open and glistening under the lights. *Holy. Fuck.*

I immediately push off the wall to close the distance between us.

"Uh, uh, uh," she says firmly, holding up an index finger to stop me. "Back against the wall, Scott. This is my fantasy."

Reluctantly, I settle back as my brain struggles with what to focus on first, her bare pussy, the word *fantasy*, or – god, help me – how she lifts her hand to her mouth and deliberately inserts her index and middle fingers between her lips.

The gentle sound of them being withdrawn from her mouth sends my already pounding blood in one direction and one direction only. My balls throb and my dick begins to strain against my zipper in earnest. Of course the situation only gets worse when she lowers her hand and makes contact with that luscious pussy of hers.

Watching her play with herself reduces any misgivings I have about the time and place to little more than a far-off whisper, effectively freeing my conscience to allow my own fingers to run along the length of my cock.

"That's it," she moans, placing a hand behind her on the counter to lean back and give herself better access. "That's my fantasy."

I freeze. Damn, my brain cells are barely working. "What?" I croak. "What is?"

She curls her fingers into her slit. "You," she breathes. "Touching yourself, jacking yourself while I watch."

Sucking in a surprised breath, I try my best to organize my thoughts despite what's laid out in front of me. *She wants me to whack off? In front of her?* What in the ever-loving . . . this girl is incredible.

"Is that right?" I make a show of dragging my fingers along my dick a few times before I undo my belt and the button of my pants. "This what you want to see?" I ask, trying to keep my voice steady as I leisurely lower the zipper.

"Yes," she rasps, the heat behind her half-masted lids leaving me rock-hard within the uncomfortable confines of my underwear. To ease the strain, I arrange myself to lie diagonally toward my hip, but keep myself covered.

She pulls her now shiny fingers free of her opening and returns them to her clit. "I love the idea. Me watching you. You watching me. Getting off. Together."

Yeah, I'm definitely onboard with that. I pull my dress shirt out of my pants to get it out of the way. Then slowly, I undo each and every button, starting from the top and working my way down, never once taking my eyes from her.

"Oh, this gets better and better," she whispers, her hips twisting slightly on the countertop, I'm assuming because she hits a particularly sweet spot.

Then to tease her . . . or is it me . . . I run a single fingertip up and down my length through the opening created by my gaping fly. Shivers run down my spine from the gentle friction and the sight of the languid circles my girl is rubbing into her clit.

"I've shown you mine, Scott. The least you can do is show me yours." The inveigling command of her tone does weird things to my stomach, and the fear that's been running in the back of my mind that her father is about to walk through the door disappears completely. My dick is so hard I doubt anything besides coming would bring me any relief at this point. I just continue to drag my fingers up and down, up and down though.

"Fine, if you're not interested," she says sullenly, pulling her fingers away and starting to close her legs.

"Keep them open."

She glares, but obeys.

"Wider," I order. In fact . . . "Put your heels up. I want to see everything."

"I'm not giving you something for nothing."

I feel my lips pull into a smirk. *That's my girl.* Widening my stance, I push the band of my briefs down to free my raging hard-on and then reach in to cup my balls and bring them forward. Slouching back against the wall, I lift my hands away in an *Is this what you wanted?* gesture, letting my heavy dick struggle with gravity on its own.

Her only answer is the clatter of her shoes falling to the floor. Lifting her heels to the edge of the counter, she lets her knees fall farther open. The vista, which now includes a glimpse of her back passage, improves tenfold.

She traces her slippery pussy. "I want one of your hands wrapped around that incredible cock of yours, Scott."

Shit, no matter how much I like to be the ones giving the orders, I'm not about to quibble. The familiar, rough feel of my palm contrasts sharply with the forbidden context of our surroundings as I give myself a decent squeeze. I stroke once, twice from root to tip. My head falls back against the wall, momentarily overwhelmed by the foreign feel of doing this with her eyes crawling all over me. Despite the flush tinged with the tiniest bit of shame that's creeping up my neck, I have no desire to stop what I'm doing. It feels too good.

Ellie's breathing picks up, calling my attention back to her. I watch, fascinated, as she works her pussy, alternating between circling her clit and sliding two fingers into her herself. Despite the lack of any kind of lube, I have to hold back from jerking myself to a quick end, a situation that's not helped by my mind supplying images of me replacing her hand with my mouth; my tongue inside of her, my lips suckling her clit, my teeth nibbling at her. So fucking hot. And all that is before I notice how her voracious gaze is locked on my own hand, which has paused its stroking to smear the precome over the head with my thumb. The combination sends a bolt of lust through my balls which are already as tight as drums. I go back to stroking, harder now.

"You close?" I groan. "I'm close. So fucking close."

A whimper falls from her lips and punches through me. I know that sound, know what it means. Her head falls back on her shoulders.

"No," I gasp. "Let me watch you."

Her chin comes back down and our eyes meet for a split second before I watch the bliss take over her features. Like a toppling domino, she sets me off. I have just enough sense left to angle myself to spill into my free hand instead of making a mess everywhere.

Shaking off the stupor doesn't take long, mere seconds probably, because that was only the appetizer and I want my main course now. Shoving off the wall, I lean into her ear. "Do not move, Opal."

The smug triumph on my girl's lips holds me captive as I wash my hands, towel them dry, and then get a condom out of my wallet. With practiced ease, I roll it down my still hard shaft.

She scoots closer to the edge of the counter and I notch myself at her entrance. Her knees grip my ribs and I take hold of her hair at the nape of her neck. "This is going to be hard and fast," I whisper. "And I want you silent."

"Shut up and get on wi–"

I shove myself deep, and her sharp, surprised intake of breath becomes a drawn-out exhalation of pure wantonness; it's music to my ears. I set a brutal pace that's fueled by the twisted feelings she's drawn out of me over the last ten minutes; the strange indignity of jacking off for her, the guilt of lusting after a teenage Ellie, the mortification of screwing her in her parents' house. But fuck if it doesn't make for another incredible climax for both of us.

We're panting and floating on a high by the time we're done. I barely remember flushing the condom or righting my clothes. Of course, when who's downstairs waiting for us re-registers in my brain, I sober up pretty quickly.

We're leaving the bathroom when Ellie sighs. "Happy graduation day to me."

"Elsabeth Frances Summers. Did you plan that whole thing?"

"Maybe," she says, smiling, still a bit loopy. "But I needed some kind of incentive to show up here."

Pulling her close, I kiss her temple. "We'll eat dinner and run, okay?"

"Okay."

As we head down the stairs, hand in hand, I add, "And you'd better lose the doe-eyes if you don't want everyone to know what we just did."

She swats at me. "Doe-eyes, my ass."

But her brother, Matt, takes one look at us as we re-enter the room and chuckles. "Did you find Amelia?" he asks, his tone all mock innocence as if he knows exactly what we've spent the last twenty minutes doing.

"Did I hear my name?"

A small, older lady walks in and heads directly for Ellie. *"Mi amor,"* she says warmly as Ellie bends to kiss her cheek. "And you must be the young man I've heard so much about," she tells me in Spanish, gesturing for me to lower my own cheek. "It's nice to finally meet you."

She addresses me in Spanish, so I answer in kind. "Same here. Ellie has nothing but wonderful things to say about you."

"Oh ho, the plot thickens," Matt drawls, and it takes me a second to figure out that he's not referring to what I said, but that I said it in Spanish.

I watch Amelia give him a sardonic look, but he responds with a mischievous wink. "What do you know about this guy, Amelia? Is he good enough for my little sister?"

"I know you'd do well not to interfere in your sister's love life," she says dryly, though her affection for Matt is obvious.

"*Love* life seems to be exactly the right word," Evan says, waving his high ball glass around. "It goes well with all the little red hearts that are floating magically in the air around Ellie's head."

Ellie scoffs but no one notices because Matt's next statement draws everyone's attention. "You know what? I'm calling it, right here, right now," he says loudly. "Married in one year," he appears to think it over, "and three months."

"Oh my god," Ellie sputters derisively.

"I'll take that action," her eldest brother Chris says, talking right over her. "I'm calling two years from now."

"What the hell, you guys?" Ellie protests from beside me, while Amelia laughs, clearly enjoying herself.

Smirking knowingly, Evan says, "I'm going with less than a year."

"Be reasonable," her dad quips. "I'll go with eighteen months."

Sophie claps excitedly. "I'm going with –"

"No. Uh uh," Matt stops her. "The chances of you having insider information is too great."

"What?!" Sophie and Ellie say in unison.

"Your brother's right," her dad of all people says. "You're out." And then he turns to me. "But it appears that you're in. Welcome to the family, son."

"Don't listen to them," Ellie tells me, shaking her head like her entire family have lost their marbles. "Since, we've only been together for a few months," she intones sarcastically, "you don't have to marry me."

If this unexpected teasing hadn't lit such a fire in my girl's demeanor, I'd probably be freaking out. But since the whole scenario reeks of the same kind of playful harassment that my family dishes out, there's a grin on my face. "Uh, I'll keep that in mind." Apparently, that was the right thing to say, because in response, I get a glowing smile from my girl and a few slaps on the back and a shoulder shove from her brothers.

"All right, give him some space," Ellie instructs.

"What's going on?"

We all turn and there's Ellie's mom, tall and elegant, her beauty masked by the same cool reserve I recognize from the charity gala.

Ellie's father is still chuckling as he goes to his wife. "Nothing at all. Just some joshing between us boys." He places a hand to the small of her back, drawing her further into the room.

"Hello, Ellie," her mom says, while Sophie nods encouragingly in my peripheral vision. All I know is that she's not using *Piper*, so it's a win. Something Ellie also notices because there's not a trace of irony when she responds.

"Hi, Mom. Thanks for doing this for me."

She reaches out to rub her daughter's arm awkwardly. "Of course."

"You remember Scott, right?"

I swear, the whole room stills for a moment. "I do."

"Thanks for having me, Mrs. Summers," I say politely.

She nods, and then turns to Amelia. "Do you know what's holding dinner up?"

"Amelia's not working tonight," Ellie says frostily, making her mother press her lips together until they almost disappear.

"I suppose *I'll* go find out what's going on then."

As she turns to leave, the woman in the maid's uniform appears in the doorway, "Dinner is ready, ma'am."

Ellie's mom lets out a very unladylike noise that rings with disgust and is overlapped by a snicker from one of Ellie's brothers. "Very well, thank you." She draws in a deep breath as if to fortify herself. "Shall we?"

We file out in pairs and behind us, I hear her two oldest brothers laughing. "You paid the caterer to call her ma'am, didn't you?"

"Maybe."

Over her shoulder, Ellie whispers with a bit of glee, "You guys are so bad."

"What?" I whisper. "I don't get it."

"Mom doesn't like being reminded of her age," she says like she can't quite believe how juvenile her brothers are, but neither can she resist enjoying the results.

Dinner is surprisingly fine; the food is good, if a little bland for me, and there are no insults or heated debates like I'm expecting. Amelia tells stories about Ellie's constant search for trouble when she was little while her mother's lips remain mostly sealed. Ellie's dad and her older brothers talk about some kind of patent case they're working on, which has Matt meeting my eyes as if to say welcome to my mind-numbing world. And Sophie supervises the entire table; she asks all the right questions to keep the multiple conversations going and she quashes any topic that hints at discord. There's a bit of a tiff between Sophie and her mother, though, when we toast with sparkling apple juice instead of champagne. I can only shake my head at that. What mother wouldn't support her daughter's desire to stay sober?

All in all, it turns out to be a pleasant experience . . . until the real show starts after dinner when the doorbell rings and some guy is admitted to the living room. "Sorry for my tardiness, everyone."

Ellie's mom floats forward with her arms extended. "Peter! So nice you could join us."

From beside me, Ellie grits out, "Oh. My. God."

"What's wrong?" I ask, but Ellie doesn't hear me, or she chooses not to, because she takes a few steps and it's her mother that she addresses.

"You have *got* to be kidding me."

Sophie comes up beside me. "Who's that?" she asks, sounding panicked.

"No idea," I tell her.

"Ellie," her mother says imperiously. "There's no need to be rude. Peter is here to say hello and congratulate you on your milestone."

"Bullshit."

The horror on her mother's face would be comical if Sophie wasn't getting so worked up with her whispered refrain of, "No, no, no, no, no."

"Ellie! That language is uncalled for."

Ellie's hands plant themselves on her hips. I certainly wouldn't want to be in her mother's shoes at the moment. I've faced her daughter down before and I'm very familiar with how intimidating she can be. "Oh, I think it is, Mom. Why would you invite him," she jabs her finger at the guy in the doorway, "when I came here tonight with a man I'm in a committed relationship with."

"Don't be silly. I'm simply keeping your options open."

Ellie pulls in a deep breath and holds it.

"Dad," Sophie hisses. "Aren't you going to do something?"

The poor guy seems resigned. "Such as?"

Ellie finds her voice, which comes out low and cutting. "I don't want or need your options."

"It's my job as your mother to stop you from making the biggest mistake of your life."

"Is that a joke?!"

"He's not good enough for you!"

Well, that escalated quickly, I think to myself, taking in the wildly sincere, yet very offensive gleam in her mother's eyes.

"No, Mom, I'm not good enough for him."

"That's preposterous. He's a *laborer*," she says like it's akin to *murderer*.

"That's right, mother. He works construction."

Despite their truth, Ellie's words are launched with so much gusto that I flinch. "Geez," I grouse under my breath. "She could at least mention I'm the boss."

"She told me," her dad says quietly. "Ellie speaks very highly of you."

*She does?* The sting of my girl's words lessens.

"And you know what else?" Ellie says loudly, ready with the next salvo. "He's Latino, and he has three children, all of whom have different mothers."

Her dad turns an aghast expression on me. "That, she didn't mention."

I grin, suddenly recognizing Ellie as a child provoking her parent on purpose. Fine, she can throw me under the bus. "*Technically* it's true," I say.

At my attitude, he realizes there's more to the story, so he relaxes.

91

"Have you lost your mind?" her mother screeches.

"I'm not finished! He's also five years younger than I am."

I almost laugh at the way she says it, as if to say *How's that for inappropriate?*

"And you're proud of this, Piper?!"

"Do not call me that," Ellie says from between clenched teeth. "And no, I'm telling you this because *I know* he couldn't be more wrong for me."

I hear a chuckle from Matt. "It's like déjà vu. It's ten years ago and Ellie's brought home the guy most likely to make Mom crazy."

"Our sister has returned to the fold," Chris says cryptically, but then I'm yanked back to Ellie's next words.

"But even if we're completely wrong for each other, I *love* him. And he loves me. Scott accepts me and my flaws, and I do the same for him. And we don't need your permission or your approval to live our life."

Beside me, her father murmurs, "She's fighting back." I frown because he sounds surprised. *Since when does El not fight back?*

"Scott is a good man," she continues. "He likes that I'm idealistic, he's not put off by my past, and he doesn't parade me around like a show pony. I couldn't ask for better."

"You couldn't ask for better?" her mother mocks. "Please, *Ellie*. Nobody wants to live like a pauper."

"A pauper?" Ellie scoffs. "First of all, I've lived around *this* kind of money my whole life," she gestures to the room, "and it's never brought me a single minute of peace. And second of all, being middle class is not a crime."

Okay, so it's possible my girl is upgrading me. Not that I'm going to interrupt to mention that I probably wouldn't qualify as middle class. But damn, her words make me feel pretty good.

Her mother's not finished making her points though. "It may not be a crime, but it's not what I want for my daughter."

"Okay," Ellie says calmly. "But I'm not you, Mom. I can take care of myself. I can build a career and make my own money. I don't have to depend on a man to support me."

Indignation radiates from her mother. "Are you saying that I shouldn't have married your father because he had an established source of income?"

"No, I'm saying that since you loved him, it didn't matter if he had an established source of income. You were free to make your own choices and I want the same."

"You're making a mistake."

"That may be. But it's mine to make," Ellie says flatly. "I came here tonight because I'd like to have a relationship with my family, but if you can't respect Scott, let alone me, we're done."

Sophie, who now must sense impending doom, opens her mouth to say something, but her father puts a quelling hand to her elbow; he's as interested in his wife's response as the rest of us.

The icy mask her mother always keeps in place begins to waver. "But he's . . ." Her voice trails off as if searching for the right word to fill in the blank.

"He's the love of my life," Ellie finishes.

# Chapter Seven

## Ellie

I meant every word. Scott *is* the love of my life. And I'll be damned if I'll stand here and listen to my mother badmouth him.

I've never been sure of who I am; whether it was the high-school rebel, or the perfect college girlfriend, or the too shiny party-girl, I've never been comfortable in my own skin – until now. And I know that's not *because of* Scott . . . but because he's given me a place at his side where I'm able to breathe freely. I like who I am when I'm with him. I don't have to put on a show for anyone, I don't have to censor myself, and I certainly don't have to let my mother bully me.

So I stand my ground and watch my mother's stiff posture wilt slightly, not with defeat – my mother would never surrender – but with resignation.

"I want the record to show that you're making a mistake," she says with a little harrumph at the end.

I cross my arms. "Not good enough."

"Fine. I want the record to show that *I think* you're making a mistake."

Surprise pierces the obstinate expression on her face when I move toward her. "Give me a hug, mother."

"Really, Pi–" She stops the name from leaving her mouth, but she sidesteps my attempts to embrace her. "Really, Ellie. Your behavior tonight is–"

My dad interjects, "Her behavior tells me our girl is back on her feet."

"Back on her feet?" my mom says, her tone bordering, once again, on outrage. "Because she's choosing a man who's beneath her?"

My jaw sets. I've been ducking her blows for years now, doing my best not to engage with her, or if I did engage, it was on a superficial level. But at this point, staying out of her way is no longer good enough. It's not *me*. Well, at least not the *me* of late. My dad's right, I am back on my feet. And if I want to continue with them firmly planted on the ground, I'm going to have to meet her head-on.

"I love you, Mom," I tell her quietly. "But I'm a grown woman and I won't allow you to belittle the man I love."

"I just want what's best for you."

Holding back my retort of '*you mean what's best for you?*' I go with, "I know. But since we can't agree on what that is, I need to know that you'll respect my choices. I'm offering you an olive branch here. If you don't want it, say the word and we'll leave."

A slight crease forms between her brows, another indication her habitual armor is slowly coming apart at the seams. That doesn't stop her from making one more attempt to make me see sense. "His family," her head jerks in the direction of Peter, "has *hundreds* of millions."

I remain unchanged.

Her shoulders slump. "You've always been the most difficult child."

This time when I approach, she doesn't pull away. Squeezing her tight, I tell her the truth, "I learned from the best."

"Okay, buddy." We all watch as Chris takes hold of a very nonplussed Peter and turns him in the direction of the door. "Smelly Ellie has spoken. You're out. The pauper's in."

Matt starts laughing. "Smelly Ellie. Now that's a name I haven't heard in *years*."

I look to Scott and the love and bemusement I find there reels me to him. Sinking into the comforting safety of his arms, I whisper, "Should we get out of here?"

"Sure. But first I have to hear the Smelly Ellie story," he says, chuckling softly, moving me closer to where my siblings are mocking my childhood self. I don't mind though, I loved eight-year-old Smelly Ellie. She didn't let anyone hold her back.

In more ways than one, I have Scott to thank for giving me back my family. If he'd let me cancel the dinner party, I'd never have stood up to my mother, and without the need to protect him, who knows how long I would have continued to side-step the woman. The possibility of now having a warmer relationship with her appeals to me more than I could have anticipated.

One thing that becomes very apparent over the next few months, though, are the differences between my family and Scott's family. There may be the same amount of teasing in Scott's house, but there's a lot less of a tendency to jump to indignant conclusions. It's not even that they forgive each other more easily, it's that there's never the assumption of malicious intent. Passive-aggressive behaviour just doesn't come up. It's wonderful, and over the summer I get to experience it every Sunday after work when I'm invited for dinner. This sense of belonging is only amplified when the girls and I fall into the habit of my reading aloud to them in Spanish after dinner in our quest to improve their vocabulary, usually with Scott in attendance.

And Scott and I? Things have been good. So good. Not exactly smooth sailing, but nothing like our bigger bumps in the road. We're learning the ins and outs of each other's personality. Yes, he gets annoyed when he finds day-old dirty dishes in my sink or a wet towel on the bathroom floor, but by the same token, I get annoyed by how uptight he can be about things that don't matter to me. I don't, however, complain when he washes and vacuums out my car, or when he solves the mystery of the check engine light, which turns out to be cracked gas cap and is easily fixed. A girl should know when to be suitably grateful.

We've found that rough patches are best ironed out the old-fashioned way, with S-E-X. Make-up sex, angry sex, rough sex, celebratory sex, languid making-love sex, quickies, marathons – it's all delicious. And instead of becoming routine, it only gets better and better.

With my personal life going so well, I can almost ignore my growing worry over my professional life. Almost. Despite my best efforts to find myself a 'real' job, by August I'm still working at the cafe. I've been offered a few low-paying internships locally, but since I'm not a fresh-faced twenty-one year old, I decide to hold out for something more substantial. It's hard to tell if I'm just postponing the necessary, painful first steps of a career or if I'm being smart. At least it's only a risk to my sanity and not my bank account.

My patience finally pays off on a random Tuesday in August when an email pops up on my phone while I'm sitting in the break room at work. It's from an organization called *the Settlement Project* which provides assistance to asylum seekers. They're requesting a copy of my CV if I'm still looking for employment. Holy shit! A combination of joy and nerves hits me like a one-two punch.

I immediately send Scott an emoji-laden text to convey my excitement. Even though he's working and probably won't be able to answer me right away, having someone to share the news with makes the situation all the more real.

As soon as I get home, I start my research on the company. It turns out to be a non-profit with a very healthy operating budget that does work all over California, Arizona, New Mexico and Texas. Without hesitation, I sit my ass down and compose what I hope is a kick-ass cover letter and send it along with my CV that very same night. I don't even care that the invitation didn't include a specific job description. The company is legitimate and my days of being picky are done. Decently paid or not, if they offer me a job, I'm taking it. If I can't survive on what they pay me, I'll ask my dad for a loan.

The next day, I receive a reply asking me to choose from a variety of available days and times for an interview, and by Friday, I'm parked at a respectable strip mall in San Jose, taking deep breaths in an attempt to calm my nerves. My phone buzzes in my hand.

**Scott: Knock em dead, Opal. Love you.**

Some of the anxiety loosens inside of me.

**Ellie: I will. I'm going in this very second. Love u too.**

Slipping my phone into my purse, I lock up my car and head for the front door. I've got this.

Inside, the chairs in the reception area are unexpectedly filled with people, and my steps falter. Approaching the receptionist, I smile. "Hi, I'm here to see Mara O'Brien."

Behind the desk, the woman looks a little harried, but she returns my smile as she picks up her phone. "I'll let her know. I'd tell you to take a seat, but . . ." She gestures vaguely.

"Not a problem. I'll be over here." I point to an empty spot against the wall.

On closer inspection, I realize the people waiting are mostly families. The children are all unnaturally quiet and well-behaved, leaning against the adults or even holding other children who are younger than they are. It hits me that they must be refugees. When I read *asylum seekers* on the website, I don't know why images of journalists, political activists, and athletes from repressive regimes came to mind instead of the many families who flee violence in Central America.

A toddler slips off her mother's lap and teeters her way over to me. She tilts her head way back to peer up and then offers me the small stuffed animal that's in her hand.

I crouch down as best I can in my skirt and heels. "Hi," I say quietly in Spanish. "Is that your tiger?" Her eyes light up as she nods.

Her mother is at our side seconds later. *"Perdón,"* she whispers, taking her daughter by the hand.

Straightening up, I tower over the woman, and I wish I'd worn flats. "Not at all. She's beautiful," I say, still in Spanish, with my most disarming smile.

The mom blinks at me several times in surprise.

"How old is she?" I ask.

Some of the wariness drops from her expression. "Twenty-five months."

"She must keep you on your toes."

Now she brightens. "Definitely."

"Elsa?"

I turn, cringing at the sound of my proper name. "Yes?"

"I'm Mara. I'm ready for you now."

After a hasty goodbye to the little girl and her mother, I follow Mara down a short hall and then into an open space filled with desks and people on either side of them. It's busy and a bit chaotic and I hear snippets of English, Spanish, and what I think is Arabic.

Mara leads me into a small office on the far side of the main room and shuts the door. The muffled quiet focuses me on my interviewer who gestures for me to take a seat.

Mara O'Brien, whose last name is Irish, but is clearly of Latin descent, wastes very little time on pleasantries before she dives right into the harder questions. I can't say we hit it off right away. I get the impression that I'm not what she expected, though what those expectations were, I couldn't tell you. It's not until well past the mid-way point, when the interview has switched over to Spanish, that her attitude seems to thaw somewhat.

Unfortunately, she's incredibly hard to get a read on. By the end of the interview, I do find out about the actual job though. I'd basically be her assistant and my duties would include whatever needed doing from getting coffee to writing reports to translating for the law students and lawyers who don't speak Spanish.

"So," Mara says. "I think I'm willing to give this a try on a temporary basis." My heart jumps. *Is she offering me a job?* She goes on, "By the end of the day, I'll have human resources send you over a proposal. Once you get that back to us, we can start on the background check. When do you think you could start?"

She watches me coolly while I do my best to contain my rising elation and at the same time consider her question. "I'd like to give my boss two weeks' notice, but if you need me sooner, I could probably swing both jobs for a while."

"That won't be necessary. Next week we're moving to larger offices about five miles down the road, so it should work out." Finally, her hard facade cracks slightly and a sliver of enthusiasm shows through as she jots down an address on a post-it note for me. "We recently received a very significant, long-term grant."

She stands, so I do the same. "Out of curiosity," I say, "how did you get my name?"

Her lips twist fleetingly, making my stomach dip. But it's so swift I almost doubt I saw it. "My boss sent me your CV," she announces, almost sounding disapproving. Then she sinks back into her chair and clicks away at her keyboard for a bit. "And it looks like she got your name from," her eyebrows rise, "Chloe Hutchins. Seems you have friends in high places."

The explanation fills me with relief as everything falls into place. "Not exactly," I say ruefully. "I stalked Ms. Hutchins at a fundraiser a few months ago, hoping to get an interview with her."

For some reason this appears to mollify Mara. "Well, you must have made an impression then. Well done, you."

My prospective new boss' approval gives me even more of a boost as I'm led back out to the reception area where I shake Mara's hand and practically float out the door.

---

Later that night, the sound of Scott's key in my apartment door has me rushing for the hall. I see him and squeal with happiness. The intensity of his smile is like the sun itself, the source of everything good in the world. Throwing myself on him, I delight in the radiating warmth.

Laughing, he says, "Did you get any details yet?"

"No," I moan, leading him into the kitchen. "I'm still waiting." I check the time on my laptop that's open on the kitchen island. "It's late now. Do you think they'll make me wait till Monday?" I hit refresh on my email account for the thousandth time today. "Holy shit!"

He peers over my shoulder. "Is that it?"

"What else could it be?" Anxiety swiftly crashes over me. "You open it."

"Opal," he chides. But I can't do it. My very future is riding on this. Pulling away from him, I start pacing.

"Please," I plead. "Just read it."

"Okay."

The click of the mouse echoes like an explosion inside my chest.

"Dear Ms. Summers," he begins. "Please find enclosed–"

My nerves get the better of me. "Scott! Please get to the important bits."

He huffs with humor. "Yes, ma'am."

From the other side of the island, I watch his eyes scroll through the email until his brows pop up.

"What?" I demand.

"Well," he drawls, stretching my patience so thin it's about to snap. "It would appear that you're a keeper, Ms. Summers."

"What? What does that mean?"

"It means that you pulling in more cash than I do is pretty hot."

"What?! Shut up!" Scurrying back around, I practically hip check him out of the way.

And there it is in black and white. A real salary, one that may not be gigantic considering the cost of living in California, but one that will pay my rent and put gas in my car and allow me to eat real food.

Turning wide eyes on my boyfriend, I tell him in my most earnest voice, "I'm *never* eating Ramen noodles again."

"Congratulations, sweetness." He pulls me close and I bury my nose in his neck. Since it's Friday, he came straight here and I revel in his scent after a day of work. "We should go out to celebrate."

"We should . . . but, is it weird that all I want to do is celebrate with you . . . possibly in the bedroom?"

He chuckles. "A celebration with me between your thighs?"

I nod against his neck. "Exactly, you know me so well. And then I want Chinese takeout. And then maybe a few more orgasms for dessert."

"Your wish is my command."

My career as a gainfully-employed adult begins on the Tuesday after Labor Day at eight am sharp. My first days are like being adrift in a vast sea of newness; people, policies, procedures, responsibilities. I do a lot of smiling and nodding all while trying to scale a seemingly impossible learning curve. But I love it. This job, which entails helping people who really need it, is everything I've ever wanted for myself, something worth getting up for every morning and I give it my all.

Slowly, as the weeks pass, I find my sea legs. Even Mara and her frosty demeanor seem to warm to my work ethic. While I still haven't been able to impress her, her mild scorn has tapered off. I've decided it's just the way she's wired as a no-nonsense type of woman. When she's at work, she works. I mean, on my first day when I tried to make casual conversation with her, she headed it off by giving me a succinct rundown of her life – *"I was born in El Salvador. I came in the 80's to escape civil war as an eleven-year-old."* – the implication being that was all I needed to know about her dedication to her job. I totally respect that.

Some of my co-workers I like better than others. I soon learn that as Mara's assistant, I sign off on donated hours – which are degree requirements for many of the interning law students. Curiously, this translates into my having to turn down numerous 'gifts' and dinner invitations. In fact, by the second week, I take to wearing my grandmother's wedding band at work to avoid the topic of dating the male law students altogether.

Though Scott is happy that I'm enjoying the challenges of my new job, he isn't thrilled with the need for the ring or with the amount of hours I've been putting in. But I grew up watching my dad work more than a hundred hours a week. I understand how the salary system works. And if my sending another email at the end of an exhausting twelve-hour day helps to coordinate decent temporary housing for one more family, who am I to argue?

I'm five weeks into my twelve-week probationary period when things take an unforeseen turn. It's after seven and the office is almost empty for the day. Since Scott won't be over until around 8:30 or 9:00 after the girls are in bed, I decide to clear out my email inbox, or at least form a plan of attack for tomorrow.

I smile to myself when I see the name of Mara's boss's boss as one of the senders. I'm moving up in the world, even if I'm only CC'd. I click on the email and read about the annual report that Mara will be contributing to. As her assistant, I'm sure I'll be compiling a lot of the information for her so I go through the email carefully. I'm about to move on when a name in the long list of CC recipients catches my attention.

*mccarthy_richard@mccarthyholdings.com*

I stare at it for a long moment, a furrow forming between my brows. Why would Scott's grandfather be receiving information about the Settlement Project? Because it's definitely him. Though Scott wasn't interested in learning anything about the man, when Richard McCarthy started contacting me, I went through everything I could find online. I know he's the largest stakeholder in McCarthy Holdings. I also know the company contributes to many non-profits, but I don't recall the Settlement Project being one of them. Plus, my pre-interview research on my employer didn't turn anything up either, because obviously, that would have stood out to me.

So, why? Why am I looking at Richard McCarthy's name?

It's a coincidence I tell myself. He's an extremely wealthy man. I'm sure he has his hands in a lot of different projects that aren't included on his company's website.

Why, then, is my heart thumping painfully in my chest? After all, this can't have anything to do with me, I'm just a lowly administrative assistant . . . an administrative assistant who didn't have any prior experience, one who's being overpaid, one who didn't even apply for the job.

My insides start gymnastics-worthy contortions. *If it's too good to be true . . .*

No, no, no.

I'm being utterly self-involved. I have to be. And there's a very easy way to find out one way or the other. I reach for the mouse and click on the man's email address. I'll ask him outright. But then my fingers hover over the keyboard. Ask him what? Did you make an anonymous contribution to the Settlement Project to provide me with a job? That sounds completely asinine. Clearly I'm overtired, so I shut down my computer for the night.

On the drive home, though, the idea sits in the back of my mind and festers. Every instinct I have is telling me that something isn't right. And on top of everything, it's dark and raining and traffic is a total bitch.

By the time I drag my weary ass out of my car and make it inside, Scott is already here.

"Honey?!" he calls and I can hear the amusement in his voice. "Are you home?"

Despite my grumpiness, I feel my lips forming a smile as I turn the corner and find him rummaging around in the fridge. Letting my purse, slide off my shoulder to the floor, I lean on the island to watch him. With the trash can beside him, it would appear he's doing a fridge clean-out.

Pulling his head out, he turns to me with an old takeout container in his hand and a wry expression on his face. "Woman, is this the Indian food we ordered like two weeks ago?" He chucks it in the trash. "If you didn't have me, you'd have to call in a hazmat team twice a year."

"Oh, probably."

Flipping the fridge door closed, he saunters over, giving me a head-to-toe once over as he approaches. Silently, I thank the powers that be that his mood is the exact opposite of mine.

His hands settle on my waist before he leans in to kiss me. Of course, what begins as an innocent peck heats up and all thoughts of Richard McCarthy are eliminated in favor of nothing but lurid notions involving his grandson. That is until my stomach grumbles loudly.

Our lips freeze and we laugh.

"Come on," he says, pulling me toward a bar stool at the counter. "Let me feed you." He gets a plate out and fills it with something from a Tupperware container on the counter. "My abuela made *bisteces a la Mexicana* with her secret-recipe rice," he says, giving me a meaningful look. "We both know that shit's the bomb." He shoves it in the microwave. "Oh, and the girls wanted me to give you this." He pushes a large sheet a paper toward me along the countertop and then turns back to hunt for a fork.

The paper turns out to be folded several times and when I've got it fully extended, it's the size of a small poster. "Oh, wow." It's a giant peace symbol, and each of the three sections it creates has been filled by one of the girls with the things they like to draw and color, like hearts, stars, animals, etc.

"Pretty cute, right?" Scott says, coming to stand next to me. "Mari helped with the idea of giving them their own space because the first one they worked on ended in some serious bickering."

"I love it," I whisper.

Probably responding to the unwarranted amount of emotion in my voice, he asks, "Hey, you okay?" He puts a finger under my chin to examine me more closely. "You haven't said much. Did something happen at work?"

His eyes drop to my left hand, but there's nothing to see because I leave my grandmother's ring locked in my desk at work. I shake my head in mild irritation at his assumption that my bad day has something to do with a male co-worker.

"No. Nothing happened," I say with a ghost of a smile, but then I sober. "Well, I don't think anything happened. It might be nothing . . . it's *probably* nothing."

"But you're going to tell me about it anyway." He doesn't phrase it as a question, the bossy man.

"Yeah, I'm going to tell you anyway."

The microwave beeps but he ignores it, his gaze concerned.

"It's nothing bad," I begin, re-folding the poster and setting it aside. As I recount the tale, I realize how little substance there is to it, and his lack of reaction except for the momentary dip of his eyebrows at the mention of his grandfather is telling.

When I finish, he just gets my dinner out of the microwave and sets it in front of me. "You should eat something."

I shake my head. "I can't eat anything until I hear what you think."

"I don't think anything, El. I'm not even sure what your point is."

If he mocks me in my current state of mind, I don't think I'll take it well. But I confess anyway. "I think your grandfather got me my job."

# Chapter Eight

## Scott

My head jerks back with surprise. "What? Because his name was on an email?" I study the worry etched into her features as I consider the idea. "Kind of a stretch, don't you think?"

"Maybe," she concedes. "But my gut is telling me maybe not."

Watching her pick up her fork, I resign myself to the prickling discomfort that always shows up when thoughts of my grandfather invade my mind. Over the last four months, since I came face-to-face with him, his son and his two grandsons, it's become a familiar sensation. *Why can't I just forget about them?*

Ellie's voice pulls me back to the present. "It explains so much," she says dejectedly. "Mara's attitude, my salary, the fact that they approached me."

"It's still a stretch. And I think you're selling yourself way short. You're more than qualified for that job." I turn my attention to placing the lid back on the Tupperware and returning it to the fridge to mask my irritability with her self-doubt. "You have an Ivy League education, El, your Spanish is excellent, and you can build a rapport with almost anyone out of thin air." I pause, hearing how true every point on that list is. "Bull*shit* he got you that job. You're the most capable person I know."

She just stares at me.

"Don't look so surprised," I say, almost sounding affronted, but then my tone turns to honey. "You and I both know that you're an incredible woman." I wander around the island and slide my palm along the warm, smooth skin of her jaw.

"Thanks for believing in me," she whispers. "A girl can always use a good pep talk."

My lip twitches. "Finish your dinner and I'll give you more than a pep talk."

I go back to sorting out her fridge, my thoughts turning this way and that, not about Ellie's ludicrous conspiracy theory, but about the even more ludicrous idea that I have brothers. *Brothers.* I barely had a chance to glance at them at the fundraiser, let alone *look* at them. *Are they as tall as I am? Are they blond? Are they rich, pompous assholes or –*

"So what should I do?"

"Huh?" I turn, inspecting some very questionable limes from the crisper before chucking them in the trash. "About what, sweetness?"

Her eyes widen as if to say, *what do you mean about what?* "Scott, I can't sit back and do nothing. I'd feel like a fraud at work."

She seems serious so I refrain from telling her she's being ridiculous. "Not sure what you could do."

I watch her worry the corner of her lip with her teeth. "Well," she says slowly. "I was thinking about emailing your grandfather."

Her words slide into my gut like wet concrete, and she must notice because she quickly tacks on, "But if you don't want me to, I won't."

Honestly, I *don't* want her to contact him and I open my mouth to say as much, but nothing comes out. Didn't I promise to be less of a selfish ass? Here's an opportunity to make good on my word. "If it's important to you, then you should do it."

"You're sure?" she asks, looking adorably guilty.

The tension slackens. "Yeah, I'm sure. If it'll set your mind at ease, I won't stand in your way. Though," I pause, a smirk curling my lip, "I'm not sure what exactly you're going to say."

She must take that as a challenge because she grabs her phone out of her purse and with her own smirk, goes to work on it. Two minutes later, she announces, "Done," with her trademark confidence.

Trying to keep the sarcasm as mild as possible, I tell her, "I can't wait to hear his reaction."

Friday comes and goes with no word, much to Ellie's disappointment. Then, over the weekend, her gloominess continues. It's as if she can't maneuver herself out of a field of eggshells of her own making. I feel for her though. She loves this new job with a passion. My soft-hearted woman has definitely found a calling in all the sob stories and injustices faced by many of the refugees she meets. And to her mind, that calling is in jeopardy. Even though I'm convinced she's making a mountain out of nothing, I can't help but worry alongside her. Apparently being in love makes me more than willing to help carry her burdens, whether real or imagined.

By early Monday afternoon, the old man still hasn't put her out of her misery. I text her again before I leave work, but I don't hear back from her until I'm pulling into the driveway at home. My phone buzzes in the cup holder.

**Opal: Sorry, I was in a meeting. Nothing yet.**

**Scott: That just tells us he's got better things to do. You're in the clear.**

**Opal: Never thought you'd be the optimistic one. See you tonight?**

**Scott: lol and of course. Don't work too late.**

She sends me a line of purple hearts and kissy emojis. Despite shaking my head, I've got a stupid smile on my face, especially when I yield a tiny piece of my manhood by sending her a single red heart in return. Good grief, if it makes her happy, I'll do it.

Grabbing my lunch box off the seat next to me, I lock up the truck and head inside. For a Monday, the day went well. My boss, Dean, is happy with how well the new project is going, and now that I don't have to deal with Jorgie or Harrison anymore, my job is so much easier.

My key in the door brings the familiar refrain of, "Papá!" and I scoop Rosa up into my arms. "How's my *Calabacita?*"

"Good." Her exuberance is open and adoring and I soak it up.

"Where're your sisters?" She's the only one who came running.

Her expression becomes conspiratorial as she says, "There's a man in the kitchen."

I cock my head. "What do you mean?"

"Carmen is helping Abuela talk to him."

Worried now, I cover the short distance to the kitchen with Rosa still in my arms. My abuela is sitting in her usual spot at the table, Carmen beside her. Then my eyes swing to the other side and the instant, violent tightening of my stomach muscles nearly knocks the wind out of me.

*What. The. Fuck?*

My grandfather, the man I so briefly met all those months ago, is sitting in my house, at my table with a mug in front of him, Daniela beside him, like he's attending a fucking tea party.

Anger makes quick work of the shock and confusion, and I feel my jaw clench. I kiss Rosa on the forehead and then set her on her feet. "Why don't you guys go play in your room?" I tell the girls in Spanish.

Something in the tone of my voice must tell them not to argue, because both Carmen and Daniela slide off their chairs with uncharacteristic tractability. Daniela just pulls Rosa from the room, but Carmen stops to whisper, "I don't know why he's here," suspicion dancing upon her features.

My anger flares hotter, but I give her the reassurance she needs. "Don't worry. I'm here now."

When they're gone, Abuela doesn't give me a chance to say anything. "Mijo, come and sit down please."

"Do you know who this guy is?" I demand, though I ask it rhetorically because there's no way she'd be sharing her table with him if she did. I don't know what possessed her to allow a stranger into the house in the first place.

Her next words come out on a sad sigh. "Yes, I know who he is."

The *get out of my house* that was on the tip of my tongue dissolves and coats my mouth in a foul layer. "What?" I choke out in English.

"Please, mijo. Sit down and I will explain."

Tremors of betrayal begin to quake through me. "Explain? Explain how you *know* him?"

My ever-steady grandmother appears almost ill at ease. "Yes. But stop saying it like that. I don't *know* him, even if this isn't the first time he's come."

My mind reels and I cross my arms over my chest in a protective gesture. "What are you saying?"

She pats the table, indicating I should sit in a chair that would leave them on either side of me. A sense of foreboding starts to build as I struggle with wanting to respect my grandmother's wishes and needing to throw this presumptuous interloper out on his ass. In the end, trust in my grandmother and good manners win out. I sit.

"How the hell did you find me?" I demand in English, glaring at the man.

"Mijo!" she admonishes. "You will show proper respect. I raised you better than that. You owe him –"

"I owe him nothing." Despite my grandmother's Spanish, I stick with English so this guy understands I'm not going to sit back and let him ride roughshod over me in my own home. "And I'm asking again, how did you find me?"

The old man's eyes dart to my grandmother's before he faces me directly. "Well, I . . . my son," he swallows hard, ". . . that is, your father . . . told me where to find you."

Air discharges from my chest as if I've been punched.

*What?* I was expecting something along the lines of a private investigator. Not this. For a good, solid minute, I sit there, gaping at the man and the shame he's wearing like a second suit, trying to make sense of his statement.

"How would he know where to find me?" I finally manage, barely daring to think maybe my father was interested in knowing about me after all.

The old man's pallor is decidedly green when he answers. "Well, he . . . he's had some communication with your mother over the years."

"Years?" I breathe, suddenly light-headed. "You're saying my father knew about me . . . for years?"

He gives a solemn nod.

The implications jam in my brain like they're caught in a bottle neck. "How long?" My voice hardens to granite over the course of the two syllables.

The grooves bracketing his mouth deepen as if to hold back something distasteful. "It appears that he's always known."

*Always?* I turn to my abuela, the one person who's always been the center of my life. "Did *you* know?" I ask hoarsely, bracing myself for the other side of the sky to come crashing down.

"No, mijo. No al principio."

The relief that accompanies the initial *no* fades. "What do you mean *not in the beginning?*"

Her shoulders sag by a degree, but her expression still glitters with her iron strength. "I found out that your mother knew who your father was when Javier was killed."

Tilting my head back, I stare at the ceiling in an attempt to take in what she's saying. "My uncle died when I was fourteen, Abuela." There's a ring of accusation in my tone that I know needs to be quashed, but searing indignation makes it impossible to temper my next words. "That was more than eight years ago."

"Yes," she says firmly. "And I will stand by my decision not to tell you about your father until the day I die."

At a complete loss and drowning in betrayal, I can only stare at her.

Her chin tilts higher as she adds, "I refused to expose you to him. He is an awful man. He saw your mother and me as vermin, as blackmailers. If we hadn't been so desperate in the months following Javier's death, I would have told him to go straight to the devil."

My brain registers all the Spanish words except one. *Chantajistas?* From *chantaje?* "Blackmail?" I sputter, my heart now thumping furiously. "He accused you of trying to blackmail him?"

Despite my English, Abuela answers me with an unyielding, *"Sí."*

I turn to pin the man's father, my grandfather, with a glower.

Visibly shaken, he says, "I didn't know . . . about that." He bows his head slightly in what I'm guessing is supposed to be an apology. "I only found out about the lump sum payment that happened almost ten years ago by going through the company records."

"Wait. He paid?" My head swings back to my grandmother and I repeat the question in Spanish. "He paid? How much was I worth?"

Watching her lips purse, I feel everything I thought I knew start to slip away from beneath my feet.

Her voice is unsteady when she finally answers. "Your mother refused to tell me the precise amount, but I told her I wanted at least half, so I could provide for you kids. She gave me fifteen thousand."

I shake my head. "What?" This keeps getting worse. "She kept half? For herself?" My disgust doesn't stop me from doing some basic math. "So if half is fifteen, she got a total of thirty." I turn to my grandfather and switch to English. "Thirty thousand, is that right?"

Dread compounds inside of me at his chagrinned expression. "No, the payment was for fifty."

As if they're poison, his words leak into my already strained relationship with my mother and contaminate it to the point of ruin. My stomach roils, the dread becoming nausea.

"Fifty?" My grandmother whispers in disbelief, her accent thick around the English number.

I know the two of us are trying to figure out the same things; the whys, the hows, and the whats of the money, money that we desperately needed at the time. I think back to all the uncertainty and upheaval of that year . . . and like the cocking of a gun to my head, it all falls into place. "Robbie. That son of a bitch."

My grandmother doesn't even scold my language, she just groans like she's in pain because she knows I'm right. That's what my mother did with the money. She used it for her dead-beat husband's legal defense. A man who bullied this family both physically and emotionally after my uncle was no longer around to keep him in check. I'd always thought it was divine intervention that Robbie got collared for that robbery. I remember hearing predictions of his going away for life. The list of charges had been long and serious and it was his second strike. But he'd had a good lawyer who'd got him a deal. Jesus, he's up for parole next year. Thanks to money meant for me and my family.

The old man shifts uncomfortably in his seat, and I don't blame him. Our family drama can't be of interest to him. "Why are you here?" I ask, feeling wrung out.

"I want to know you, Scott."

"Why? If my own father wants nothing to do with me, why would you?"

"My son has acted deplorably. I want you to know that his actions don't reflect the feelings of the rest of *your* family. Your brothers and I would very much like to get to know you."

I rub the back of my neck, not liking how the phrases *your family* and *your brothers* make me squirm when I'm already feeling like I've gone ten rounds with a professional fighter in an octagon.

"But I can see how tonight has come as a shock and I don't expect you to make any hard and fast decisions." He hesitates, but then pushes on. "All I ask is that you consider taking my calls." It comes out as a question, making him sound remarkably vulnerable.

Maybe it's the shock or maybe it's how my grandmother's hopeful expression is eerily similar to that of the old man's, but I hear myself say, "I . . . I guess so. Do I . . . Are there just the two . . . brothers?"

A spark of eagerness ignites in him at my interest. "Uh . . . well . . . yes. Just Eric and Shane. They have cousins on their mother's side, but on our side there's only my one child . . . your father."

I nod automatically, because what else would I do?

"They've both expressed their desire to meet you, Scott. They're very curious."

Again, I nod, this time because I understand exactly how they feel. I haven't been able to stamp out my curiosity no matter how hard I've tried.

As if not wanting to upset his good fortune, my grandfather carefully stands to go.

"One more thing," I say, fixing him with a serious look. "Did you get Ellie the job?"

If the answer wasn't written all over his face, the way he sinks back into the chair would tell me all I need to know. I blow out a frustrated breath. This is going to hurt my girl.

"Yes," he admits after a moment of silence. "But I had only good intentions." His attention flicks to my grandmother's and I frown. "It was suggested that I contribute to the Settlement Project and put Ms. Summers' name forward for employment as a way to . . ." he searches for the right word, ". . . to make amends for my son's callousness. It was never my –"

At this point, I'm completely drained, so I cut him off. "Suggested by who?"

His gaze leaps away from mine and settles on my grandmother's – again. And I can't stop a weak, incredulous laugh from escaping my throat. "You two have been scheming?"

I doubt Abuela caught the meaning of the word *scheming*, but she knows I've made the connection between them, and she's the one who answers the question.

"Mijo, when he came here looking for you months ago, I was angry. I told him if he really wanted to prove he was deserving of getting to know you, he could do some good for our community, and, by extension, for *la güera*. I never expected him to follow through."

Farcical images of them struggling to communicate with each other, hand gestures and all, are interrupted by my grandfather's need to defend his actions. "Ms. Summers has proven beyond a shadow of a doubt that she's a very capable employee. And she was very loyal to you in her steadfast refusal to engage with me via email. I hope neither of you will hold this against me. I only wanted to help."

Reeling and unsure why my anger isn't as sharp as it was when I first found him in the kitchen, I scrub my palms down my face.

"I have to give the girls their dinner," my grandmother announces, ever practical. "Invite him to stay."

I scoff. "I'm not inviting him to eat with us. What would we tell the girls?"

"The truth?" she says with a hint of sarcasm, tipping my world further on its axis.

"I'm going to go," my grandfather says quietly. "Thank you for the chance to talk. I'd very much like to do it again sometime."

Nodding absently, I almost miss my grandmother's nudge to my arm. With a frustrated grunt, I tell him, "She'd like you to stay for dinner."

I watch his demeanor brighten as he inclines his head toward her in thanks. *"Gracias, Señora,"* he says, the Spanish words awkward in his mouth, but I appreciate his effort. "Maybe another time when things are more settled. Then I would be honored."

Damnit, I also appreciate that he directs his English words to her, not treating her like she's dimwitted because she's hesitant to use her second language.

"Okay," she says simply, giving him a nod.

"I'll show myself out."

The sound of the front door closing spurs my grandmother into action. While she bustles around the kitchen, all I can do is sit on my ass and let my mind spin through the revelations of the last hour.

"Go get the girls, please, Scotty."

At least I seem to be able to follow orders.

When the five of us are seated around the table, the girls start in with their questions, which I let my grandmother field. I like the calm, matter-of-fact way that she announces who the man was, and how in turn, the girls take their cues from her. They certainly take the appearance of a ready-made grandfather much better than I did those months ago. Even now, as they try to draw me into the conversation, I can't muster more than one word answers while I push my food around on my plate.

A knock at the front door sends the girls into a tizzy.

"Make sure you check to see who it is," my grandmother calls.

"It's Ellie!" Daniela exclaims from the living room.

While I listen to them excitedly tell Ellie everything about the afternoon, I can't help but sink into the deep relief her arrival brings. Her presence is exactly what I need. "You called her?" I ask, watching my grandmother put a plate together for the woman I love.

"I did."

I blow out a breath. "Thanks."

Ellie breezes into the kitchen, all smiles as usual, first greeting my grandmother with a *buenas tardes* and a kiss on the cheek, then accepting the dish with thanks. She sits beside me. "Hey," she says softly, leaning in to kiss me chastely. Pulling back, she looks me over, seeming to catalogue everything from the set of my jaw to my sagging posture.

While she eats, they talk about grandparents, of which Ellie doesn't have any who are living, but she answers every single one of the girls' invasive questions. I love how she treats them, like they matter, never judging them, never criticizing. I'll admit to some flare ups of jealousy over the summer, but I really couldn't hope for a better role model for them. A better mother. The idea grounds me. No matter what else is going on in my life, I need to stay focused of what's important; Ellie and the girls.

As soon as Ellie has taken her last bite, my grandmother attempts to usher the girls away to give us some privacy.

"What?" Daniela squawks in outrage, bringing a weak smile to my lips. "But Ellie's here!"

"No arguments. Let's go clean your room."

When it seems like all three of them are going to revolt, Ellie tells them she'll tuck them in when it's time for bed. Somewhat mollified, they finally agree.

"You're so good with them," I tell her as the quiet of the room settles around us.

She hums her cautious agreement, but changes the subject. "Quite the surprising turn of events tonight. You okay?"

"I guess."

"I assume it was my email that prompted his visit?"

Nodding slowly, I do my best to maintain eye contact. "Probably, yeah. You were right about the job. I asked him straight up."

A soft, resigned sigh passes her lips. "It was always too good to be true," she says, then gives a hollow laugh. "You think I can swing a reference from Mara . . . maybe if I give her two weeks' notice?"

"Two weeks' notice?" Anger burns away my apathy. "You're quitting that job over my dead body."

# Chapter Nine

## Ellie

Over the last few days, I've been considering things at work in a new light. Mara's attitude may have thawed toward me over the weeks, but her disapproving looks and impatience make a lot more sense now. It's obvious how my lack of experience slows everything down, forcing me to constantly pester my co-workers for advice. I've even been imagining the person whose job I've taken. Am I taking food directly out of the mouths of a family whose mother or father isn't working because of me?

I kept covertly checking my personal email account today, desperate for Richard McCarthy to drop me simple note, telling me he has no idea what I'm talking about. It didn't come. And then Scott's grandmother called me from their home phone, asking me to come for dinner if I could. She wouldn't tell me what was going on, only that Scott would appreciate my presence.

After the girls ambushed me at the door and spilled the beans, I had approximately thirty seconds to assimilate the information before I had to face Scott in the kitchen. One glance at him, and I knew this wasn't only about my job. I've never seen him so defeated . . . until I say I'm quitting.

"You're quitting that job over my dead body." His harsh tone takes me by surprise and it must show on my face because he goes on. "You love that job. You're not quitting."

"Scott —"

"Nobody gets their first real job on merit alone, El." Then, as if his own words have convinced him of the soundness of his argument, with finality he reiterates, "You're not quitting."

We glare at each other, an undercurrent of challenge simmering between us until it occurs to me that my job is probably the least of his worries. "Tell me what happened."

The defiant set of his jaw loosens with an onset of obviously unwanted emotion. Twisting in my chair, I lean my forehead to his bicep in a show of silent support as his chest rises with a deep breath. "He knew," he murmurs. "My whole life he knew."

I pull back. "What? Who?"

"My father."

Hearing my sharp intake of breath, he lifts his gaze to mine. "He even knew where I lived." He swallows hard. "I just . . . I don't understand. If I had a child, I would want to know him. I would want to know that he was happy and healthy and *safe*."

"Oh, Scott."

"Because I haven't always been safe. God, my mother's hair-brained ideas when I was small . . ." He shakes his head. "It doesn't make sense to me."

Of course it doesn't. Scott is the most caring man I know. His dedication to his girls is absolute. "So your mom was able to let him know that she was pregnant?"

He shrugs. "He used the word *always* when I asked how long my father's known about me." The slow shaking of his head becomes jerkier. "My mom has always sworn up, down, and sideways that she had no idea how to find him. It was total bullshit. Apparently, after my uncle died and we were so pathetically desperate, she got fifty G's out of him."

I feel my jaw go slack.

"And now that I think about it, I bet that wasn't the only time she approached him for money."

Doubt hits me. "You mean, in a way, he paid child support?"

His lips twist into a sneer. "More like mother support. Of the fifty, we know she kept thirty five for herself."

"What?" I say breathlessly. I can't have heard him correctly.

"Yeah, you believe that shit? She gave my grandmother fifteen to keep all of us fed and clothed, and I'm almost positive she used the rest to hire that scumbag husband of hers a lawyer."

His palm hits the table and I jump.

"There I was, fifteen years old with two jobs, working after-school and on the weekends, killing myself, and she's giving away money that was meant for me to a man who did nothing but make our lives a misery. I mean, what the fuck?!"

He turns to me expectantly, like I should be able to explain his mother's actions. "I wish I knew what to say," I tell him quietly, stroking the hair at the back of his neck. He leans into my touch, so I move closer and put my arms around him as best as I can. "What she did was disgraceful. I can't tell you how sorry I am."

For a few moments, there's only silence while I hold him. Then I hear an unexpected, low chuckle from him.

"*Disgraceful*, Opal? Really?" He sits up. "That's the word you're going with?"

Feeling sheepish, I say, "Well, she's your mom. I was trying to keep it classy. Would you prefer I call her a duplicitous snake?"

"Better." I see a flash of a grin come and go. "But I guess calling her names doesn't change anything."

"No, it doesn't, but you have every right to be angry."

I watch his hand clench into a fist on the table. "I wish I was only angry. But my own mother sold me out, El. She *betrayed* me. I mean, I've always known she was never all-in on the motherhood thing. But this? I was fifteen. I could have stayed in school for a while longer, maybe squeezed in another year of childhood. I could have spent more time with Rosa when she was a baby. I could have slept more instead of lying awake every night, worrying about how we were going to pay the fucking electric bill."

His raw, indignant pain causes goosebumps to break out along my arms and I feel the first sting of tears.

"Stop that."

I blink. "Stop what?"

"Feeling sorry for me."

"I'm not feeling sorry for you. I . . . I want to go back and shoulder some of that responsibility for you. It wasn't fair."

"Life is never fair." The melancholy on his face wanes. "And besides, when I was fifteen, you were twenty. I think that kind of thing is frowned upon." The quirk to his lips mitigates some of the sorrow that's weighing me down.

"Actually, that kind of thing is illegal, and orange is so not my color."

He barks out a laugh, reaching a hand out to hook my neck, pulling me in for a kiss. "I'm sorry for being such a whiner."

"You're not whining, you're sharing. That's what I'm here for. I love you, Scott."

"Good, because I love you too, Opal." Leaning back in, he kisses me soft and slow until he recalls that we're in his grandmother's kitchen. "We'll have to finish that later," he murmurs with a last, lingering kiss as he gets to his feet. "Let me see what's going on with the girls. Maybe we can leave now."

"Hang on," I say, putting my hand on his arm. "You haven't told me the rest of the story. Richard McCarthy turned up here at the house?"

He plops back down on his chair dejectedly. "Yeah, turns out he's been around to see my grandmother before today. It was her idea to get you a job."

"What?" It comes out heavily laden with disbelief, because, *what?*

"That was my reaction too."

The few details he has do nothing to erase my surprise. Even though my outrageous theory turned out to have merit, I'm no less flabbergasted. Then he finishes with an even more surprising confession.

"I don't know," he says almost hesitantly. "He seemed like a stand-up guy. I kind of agreed to talk to him at some point in the future."

"Oh?" I ask carefully. We've waded into these waters before and they've proven to be shark-infested, something along the lines of me floating the idea of giving his grandfather a chance only to have it instantly pulled under and thrashed to within an inch of its existence.

"Oh?" he mimics, definitely mocking my neutral tone. "Don't pretend you're not thrilled."

"It doesn't matter if I'm thrilled. What matters is how you feel about it."

His amusement dims. "You don't think getting involved with them will be a mistake?"

I don't want to be obtuse or pretend like he shouldn't have misgivings, but frankly, I've never understood his dread. "A mistake in the sense that they'll all be like your father?"

"Yeah. No. I don't know," he says, rubbing at his eyes. "What I'd really like is to forget about them. Permanently. But I haven't been able to do that."

"They're your family, Scott." He makes a noise of disgust, but I go on. "It's only natural to want to find out more about them. I understand you not wanting a relationship with your father, but I think maybe your brothers deserve a chance."

"I just can't picture it," he whispers. "What could we possibly have in common?"

"You'll never know if you don't try."

"Yeah, maybe." He heaves a sigh. "But how do I shake the feeling that I'm being disloyal to my *real* family."

Reaching for the hand that's still fisted on the table, I give it a reassuring squeeze. "Your *real* family love you. They'd never begrudge you this chance."

He nods like he agrees with me, but there's still doubt drawn into every line on his face.

"Whatever you decide, you have my full support. No matter what, I'm with you."

"Thank you, sweetness. You don't know how much that means to me."

The next morning, my commute doesn't go well. I try not to dwell on the irony of being late on today of all days as I slip through the rabbit warren of cubicles with hurried steps. These offices are a decided improvement over the completely open floor plan of the previous ones. Here at least clients have a bit of privacy with their assigned caseworker. That doesn't help me at all though because I can see Mara through the glass wall of her office, already at her desk, hard at work. Shit.

I get my jacket off and stow my purse in the bottom drawer of my desk before I knock on her open door. She acknowledges me with a cursory glance, not bothering to stop what she's doing. For a moment, I just listen to the clacking of her keyboard. Mara isn't one for pleasantries, so I dive right in after clearing my throat nervously. "So, did you get my email?"

At first I don't think she's heard me, but after a few more clicks of her keyboard, she turns her laptop toward me. "You mean this one?"

The subject line clearly reads *Letter of Resignation*. "Yeah."

"Please," she says, the single word weighed down with sarcasm. "Save your martyrdom for someone who's interested. I'm not training someone new."

"Mara —"

"You've proven you can do the job. So do it. I don't want to hear any more about it."

I exhale noisily, half in relief, half in frustration. "Are you sure?"

"Unequivocally sure. I may not have appreciated being told who my assistant would be, but I saw your worth from the beginning. The way you connected with that woman in the waiting room right before your interview? That can't be taught."

My mouth opens, then closes, unsure of how to respond. Turns out I don't have to.

"If you bring it up again, Ellie, I'll fire you."

A short, high-pitched noise escapes my lips. "Okay, then."

"Glad we got that sorted out," she says, moving her empty coffee mug toward me on the desk.

"Coming right up, boss."

I spend the rest of the day wrapped up in a sense of unreality, wondering if I should be feeling guiltier or even saddened that my principles aren't as solid as I thought they were. Instead, all I can think about is what a relief it is not to have to go back to job hunting.

On my lunchbreak, I text Scott.

**Ellie: Mara wouldn't accept my resignation.**

**Scott: What? I told you not to quit.**

**Ellie: I don't do well with commands.**

**Scott: Ha. We both know that's not true.**

**Ellie: Very funny. I'm relieved though.**

**Scott: SMH. Stubborn woman. Maybe I'll spank it out of you this weekend.**

I smile at that. Scott and I have big plans this weekend. We're going to cook for ourselves at my apartment, and then he's staying the night – the whole night – for the first time. And I have Rosa's mother, Lolita to thank. After the choir performance debacle, she disappeared from Rosa's life over the summer, but resurfaced when the school year started. She'd completed an out-patient rehab stint; I was thrilled for her, but Scott was suspicious as hell. He's only allowed Lolita supervised visits at their house . . . until now. This Saturday will be Rosa's first overnight visit with her mom, and we're taking advantage of it.

**Ellie: You can try.**

**Scott: Challenge accepted.**

I chuckle low. Oh, it's on, Mr. McCarthy.

---

The timing of our Saturday together isn't ideal. It follows too closely on the heels of Richard McCarthy's visit to the house, a visit that Scott claims to have moved past. But I know better. He's been off; a little down, a little withdrawn. Even if I know he needs time to process and come to terms with what he learned, I wish I could help him. It can't be easy to accept that both of your parents lack whatever gene gives impetus to the instinct to put a child's welfare first.

When we drop Rosa off at Lolita's mother's house after lunch on Saturday, he seems fine, though. Then the trip to the grocery store to get the ingredients for our cooking project is mostly upbeat. But as the afternoon wears on, it becomes more and more obvious that Scott isn't himself. A lot of little things are irritating him or even out-right grating on his nerves, and I waffle on whether I should challenge his attitude or ignore it.

My indecision doesn't pay off.

We're side by side at the kitchen island – I'm chopping the celery and green pepper for our attempt at making chilli, and he's chopping the onion – when life gives him a nice firm shove off the edge of reason.

He hisses, making my head jerk up. The blood welling on his index finger sends a shot of tingly adrenaline to my fingertips. "Are you okay?" I cry.

Grimacing, he shoves the injured finger into his mouth.

I pull on his wrist. "Let me see."

We both examine it. "It's fine," he says tersely, but the blood's welling up again.

I'm not squeamish, but neither am I a huge fan of bleeding boyfriends. "It's not fine."

I go for the bottle of peroxide and a bandaid from the bathroom. "Here, let me help." Leading him to the sink, I rinse the cut under the water. "It's not that deep," I say after taking another look.

"I told you it's fine."

"You should be more careful," I say as I pour peroxide over the wound.

"Geez, thanks for the advice. I never would have thought of that on my own."

I dab at his finger with a paper towel. "I'm just trying to help." God, this man has been rebuffing me all afternoon, I think churlishly, but then I remember he's had a rough week. "Are you worried about Rosa?" I ask softly. "I'm sure she's fine."

"That's easy for you to say," he mutters under his breath, making me pause mid rip of the bandaid wrapper. *What does that mean?* is on the tip of my tongue, but I manage to swap it out for, "At least you won't need stitches."

Once his finger is wrapped up, he grumbles out a sullen, "Thanks."

I turn the stove on to preheat the pan and he goes back to his onion. Seconds later, he announces, "I should have gotten her a cellphone."

"Who? Rosa?" My eyebrows shift up as I return to the green pepper. "She's seven, Scott." The slightly deadpan tone of my voice makes me cringe, but luckily he doesn't notice.

"But if she had a phone, she could call if she needed help."

That gives me pause. I don't like the idea of Rosa needing help any more than Scott does. "She has your number memorized, right?"

"Yeah," he concedes, glancing at his cellphone that's sitting two feet away on the counter. "But that's not going to work unless she's near another phone."

I relax. "She will be though. You said they're not planning to go anywhere."

He huffs. "Whose side are you on?"

"Rosa's," I say, adding an unintentional barb to her name. Is he implying that Rosa's well-being isn't important to me?

He turns back to his cutting board, but not before he shoots me a glare, clearly aggravated with my inability to empathize with his fear, no matter how unlikely. And he's right. He doesn't need logic from me, he needs understanding.

"Sorry. I know this isn't easy for you." Accepting the cutting board from him, I scrape the chopped onions into the pan. "But you know that I worry about her too, right?"

"Not half as much as I do," he declares.

My stirring of the pan's sizzling contents halts at the jab. Keep calm, I tell myself. He's not being cruel on purpose.

He's just indulging in a little knee-jerk reacting, which is understandable with all the stress he's been under. "You're right. You're her father." *And I'm not her mother.*

"Exactly," he says emphatically and the jab becomes a slicing pain that penetrates my sternum. Resisting the urge to rub at my chest proves impossible as I remind myself that I haven't earned the right to be hurt by the implication of his words. I have a long way to go before I'm mother material. Blowing out a slow breath, I go back to the task at hand.

"You don't know how many times Lolita has fucked up, or not shown up, or gone back on her promises."

Okay, that was a large shift in topic. Maybe he's not unhappy with me, but with Lolita. I busy myself by adding the ground beef to the pan so he won't see the relief on my face.

"You have no idea," he continues, "how sick of her I am."

"That's a little harsh." The words sail from my mouth before I can stop them. But once they're out, they ring true. "From what you've told me, she's doing much better." I glance over my shoulder to find him staring at me like I've completely lost it.

"She's always improving, or making an effort, or working toward a goal, but in the end, she always slides back into the gutter."

His ugly bitterness not only startles me but raises my hackles. "Don't say that. She's the mother of your child." I have no idea why I'm standing up for a woman who's failed her daughter on too many occasions to count.

He scoffs. "Only when she feels like it." He's pacing now on the other side of the island, anger coming off of him in waves.

I turn back to the stove, moving the pan's contents so it won't stick. "Where is this coming from, Scott?"

"I'm fed up. It's a never-ending trip through a house of horrors. I shouldn't have to put up with it."

"Maybe not, but you do it because it's what's best for Rosa. She deserves the chance to know her mom."

Over my shoulder, I watch his face screw up with distaste. "You think Rosa has any respect for that woman? Kids should be able to expect things from their parents. The only thing she expects from Lolita is disappointment. Everyone, including Rosa, knows it's only a matter of time before she chooses the drugs again."

Pique rises in my gut as I put the wooden spoon down. "That's not fair and you know it. Addiction isn't something she *wants*."

Again, he scoffs, this time with real malice. "Bullshit. Lolita's problem is that she doesn't want anything more than the drugs."

I cross my arms over my chest, ready to do battle with him. "You don't really believe that."

"Oh, yes, I do."

"You sound like an uneducated jackass right now."

His spine snaps straight and I know immediately that I've made a mistake, a big one. "Don't pretend you didn't know that when you got involved with me," he spits. Grabbing his cell off the counter, he heads for the door.

"Scott," I call. "I didn't mean it like that."

I can hear him shoving his feet into his shoes, and my heart is telling me to stop him, but my brain is still incensed with his idiotic little sermon. The door opens.

"Scott," I call again. But all I get in response is the door thumping closed.

# Chapter Ten

## Scott

I'll show her an uneducated jackass.

My angry steps carry me right out the front doors of her building and down the street to my truck. A flyer is waiting for me on the windshield under the wiper, and I rip it away and chuck it to the ground. Some old guy walking his dog shoots daggers my way, but I couldn't care less.

My little girl probably needs me right now and I'm arguing semantics with a woman who doesn't understand the situation. Why is she defending Lolita anyway? She should be on my side. She's *my* girlfriend and Rosa is *my* daughter. And dammit, I despise this all-too familiar feeling of helplessness that laces itself through my ribs and then pulls tight, squeezing the life from my lungs every single time Rosa goes with Lolita.

Determined to get my kid, I get in my truck and drive to Lolita's mother's house. I should never have agreed to the sleepover in the first place. I should have ignored Rosa's hopeful eyes and shut that shit down from the start – except I couldn't . . . but I don't want to think about that because I'm already beyond pissed with Lolita.

Within minutes, I'm approaching my destination, but of course there's nowhere to park because the house sits on a busy street. I circle the block with satisfying thoughts of banging on the front door running through my head. On my second pass, to my utter frustration, there's still nowhere to stop, so I double park and hit the hazard lights. A glimpse of the house shows me the curtains in the front room are partially open and I catch sight of movement in the window. I pause with my hand on the door handle. There's more movement. I see Rosa and then Lolita. They're laughing. *What the hell are they doing?* And then I remember Rosa's excited chatter about their plans to play *Just Dance*.

Like someone's pulled the plug, my outrage and resentment begin to circle the drain. What am *I* doing? I'm not thinking straight. Heaving out a breath, I let my head fall back on the headrest, and slowly the scattered pieces of the last hour coalesce into a fully formed picture of . . . an uneducated jackass.

*Fuck.*

I'm a fool. And I've done it again. I lashed out at El for no other reason than she was there. I don't even bother to fight the shame that fills the void left by my dwindling outrage.

A car honks behind me, forcing me to throw my truck into gear. I drive around blindly for a while, letting my self-disgust distract me from where I need to be and what I need to do. I've never been very good at owning up to my shortcomings. In fact, before Ellie, I'd been content to sit on my high horse. People look up to me anyway; I'm the oldest sibling, I'm the boss at work, I'm the most responsible of my friends . . . I've always taken care of everyone and everything, secure in the knowledge that I rarely take a wrong step. But now, with Ellie, I seem to be messing up a lot and having to return to her with my tail between my legs.

I pull over when my phone vibrates in my pocket. Digging it out, I read the screen with trepidation.

**Opal: I'm sorry. I shouldn't have said any of those things.**

I shake my head, recognizing full well that I don't deserve the apology. Why can't I learn not to use her as a target? If I don't watch myself, I'll end up hitting a spot that won't just hurt her, but will show her how much better she deserves. My mouth goes dry at the idea.

I check the time. I've been gone for almost an hour.

**Scott: I'm the one who should apologize. Coming home now.**

My breath seizes in my chest at the word *home* as I hit send. But that's what she is to me. Home. I'm such an idiot. Afraid that another apology for another fuck-up isn't going to be enough, I run to the corner store to get her some flowers and a pack of Twizzlers.

When I'm finally outside her apartment door, I falter, almost wanting to knock instead of using my key. But that's not a precedent I'm going to set. I want this thing behind us. I'll grovel if I have to.

The sound of the lock turning and the door opening brings her to the entry hall. We stare at each other across the five feet that separates us. Standing there with the mass of her curly brown hair pulled over one shoulder, running the opal pendant I got for her nervously along the chain, she'd be more beautiful than ever if it weren't for the uncertainty in her stance. Uncertainty that I put there.

Hesitant to speak, I hold the flowers out to her, hoping they convey the depth of my remorse. Thankfully her expression softens enough that I can fill my lungs again before she crosses the distance between us and puts her arms around my neck.

As my arms fold around her, I whisper, "I'm sorry. So, so sorry."

She nods against my neck, squeezing me tighter. After a few moments, she pulls back. "I'm sorry too. I shouldn't have opened my mouth. None of that stuff is my business." Taking the flowers from me, she turns and I follow her into the kitchen.

"It *is* your business, Opal."

"No, it's not," she says, grabbing the vase – the one the roses I got for her came in – from the cupboard and filling it with some water. "Sometimes, I forget that my unsolicited opinions are just that, unsolicited."

I'm shaking my head, but she keeps talking as she cuts the plastic from around the flowers. "You needed to vent, and I should have listened instead of judged."

I snort, prompting her to look up. "You're wrong. If you don't tell me I'm being an ass, who will? It's part of your job description as my girlfriend." The word *girlfriend* suddenly sounds hollow, almost transient . . . frighteningly transient, which sets my mind off in search of a more permanent version; fiancée, wife . . . even a corny *soul mate* makes an appearance.

She interrupts my wandering thoughts with, "My job description involves supporting you, not stuffing my opinions down your throat."

"Please, sweetness," I say, feeling my lips tug at the corners. "Let's not pretend that any girlfriend worth her salt isn't going to stuff opinions down a guy's throat." My smile gets wider at the stilted guffaw that slips from her lips. "And I expect nothing less from you. I *want* nothing less. All right? Your opinions are more important to me than anyone else's."

"They are?"

"Yeah, they are."

"Which is why you walked out while I was expressing them?" she asks with an arched brow.

I pull my lips between my teeth. *Touché.* "About that . . ." I falter, watching her finish arranging the flowers. "I'm sorry. I shouldn't have left. I was frustrated and angry and I took it out on you . . . again. And, yeah, I'm sorry."

She nods, then makes her way around the island. "You don't really think that I don't care about Rosa, do you?"

"What? No." I pull her close. "I never said that." *Did I?*

With her forehead resting on my shoulder, I feel her warm exhale on my collarbone. "Okay, I just wanted to make sure you know that I lo– that I really care about the girls."

"I know you do, sweetness," I whisper. "I didn't mean to imply you didn't."

She pulls back, studying my face as if to confirm my story. Whatever she finds there must satisfy her because she plants a chaste kiss on my lips and then slips from my arms to the stove to stir our dinner. "Where'd you go?" she asks.

I groan. "To get Rosa."

Swiveling around, she sends me a disbelieving look.

"I didn't go in. At the last minute, I realized I was making a mistake."

She tilts her head in a gesture that very much suggests she's in agreement with my assessment of the situation. I'd laugh if her expression didn't turn serious. Leaning her hands on the island that separates us, she taps her nails a few times before she says, "Since you claim to like my opinions, can I tell you something you probably won't like?"

Repressing a sigh, I nod. I have to learn to take my lumps.

"I think your dismissive attitude toward addiction is pretty shitty."

Surprise manifests itself as a tsk. "I'm not dismissive."

"Yes, you are. Just because you're not affected by it, doesn't mean that others aren't. Including Lolita. Including me."

The censure in her voice irks me. "I may only deal with it second hand, but that doesn't mean I . . ." I'm trying to weigh my words carefully when I realize that she's probably right. Exhaling heavily, I meet her gaze. "Okay, you might have a point. But even before I met you, El, I was tired. Watching my mother self-destruct when I was a kid, and then watching Lolis go the same way? I'm sorry, but I don't have any patience left."

"Okay, that's fair, but you have to understand that your patience level doesn't change what is a very real struggle for a lot of people, Scott. And spouting bullshit about loving drugs more than one's own child in front of the wrong audience would only be destructive."

I duck my head and run a hand along the back of my neck, trying to ease the prickle of shame that appears there. "You're right. That was a stupid thing to say." An impulsive desire to come clean with her spurs me to add more. "And it's possible that I'm upset with Lolita for more than the usual reasons . . . so you remember what happened at the girls' choir performance?"

She nods.

"At the time, I considered going back to court to try to get our custody agreement changed, but for a million different reasons, I didn't. Well, now, last week when Rosa asked to stay overnight and I said not in a million years, Lolita threatened me."

"What?"

"Yeah, she *reminded* me there's a court order in place and that I have to honor it."

With her brows pinched with consternation, Ellie comes back around the island to stand in front of me. "Why didn't you tell me?"

"I don't know. I was mad at myself for letting it slide."

She tugs at the bottom of my T-shirt, urging me closer. "That doesn't explain why you didn't tell me."

Awkwardness rises in my chest. "I don't know. I guess . . . I didn't want you to be disappointed in me."

"What? Why would I be disappointed in you?"

I shrug. "I'm supposed to have my shit together, remember? You said so yourself." Her lips twist into something that resembles the disillusionment I was trying to avoid. "And it's stressful," I go on. "It's bad enough that I have to deal with it."

She dips her chin, seeming to study the floor as she shakes her head and I worry I've upset her again. "What happened to us communicating?" She looks up, her brow furrowed. "What happened to standing on the same side of the divide? Together?"

My eyes dart away. "I don't know." And I really don't.

When I don't come up with an answer for her, she cups my jaw. "I don't need you to take the brunt of everything life has to throw at us, Scott. I'm here to stand beside you, not behind you. I want us to be equals in this."

I feel myself nod as I place my hand over hers, sliding it to my lips to kiss her palm. "I want that too."

"Then that means sharing this kind of thing with each other."

I frown. "I just hate the thought of overwhelming you with all my baggage."

"But you'll let it overwhelm you? To the point that you're taking shots at me?"

My shoulders sag.

"We need to talk more so we can deal with stuff, together, Scott."

That sounds . . . amazing. To not worry about everything on my own. What would she have said if I'd run the idea of changing the custody agreement by her? Or if I'd told her how much I've been obsessing over my father's family?

Slowly, I nod. "Yeah. I'd like that. It might take me a while to . . . adjust." I lower my forehead to hers. "But I promise to work on it."

"That's all I ask," she says, her words brushing my lips.

My hands slide around her waist, slipping under her shirt to stroke the warm, silky skin of her back. "Thanks for putting up with me," I whisper before I kiss her, soft and gentle. "I always appreciate an appearance by Sister Opal, the Wise."

With both of us fighting a smile, the rhythm of our lips begins clumsily. But soon, like it always does, our need for intimacy leads to arousal which then ignites the white-hot lust that's always burning right below the surface between us. And this time, the ignition is accompanied by all the anger and the worry of the last few hours, making it all the more intense.

By the time we make it to the bed and I've sunk myself into her core, everything has combined to create a storm of urgency. Her nails scratch at my biceps as she arches, taking my deep, forceful strokes like I'm feeding her manna. When we're spent and sweaty, I can't seem to stop kissing and nibbling and touching her as if I'm worried that stopping will cause her to disappear on me.

Finally, with her nose burrowed in my neck, she inhales sharply. "Oh, shit, the chilli."

When she doesn't immediately move, I laugh. Patting her naked ass, I encourage her to get up. "Come on, then. Let's go see what's going on."

Unhurriedly, I get rid of the condom. Then I pass her my T-shirt and pull on my boxer briefs. I follow her out into the kitchen with my attention caught on the hem of my shirt which falls to only the very tops of her thighs. Out of nowhere, a vision of my come leaking down the insides of her legs assaults me. *Shit*. Of course, my perverted imagination runs with it, expanding on the fantasy, morphing it into an image of her laid out on her back, deliciously fucked, knees splayed wide to show me my come oozing from her pussy. Renewed lust punches through me and my muffled grunt draws her notice.

"You okay?" she asks over her shoulder, stirring the chilli.

"Yeah," I say barely keeping my voice from squeaking. To cover my disquiet – because condoms are *always* necessary – I open a drawer and pull out a spoon to get a taste of our science experiment. Blowing on it, I take the bite and almost spit it back out. "Did you put any salt in it?" I gasp after I've forced myself to swallow.

She scans the counter, grabbing up the grocery bag and pulling out all the spices we bought, the packages still sealed.

We look at each other, and slowly start laughing.

# Chapter Eleven

## Ellie

**M**y first thought of the day is more of a sensation, one that can only be described as pure pleasure. *Warmth.* And the caress of soft lips placing open-mouthed kisses down my nape.

Scott.

Scott is here in my bed. With languid contentment, I stretch out my limbs, wanting him closer, savoring the heat of a very substantial erection pressing against my backside. You'd think the man would be completely spent after last night.

His soft hum of appreciation is accompanied by an arm snaking around my hips to pull me more firmly against him. When his fingers skim up my stomach and graze my nipple though, I hiss.

"You sore?" he rumbles into my hair.

"Mmmhmm." I press his hand to my breast to stop the friction and soothe the ache. I'm slipping back into sleep when his voice startles me.

"Aren't you awake?"

"Hmmm? Go back to sleep," I mumble.

"I can't. It's 8:40."

"So?"

"So, I'm going to make a coffee run." He starts getting up, letting cold air under the blankets. "You want the usual?"

"What?" I say, partially confused, partially horrified. *He's not a morning person, is he?* The possibility is disconcerting. Prying my lids open a fraction, I roll over and watch him pull on his jeans.

"Opal?"

"Huh?"

He exhales with amusement. "Maybe by the time I get back, you'll be conscious."

He saunters out of the room and I hear the bathroom door close. "Don't you know it's Sunday?" I grumble, snuggling back down under the covers. Except now I need the bathroom too. Dammit.

Scott comes back, appearing wide awake and ready to face the world. Grabbing his wallet from the bedside table, he leans over and kisses my cheek. "Be right back."

Sighing dramatically to the now empty room, I throw back the covers and haul myself into the bathroom to take care of business. After I've brushed my hair and my teeth, I'm much more awake and grudgingly look around for some clothing. I'm almost dressed when I hear . . . is that Vader's Death March?

Following the muffled sound around the other side of the bed, I crouch down and pull Scott's phone from between the bed and the nightstand. The screen is lit up with *La Suegra del Infierno (home)*.

*The Mother in law from Hell?*

There's a serious shortage of caffeine in my system so it takes a moment to make the connection between the number and Rosa. Less than a nanosecond later, I've rejected any notion of Scott's privacy and accepted the call.

"Hello?"

"Papá?" asks a small, shaky voice.

My heartrate takes off. "Rosa? It's Ellie. Are you okay?"

She sniffles. "I want to come home. Is my dad there?"

"He forgot his phone," I say, trying to keep calm despite Rosa's obvious distress. "But he should be back soon." In the background through the phone, I hear muffled yelling. "Rosa, are you . . . are you safe?"

She sniffles again, but stays mute. Maybe she's unsure. I try again. "What's going on? How come you want to come home?"

"I need to pee."

*What?!* My brain trips and stumbles. "Umm . . . Is there someone in the bathroom?"

"The door is locked. I can't get out."

*Get out?* "You mean you can't get in? To the bathroom?"

"No the bedroom door is locked. I can't get out."

My heart now pounds in my chest. *What?!* "Okay," I say, getting to my feet and hitting the speaker button so I can pull a hoodie over my head, all the while trying to calculate how long Scott will be gone and if I should wait for him or go to her now. "Umm . . ."

The arguing in the background sharpens and Rosa whimpers. "Ellie, I want to come home."

I shove my bare feet into a pair of sneakers. "Okay, I'm coming." Grabbing my own phone, I leave the bedroom. "Just stay on the line with me, okay?" I rip a sheet of paper out of an old notebook and desperately search for a pen. Scribbling Rosa's name on the paper in big letters, I leave it on the kitchen island. At the last second I add my passcode and an arrow to the paper, placing my phone next to it. It's a risk to only take Scott's phone. If Rosa hangs up, it will be useless to me without the passcode. But I can't leave Scott with no way to contact me.

With my keys in hand, I run.

"I'm in the car now, honey, okay." I put the phone in the cup holder. "I'll be there in less than five minutes."

"Okay." God, she's definitely crying.

"Where's your mom?" I ask, silently thanking the stars that I went with Scott to drop Rosa off yesterday, so I know where to go.

"She's in the living room."

"And she can't open the door?"

"She says I have to stay here until they leave."

Wondering who *they* are, I try to keep calm while I drive. "Have they been there long?"

"I don't know." A sudden burst of yelling carries down the line. "Ellie, I'm scared."

"Okay, I know," I tell her, gripping the steering wheel tighter to stop my hands from shaking. Thank goodness it's Sunday morning and there's barely any traffic. I'm still a ways from the house when I spy a parking spot. I decide to take it, pulling in nose first, not caring that my car's rear end is hanging partially out onto the street. I'm certainly not going to take the time to parallel park it properly.

Snatching the phone up, I run toward the house. As I'm coming up to the front door, I can hear the arguing. "I'm here now, Rosa. Stay with me on the phone though, okay?"

"Okay."

With a clammy hand, I knock sharply. As if someone hit the mute button, the disagreement that's raging inside stops.

I hear heavy footsteps approach. The door is jerked open by some guy who looks seriously worse for wear. If his bloodshot eyes, messy hair, and disheveled clothes are any indication, he's badly hung over.

"Who the hell are you?" he asks peevishly, giving me a once-over.

"I'm here for Rosa." I say it as clearly and as calmly as I can.

"Rosa?" He glowers, then yells over his shoulder, "Lolita, deal with this shit." He tries to shut the door in my face, but I lodge the toe of my sneaker in the gap before it can close. The door bounces back, surprising the guy. He's not happy.

I put my hands up, one of them still gripping Scott's phone, in a non-threatening gesture. "Just get Rosa and I'll leave." I make it sound simple, because it is.

I recognize Lolita from pictures as she comes up, her features hard with suspicion.

"E-ellie?" comes from the phone, still on speaker, and I watch Lolita's whole demeanor change, shocked by the sound of her daughter's distressed voice.

"Yeah, honey. I'm here. Your mom's coming to let you out now." I look Lolita dead in the eye and tell her, "Rosa needs to use the bathroom."

Before she spins on her heel, I watch a whole host emotions flicker across the woman's face; outrage, shame, panic, worry. Good. This shit is inexcusable.

Low voices from inside the house have the guy who answered the door turning back to them. "Where do you think you're going? We're not finished here."

Worried he's talking to Lolita, I step up onto the threshold and into the room. Lolita's nowhere to be found, but there are three other people in the room, two women sitting on a sofa across from the door, and a man perched on the arm rest beside them.

"I told you," hangover guy says, "no one's going anywhere until you admit to what a whore you are."

The last ten minutes and its potent cocktail of anxiety and adrenaline must make me stupid because I scoff, loudly and derisively. All this because this asshole's a whining misogynist?

He whirls on me. "You got something to say, bitch?"

My disgust must be evident to him, but I manage to keep my mouth shut, instead focusing on the noise coming from down the hall.

"I can't hear you!" My heart begins to thump at his aggression, but I don't look away as he tries to stare me down. If there's one thing Piper's experiences have taught me about douchebags over the years, it's that if you give an inch, they take a mile. Not happening here, not with Rosa involved.

A hesitant female voice calls his attention back to the room. "Maybe you should go, Daniel."

"Me?" he spits with real resentment, taking a step away from me. "Are you serious?"

The sound of a toilet flushing somewhere in the house is a relief. I don't know who this Daniel guy is to the family, but the way he feels entitled to bully and intimidate everyone tells me the sooner Rosa and I are away from here the better.

His voice becomes thunderous. "This bitch shows up and you want *me* to leave?"

No one answers because from my palm, Scott's phone starts going off. A glance at the screen tells me it's him, calling from my phone. Thank goodness. I'm about to answer when the guy twirls around, swinging his arm. I look up to find myself staring down the barrel of a gun.

"Do not answer that."

In the blink of an eye, disbelief becomes terror. My insides freeze, then liquefy, then freeze again. For long seconds the world around me disappears and there's nothing but the horrible menace of the muzzle that's little more than two feet from my face. Slowly, awareness trickles back in; I register the terrified faces of the others in the room, see their lips moving, see the guy turning to them though he keeps the gun trained on me. Then, for some reason, everyone re-focuses on me and I flinch sideways a half step.

The phone.

Though it sounds as if it's coming from miles away, the phone in my hand is ringing again. It stops and the room collectively relaxes. But the reprieve is shattered almost immediately by it going off again.

"Shut it off!"

The rigid tension in his tone cuts me right down to the bone. I scramble to hit ignore and then manage to turn the volume down with my quaking fingers before Scott can call again.

"Ellie!" Like a shot, Rosa comes running, hurling herself at me.

*No!*

I fall to my knees and catch her, clutching her to me with all my might. "You came," she breathes happily in my ear and then tries to pull back to see me, but I hold her tightly. "Just stay there," I whisper and she tenses in my arms. She must realize that something is wrong. "Just stay there," I repeat almost inaudibly as dismay ripples through the room. Even the Daniel guy hesitates as the gun pointed at us droops toward the floor.

"Daniel," the man seated on the armrest of the sofa says quietly. "Put that away. This isn't the time or the place."

Daniel's anger ignites again as he swings the weapon around to point it at the speaker, sparking titters of alarm. "You think your crack-whore sister's brat changes anything?" he rages.

"Of course it does."

"No, it doesn't!" Daniel uses the gun for emphasis and one of the women lets out a clipped shriek.

"You need to think this through, Daniel," the man continues in a surprisingly calm voice. "You don't think he'll start pulling in favors over something like this?"

I don't understand what he means, but Daniel obviously does because once again the muzzle of the gun dips. My eyes dart to the still ajar front door.

"No," Daniel says, shaking his head vehemently. "No. No one goes anywhere till we get this shit sorted."

"Daniel, please," one of the women pleads, the younger one. "There's nothing to sort."

This sets Daniel off on a long-winded rant about cheating whores and the meaning of loyalty while he paces, gesturing wildly with the gun. Every time death rounds on me and Rosa, I freeze, which is then followed by full-body tremors as soon as it moves on. The cycle is repeated multiple times. "Don't listen," I murmur to Rosa, smoothing her hair down. Against her back, Scott's phone, still in my grip, has been vibrating almost non-stop. It both adds to and lessens my worry knowing that he must be coming.

My legs start to lose feeling, sitting like I am on my heels. I don't know how much more of this I can take. It feels like tension is bleeding from my pores. Again, I glance at the door.

"I said no one's going anywhere," Daniel screams, and it takes a second to realize the reminder is directed at me. He stomps to the door and kicks it closed, making us all jump. I manage to keep Rosa's back to the man, but she whimpers loudly and I worry that she's noticed the gun. Hearing her, Daniel's rage seems to waver, and I feel a surge of hope that he's going to end this madness.

In the distance, I hear the faint wail of a siren and my attention jerks to the front window, wondering if it has anything to do with us. Daniel must wonder the same thing because his expression turns vicious.

"Did someone call the cops?!"

Silence . . . except for the ominous wail that's edging closer, getting louder and louder as the seconds tick by.

"Son of a bitch!"

"Just go," the man balanced on the armrest of the sofa suggests.

"God damn you! You were my best friend!"

I hold my breath as Daniel waves the gun around some more, unsure of what to do with the sound of that siren getting closer, piercing the air now, shrill and sharp.

"Dan. Go!" The supposedly traitorous best friend seems genuinely worried that Daniel is going to stick around for a standoff with the cops. And all I can think is *Yes, Daniel! Go!*

It's the flashing of the blue and red lights in the front window that triggers him to make a bee-line for the back of the house. Exhausted, I slide over onto my butt and pull my legs out from under me, still keeping Rosa gripped in my arms. "He's gone now," I whisper softly. "We're okay, he's gone."

Lolita rushes toward us. "Oh, Rosita, are you okay?" She tries to pull Rosa from my arms, but Rosa clings to me like a barnacle.

"No! I want Ellie."

The shocked betrayal on the woman's face would make me feel sorry for here if I weren't so off balance right now. There's no chance for reactions though as loud steps clomp up the porch. But it's not the cops like I'm expecting. After a succinct rap to the door, it pushes open without anyone moving to open it.

Scott bursts in, his face tinged with the ungodly combination of panic and murder. Sweeping his gaze in a wide arc, he finds us on the floor.

"What. The fuck. Is going on?"

"Scotty," Lolita breathes with alarm, standing as if she's going to intercept him.

Brushing past her, he drops down beside us, and Rosa releases me to attach herself to her dad. *"Calabacita,"* he coos, stroking her back. "It's all good now. I'm here."

Without Rosa needing me, without her warm, reassuring weight, I feel myself begin to splinter, especially when Scott's accusing eyes land on mine. *Oh god, he thinks I've done something.* The added strain magnifies my dismay tenfold, which must be noticeable because he frowns as he reaches for me, motioning me closer. Weak with relief, I tuck myself under his arm and rest my head on his shoulder next to Rosa's arm while he squeezes us both tightly.

"Sweetness," he murmurs, kissing the top of my head. "What happened? Why are the cops outside?"

I have no words for him though. My mind is a tangled mess.

With Rosa in his arms, he gets to his feet, pulling me up along with him. Noticing I'm unsteady on my feet, he puts his arm back around me. His presence is like a balm to my jagged nerves.

"What the hell happened?" he repeats.

Flinching, I push my nose farther into the crook of his neck, asking for a moment before I have to defend myself. His grip tightens on my hip in silent reassurance and I figure out he's not talking to me when someone else answers.

"Listen, Scotty," the male voice says. "Everyone's fine, so . . ."

"Obviously, no one's fine, Mateo," he grinds out, telling me that his not knowing what's going on is wrenching at the hold he has on his temper.

There's a knock on the door accompanied by the muted squawk of a police radio.

"I can't believe you called the cops," the man, Mateo, hisses. It comes to me that I know that name; he's Lolita's brother.

Glancing up, I get an eyeful of Lolita's loathing. "Is that a joke?" she hisses back. "I'd already called them *before* this idiot got here." She gestures at me heatedly.

"Everyone keeps their mouths shut," Mateo continues in a harsh whisper. "I'll handle this."

I hear the door being opened as Scott moves us over to the couch where he arranges Rosa on his lap with her legs resting across mine. When Lolita comes near and touches Rosa's shoulder, Rosa gives a low whine and leans away. At her daughter's rejection, sympathy weakens my need to conveniently blame her for all of this. But my over-taxed brain needs something easier than emotions to deal with, so I instead concentrate on what's being said at the door.

Apparently the 'domestic disturbance' wasn't serious at all, just an overreaction on his sister's part to his girlfriend's ex's refusal to leave the house when asked. The police aren't satisfied and request to speak to the 911 caller in private out on the porch.

"I want to go home now," Rosa says softly for at least the tenth time today, and I have to agree with her. To add my silent pleas to hers, I sit up and face him.

"Soon," he tells his daughter gently as he searches my face for more than he got from the version given to the police. "You okay?" he asks.

Automatically, my head bobbles on my neck in the affirmative.

"As soon as the cops clear out, we'll go." Kissing my forehead, he pulls me back to his chest where I allow myself to sink into the safety of his presence. As the adrenaline drains from my system, it's being replaced by exhaustion.

"Listen, Scotty," I hear Lolita's brother over my head. "We need to talk."

"Let me take Rosa home first," he says.

"I just need you to know –"

"Leave it, Mateo!" Both Rosa and I jump at Scott's harsh tone. "We'll talk later," he says, moderating his voice.

"Fine." The front door opens and Mateo doesn't give his sister a single second to collect herself. "They gone?"

"Yeah," Lolita says, pursing her lips, looking over at our huddle with longing and disdain.

"Well, what'd you tell them?" her brother demands.

Her face contorts into a scowl. "Nothing. I'm not stupid. I just said he was scaring my kid because he refused to leave. That's it. I thanked them for driving him off."

"Him who?" Scott asks, his voice icy.

"Daniel."

"Daniel?" Scott asks, confused. "Daniel, Daniel? Why would you call the cops on Daniel?" Scott must know him.

Silence. No one says a word.

"Sol?" Scott prompts, hoping Lolita's mother will be willing to tell him.

"I'm not getting involved in this."

"No, of course not," Scott grumbles under his breath, then says, "Go get dressed, Rosa, please."

"You're taking her?" Lolita wails. "I don't have to have her back until after dinner."

Under no circumstances would I allow Rosa to stay here in this house a minute longer, but I'm glad that it's not me who has to insist.

"Lolita," her brother says. "Let it go."

"Shut up! This is all your fault!" The fury that accompanies the accusation makes Rosa flinch and propels Scott into action. He urges me to my feet and then stands with his daughter still clinging to him while Lolita hurls invective at her brother.

Our movement draws her attention and her rage quickly becomes desperation. "Please, Scotty! I swear none of this had anything to do with me. Please. Don't take her."

My already rattled nerves quiver at her anguished tone, and I'm so grateful that Scott doesn't add to it by raising his voice. When he speaks, he's surprisingly gentle. "I'll come back later for her stuff and we can talk then, okay?"

"This is all her fault," Lolita cries, jabbing a finger in my direction, making me jump.

"Enough," Scott says in a way that belies the calm from seconds earlier. "We're not having this conversation right now."

Hearing the steel in Scott's voice, Lolita doesn't argue further, just concentrates on her last seconds with her daughter. "I'm sorry, Rosa. I love you so much and I'll see you next time, okay?" But Rosa turns her face to avoid her mother.

Out on the porch, when the door is shut behind us, Lolita's voice reaches us loud and clear as she launches into her brother and his girlfriend at the top of her lungs.

"Christ," Scott hisses. "Let's get out of here."

On shaky legs, I rush to keep up with his long stride as he heads toward his truck, which is parked at the end of the driveway, blocking the sidewalk. Ripping open the passenger-side door, he awkwardly gets the seat pulled forward with Rosa still in his arms. She doesn't protest when he buckles her in. He pulls his head out and then slams the door. The finality of the bang has the bottom of my stomach dropping away. Staring at the closed door, I realize I'm not going with them, that I'm being dismissed. His daughter needs him.

"El!" I cringe away from him, then gather he's been trying to get my attention. Meeting his concerned eyes, I whisper, "Yes?"

"My phone?" He's holding mine out to me, expecting me to trade it for the one that's still clutched so tightly in my hand. It feels wrong to give it up now, but I force myself to let him take it from me. "You sure you're okay to drive?"

He follows my gaze to the truck's closed passenger door. I want to tell him that I'm not okay, that I don't want to be by myself, but then I see Rosa through the window, trusting and innocent, and I know I won't because I'm an adult and not half as important as a seven-year-old. "Yeah, m'okay."

Somehow my feet are able to retrace my steps back to my car. When I'm finally sitting in the driver's seat, I hold my hands palms up over my lap, and watch them tremble. Maybe I should wait a little before I drive anywhere. But what if *he* comes back? My head snaps up and I search the sidewalk, all of a sudden certain he'll be right there, pointing the gun at me through the windshield. But there's no one, just me and my imagination until I swing my head around to the other side and spy Scott jogging across the street toward me.

Our eyes meet through the glass as he pulls my door open. "Come on," he says, reaching for my hand to pull me up. "You're not okay. Go get in the truck. I'll park your car properly."

"Thanks," I whisper, unable to keep up the pretense. "The keys are in the ignition."

Barely cognizant enough to check for traffic, I cross the street to where he's double parked and get in. I feel myself relax by a few degrees.

"Ellie?"

Rosa's soft voice further dissipates the fog. Slowly, I twist in my seat. "Yeah, honey?"

"Thanks for coming to get me."

I smile faintly. "I'll always come get you, Rosa, anytime, anywhere. No matter what. Okay?"

Her smile is much more pronounced than mine and it goes a long way to settling my nerves. "Okay," she chirps happily as Scott yanks open his door.

"What's okay?" he asks, pulling into traffic.

"Ellie saved me, Papá."

I watch Scott's lips push together in a frown. God, I'm so worried that when he hears the story, he's not going to be pleased with me. An image of the accusatory glare he'd leveled me with when he first arrived slots itself into the forefront of my mind.

"Tell me what happened, *Calabacita*."

While Rosa explains her version of events in the disjointed way of a child, embellishing some parts, downplaying others,

I keep my unseeing gaze trained out the passenger-side window and wait for her to mention the one detail which will undoubtedly set Scott off. But it never comes. All through Scott and Rosa's shared indignation about the lock on the bedroom door, and the yelling, and the curse words, there's no mention of the gun. Slumping further in the seat, I say a silent prayer of thanks that somehow, someway, she never saw it.

I've been so caught up in the account that I don't notice where we we're going. When we pull into Scott's driveway, I look at him in confusion. "You didn't drop me off."

He only grunts out a noise that rings with disapproval before he gets out and comes around to first pull me out and then Rosa who he has to carry because not only is she still in her pajamas, but she's not wearing any shoes.

Inside, our unexpected arrival causes a bit of an uproar that's headed up by an excited Carmen and Daniela. Scott allows them a few minutes to grill us about what's going on. As Rosa excitedly retells the story for her siblings, Scott watches her closely, I'm guessing to gauge her frame of mind. The girls had been eating breakfast when we came in so they eventually get shuffled back to the table and Scott pours Rosa some cereal. Once they're settled in the care of his grandmother, he pulls me out the kitchen door and into the back yard.

I'm about to be interrogated, I can feel it.

# Chapter Twelve

## Scott

What a clusterfuck of a morning. I'd be coming down hard on myself for forgetting my phone in the first place if I weren't so twisted up with resentment against Lolita right now. How dare she lock my kid up like an animal?

A soccer ball left out on the concrete patio catches my eye as I come down the steps into the back yard. I send it flying with a well-placed kick and the still, morning air reverberates with its impact against the cinderblock wall that serves as our fence. It's not half as satisfying as I need it to be, but I refuse to give in to the urge to scream in frustration where my kids can witness it.

Ellie's soft voice comes from behind me. "I'm sorry," she whispers, making me wheel on her.

"For what?" I demand, trying to keep a lid on my anger.

The way she flinches puts a dent in my outrage, but it's a small one.

"Oh, um," she hesitates, "I know I shouldn't have gone to the house, and I'm sorry for interfering."

I feel my face pinch with annoyance. First of all, she can hardly get her voice above an exasperatingly timid whisper, and second, she looks guilty as fuck. "Interfering?" I deadpan. "Am I hearing you right?"

"I understand you're upset with me. I just didn't know what else —"

"You think I'm upset? Why would I be upset that you helped my daughter when she needed it?" I can see the effect my attitude is having on her, can see it reflected in the misgiving in her expression, but I can't stop my next words. "What's going on with you?"

Something that strikes me as fear settles on her features and works to clear away some of the haze of self-absorbed assholery I'm wallowing in. Something isn't right.

Taking her hand, I guide her to the picnic table and encourage her to sit up on the tabletop with her legs dangling off the end. I step between her thighs and, in a gesture that I hope is comforting, I kiss her once, softly on the lips. When I pull back, however, the turmoil hasn't abated in the least. I cup her jaw with my palms.

"What's going on, sweetness?" My brows pull together when her eyes jackrabbit away. "I'm not that much of an ogre, am I?" I say, trying to lighten the mood, stroking her cheeks with my thumbs. But when she brings her gaze back, there's not a hint of humor.

"He had a gun," she whispers.

"Huh?" Her words are almost inaudible and obviously I've heard them wrong.

"He had a gun aimed at us."

I recoil this time and jerk her with me because I'm still holding her face. Reaching for my wrists to steady herself, she watches as I internally free-fall through every negative emotion imaginable.

"Who did?" I finally force out. "Daniel?"

Tears start to well in her big, brown eyes as she nods. "I've never been so scared. Rosa was right there, holding on to me. What if . . ?" But I don't let her finish that sentence. I can't. I just crush her to my chest as if that will annihilate all trace of such a terrifying, incomprehensible thought.

*A gun? A fucking gun?*

Even though the danger no longer exists, I have to force myself to stay calm, and all at once it occurs to me how difficult it would have been for Ellie to face the real thing. Gripping her shoulders, I push her back enough to study her tear-stained face. Her behavior makes a lot more sense now.

"Rosa didn't mention anything," I say cautiously.

She shakes her head, and then her face crumples with renewed crying. "I don't think she saw it," she says through a soft sob.

Experiencing Ellie's tears is never pleasant, but right now, it's heart-wrenching. Pulling her close, I rock her gently as she cries, murmuring soft nothings to her as I do my best to absorb the flood of relief and gratitude that's running right alongside the shock and fury.

*A fucking gun.*

Gradually, she quiets and I wipe her tears. "Sorry for being all weepy," she says, her voice still low and raspy. "I'm sticking close to standard protocol, huh?"

"It's probably a good thing to get it all out, sweetness. Are you going to be okay?"

"Yeah. I'm feeling better."

My arms fall to my sides and I tilt my head to the dull grey of the overcast sky as if looking for a way to keep the tumult swelling inside of me at bay.

She pulls a deep, shuddering breath into her lungs. "I'm just so glad that I was able to keep her back to him."

"That was quick-thinking."

"No," she says shakily. "It was instinct."

"Can you tell me everything, from the beginning?"

While she tells the tale in excruciating detail, I pace. When she's done, although my rage at Daniel *fucking* Patterson is boiling in my gut, I recognize that Ellie and the girls have to be my first priority.

With a neighbor's wind chimes jingling softly somewhere, I tip her chin up and say my next words with more than a little conviction. "Thank you. That you went for her like that means more to me than you can imagine."

She gathers her hair away from her pale face in a nervous gesture. "I don't know. If I hadn't gone, Rosa wouldn't have been in that room at all."

"No, she'd have been locked up, alone and scared. You did the right thing, El. Please, don't doubt that." When she's still unconvinced, I add, "Under the circumstances, I would have done the same thing. It's so good to know that I can count on you in an emergency." My beautiful girl, who's clearly still shaken up, gives me the ghost of a smile. "Come on, let's go inside," I say, helping her hop down off the table.

After getting her installed on the sofa in the living room where the girls are still in pajamas watching cartoons, I pour two cups of coffee and go sit with my girls, all of them.

I wish I could say this quiet time was enjoyable, but I'm antsy as fuck. Not only am I trying to reconcile the idea of a gun being in any proximity to my daughter and my girlfriend, but Ellie is understandably, yet uncharacteristically quiet. And on top of everything Lolita is blowing up my phone with texts and calls. Finally after the tenth text, I angrily slam my thumbs down on the screen, telling her to give it a rest for a few hours.

"Is that Lolita?" Ellie asks quietly.

"Yeah."

"I can't believe I'm saying this, but I think she did what she thought was necessary to keep Rosa safe."

Angrily, I whisper, "She should have called me."

Ellie nods, but I can tell she has more to say.

"What?" I ask, unable to keep the snap from my tone as my gaze flicks to the girls who are only a few feet away. I turn the TV up a notch

"Just, I think she wanted to prove that she could take care of Rosa on her own."

"And look how that turned out. No, I'm calling the lawyer first thing in the morning."

"I don't think you should. I think you should wait, at least for a few days."

A garbled noise of disbelief is my only response.

Ellie seems saddened, but it's like water off a duck's back for me at this point. Honestly, the steps I need to take to put this morning's events to rights are the only things holding me together. Constructing a mental checklist keeps my mind from fixating on the unthinkable.

And that's how I get through the day, step by step. First, I sit Rosa down and get her talking about what happened again. Without asking her outright, I confirm she had no idea Daniel had a weapon.

Then in the afternoon, while my grandmother is at Mass, I leave the girls with Ellie and go back to Lolita's mother's place to pick up Rosa's things. Listening to Lolita's passionate defense of her actions does nothing for me. My patience where she's concerned has officially dried up. Her brother, Mateo, at least keeps quiet and doesn't bitch when I ask him to help me drive Ellie's car home. He breaks his silence though when I'm running him back.

"He wouldn't have done it, you know that, right?"

I just grunt, keeping my focus on the road. It's telling that he doesn't plead Lolita's case, but Daniel's. It's a good thing the trip takes less than five minutes. If I'd had to share such a small space with him for longer, I'd have completely lost my shit.

The hardest part is yet to come though, when I'm forced to leave Ellie in her bed by herself. It's always bothered me, not having all four of them in one place, under one roof, where I know they're all safe, but today it's unbearable.

Poor Ellie hasn't been herself all day. She's been edgy, seeking out my touch, my approval in subtle ways that make me crazy, not because I begrudge her the attention, but because it's not like her. I hate that this has hurt her, maybe even altered her in some kind of fundamental way.

As I tiredly tuck her blankets around her, I watch her watching me. She may not ask me to stay, but the pleading in her eyes is louder than any words. And I break.

"Come back home with me."

The complete lack of privacy waiting for us in my grandmother's house kindles . . . not shame, exactly, but maybe embarrassment at not being able to provide her with a suitable place where she'd be safe. But I'd face it for her. Anything for her.

Her lips push together in a small grin. "I love you for offering, but I wouldn't do that to you. Can you imagine your grandmother's face when she finds me wrapped around you in the morning?"

The band already squeezing my lungs pulls tighter as I sink down on the edge of the bed beside her. "I know it's not an ideal situation . . . but I can't leave you here, El."

I get a reassuring flash of a true smile. "Yes, you can. You and I both know there's no danger here," she says, pulling her arm from beneath the covers to gesture at the room in general. "Any kind of . . . insecurity we're feeling isn't rational, and if I give in to it, I think everything that's happened will dog me for longer."

Feeling helpless, I search her face for any hint that she's not being completely honest with me.

"It's mind over matter," she continues, but I place my index finger gently over her lips. When it's clear she's going to let me talk, I cup her cheek and sweep a thumb over her cheekbone.

"See, I'm not sure if you're trying to spare me here, Opal, or if you're really okay with me leaving." Her expression gives nothing away. "Because if you need me, we stick together. No matter what. In fact, I'm tempted to throw you over my shoulder and haul you out of here regardless."

And just like that, her entire countenance changes and a tiny giggle fills the air. "Oh, yeah? Will you bind and gag me too?"

A short laugh at her eager tone sounds between us. "All jokes aside, I need to know where you're at, my beautiful girl."

She licks her lips nervously. "I meant what I said. If I don't . . . handle this tonight, if I don't push through, I think it might become a problem."

My thoughts start flip-flopping inside my head, trying to decipher what she means.

"I know myself," she goes on. "I'm more than capable of using you as a crutch. And I have no intention of turning you into my new dirty martini."

*Dirty martini? What?* And then her meaning rushes me, spiking my pulse like a bouncy ball.

Her hand covers mine against her cheek. "So, you're going to go and I'm going to promise to call if I need you."

With a defeated exhale, I slide down beside her on the bed so we're lying face to face. "You're sure?"

"Very sure." Her lips find mine. "Now go before I start wailing and clinging to your leg in highly dramatic fashion."

A weak grin teases my lips. "Okay," I say simply, trusting her to know what's best for her. I kiss her reluctantly one last time.

I call her in the morning and she claims to be feeling much more like herself after getting some sleep. That's more than I can say for myself. I did nothing but toss and turn all night while the day's events and their *what ifs* sank their claws deep into my flesh.

Mondays are never my favorite, but work turns into an exceptionally long, arduous affair. And worse, Jorgie, who I exchanged texts with yesterday afternoon, doesn't get back to me until after dinner.

**Jorgie: Pick you up in an hour.**

My stomach dips. I've been coming out of my skin waiting for this text. I should count myself lucky, it could have come two or three days from now, a week even. And now that I've read it, Sudden misgivings seep into my resolve to see this through. Plus, in an hour I'm supposed to be at Ellie's place.

Indecision peels away another layer of my sanity. Nothing should be more important than Ellie's well-being. Except maybe I can do both. I'll get this done and then I can see her after. An hour's not going to matter one way or the other. Before I can change my mind, I text her.

**Scott: I'm going to need an extra hour. R U good with that?**

**Opal: I'm sure I'll survive. Everything ok?**

**Scott: Yeah, just**

*Just what?* My thumbs hang over the keyboard. When they return to type, a sick feeling spreads through my chest.

**Scott: Yeah, just a homework problem.**

**Opal: Ok, take your time.**

By the time Jorgie shows up, my brain is still trying to justify lying to her, but no amount of rationalization seems to be working. I hope I know what I'm doing.

When I get into Jorgie's car, he doesn't help matters.

"You sure about this?"

Jorgie and I finally put our differences aside last month when he showed up on a Sunday morning with coffee and an apology. Personally, I thought he should have grovelled a bit more, but I figured twenty years of friendship wasn't something to give up on lightly.

I turn a stony glare on him. "I'm sure. Where we going?"

My heart falls when he names a place at least forty minutes away, but I'm not backing out now. I don't think I could even if I wanted to.

We drive mostly in silence, listening to tunes while I brood in a mix of angry anticipation and dread. When we pull up in front of a small house in a sleepy suburban neighborhood, Jorgie shrugs at my questioning glance. "I'm only the messenger."

He doesn't knock, just walks in the front door like he owns the place. The living room is eerily void of furniture, but we follow the sound of voices into the kitchen. Around a table are five guys, drinking beers and smoking.

"About time, Junior," Niner gripes, getting to his feet, stubbing out his cigarette. "You drive like a fucking old lady, or what?"

Jorgie snorts. "At least I'll make it to old age. You assholes will all be dead soon from sucking on those cancer sticks."

My eyes land on Alejandro, who's ignoring everything else in the room but me. The way his scrutiny rakes over me is unnerving. He knows I'm in way over my head here, and I'm suddenly afraid he's going to call me out for wasting his time.

Only a very unwise man would waste Alejandro Bernal-Acosta's time, and I wonder just how close to empty my goodwill with Alejandro is running. He may have known me my whole life, but his best friend, my Tío Javier, has been dead for going on a decade . . . and surely he's got better things to do than babysit me and my petty grudges. Drug syndicates don't run themselves after all.

But then he says, "Clear out. Go get dinner or something. I want to talk to Scotty." And by the tone of his voice, I can tell that he's not pissed off with me, just curious.

The guys get to their feet without complaint and leave one by one, mumbling greetings and administering a few cuffs to our shoulders as they go.

"You too, Jorgie."

Jorgie checks with me briefly, but he does as he's told. "I'll be on the back steps."

When we're alone, Alejandro says, "Grab a beer from the fridge."

For a moment, I consider it. A beer might do my nerves some good, but Ellie smelling it on me is one of the least appealing things I can think of.

"Nah, I'm good."

He gestures to the chair in front of him so I take it.

"Thanks for doing this," I begin, but he holds up a hand to stop me.

"You've never asked me for anything, Scotty. I'm happy to help you out." In the almost seven months since I last saw him when Ellie and I went to pick up my mom from that bar, he looks like he's aged years. He's tired, that much is clear, and I'm tempted to ask if he's okay until he says more. "But I need to know what you're thinking here."

"I just want to talk to him."

The tick of his eyebrows tells me he knows that's bullshit, but I keep my mouth shut.

"I sent Luis to pick him up."

My gaze snaps to his in alarm. If Alejandro is the devil, Luis is his wrath. Luis takes care of shit when shit is serious, I know that much. I bite back the apology that's forming on my tongue because he's still talking.

"The kid was expecting us. Didn't so much as say a word when he was told to get in the truck."

My earlier misgivings begin to refashion themselves into something that feels more like the sting of conscience. "I just want to talk to him," I repeat, though it feels like less of a lie than it did thirty seconds ago.

"All right then." He gets to his feet and I follow him to a door off the kitchen. As we go down into the basement on creaking, wooden steps, nightmarish visions of Daniel tied to a chair assault me, but when Alejandro flips the switch, I don't see him at all. Movement pulls my attention to the other side of the room where Daniel is sliding up the wall from where he was sitting on the floor. He squints against the light.

The unfinished basement is completely barren and cold as fuck, but that doesn't stop the heat of my rage from surfacing when I see him. My knuckles crack with how hard I clench my fists.

I remind myself I only want to talk.

Except not a single word occurs to me. Not that I could get it out anyway with my teeth grinding together like they are.

"Listen, Scotty," Daniel croaks, his eyes bouncing nervously between me and Alejandro.

My head tilts, wondering what he could possibly have to say for himself. Turns out he's got nothing because his mouth snaps shut and stays that way. I've known Daniel Patterson forever. He's Lolita's brother's best friend. Though Daniel and Mateo are two years younger, we crossed paths often as kids and then teenagers. I have fond memories of kicking their asses at Mortal Kombat. It's been years though. Who would have thought that little kid would grow up to be this grubby, disheveled piece of shit who nearly annihilated my life as I know it?

Alejandro interrupts my thoughts by moving to lean against the wall to my left. He crosses his arms over his chest and lifts an eyebrow at me as if to say, *now what?*

That's a very good question. What am I doing here?

"I'm listening," I tell Daniel simply, but I can hear the underlying threat in my tone.

"I wasn't thinking," he pleads, rubbing his hands down the front of his jeans in a nervous gesture.

I glare at him. He's going to have to do way better than that.

"I . . . I didn't know who she was."

My head shakes of its own accord in disgust. "Didn't know who she was?" I mock. "My daughter or my girlfriend?"

He doesn't know how to answer that and his silence begins to gnaw at my patience. "Why the fuck would you have a gun anyway?"

"I need that shit for protection, man! The streets aren't safe." His attention jumps to Alejandro as if he's worried he's offending the owner of said streets.

"No, Daniel," I say, the volume of my voice rising, jerking his focus back to me. "Why would you have a gun in Mateo's house?"

"I loved her!"

My face screws up. "Who? Angela?"

"Yeah, how would you like it if your best friend was fucking your woman behind your back? For months!"

Anger spikes through me like lightning, pushing me to cross the space separating us. "You pulled a gun because of a fucking love triangle?!" My hand takes hold of his T-shirt. "Are you stupid?!"

He flinches away. "I, I wasn't thinking," he stutters. "I was just so pissed off and that girl showed up and –"

"That girl?!" I rage at him. "That girl is going to be my wife!" My right fist slams into his face even before I have a chance to think about it, filling the room with a very satisfying *thunk*. "Now she's traumatized because of you." I hit him again, but this time he's not so docile.

"Get off me!" He throws a punch that glances off my chin, but I barely feel it. I pummel him with two more quick shots and he sags in my grip.

"And then my daughter shows up and you don't stand down?! Huh?" I shove him back into the cement wall and he manages to catch himself before he goes down. "What the fuck is that?"

Disregarding the remorse in his expression, I continue to rant. "You think I've worked so hard in life for an asshole like you to take it all away from me?!" I move in and grab his shirt again. "What if the gun went off?" His arms come up to protect his face, so I hit him in the gut. "What then?!" The mere possibility of Ellie or Rosa being gone swallows me whole as I hit him again and again. When I finally let him go, I get in a last shot to his ribs on his way down. The distressed whoosh of his breath leaving his lungs doesn't even faze me. It's only fair. He didn't show any concern for my girls' welfare, I won't show any for his. I'm about to kick him when something grips my arm. I spin around, coiled tight, poised to deal with the new threat.

"Scotty! I said that's enough!"

Jerking my arm out of his grasp, I barely refrain from taking a swing at Alejandro. Adrenaline buffets me from all sides, and despite my heaving chest, from one second to the next, I feel like I'm suffocating.

"Scotty," he says calmly. "Right here." He points to his face. "There you go. Take a deep breath."

My constricted airways loosen slowly, but enough to get some oxygen circulating in my system again, allowing me to focus on Alejandro. "You're done here," he says, his tone leaving no room for argument. "Go home."

I take in the aftermath of my actions; Daniel sprawled on the concrete floor, trying to catch his own breath, blood oozing from his nose and one of his eyes already beginning to swell shut. Instead of horrifying me, the sight only serves to enrage me again. I draw my foot back, ready to unleash more of my frustration on this piece of shit, but Alejandro plants a heavy palm in the center of my chest and pushes me away.

"Go. Home."

I stumble back. The thought of slamming my fist into Alejandro's face briefly flits through my mind, but it seems my sense of self-preservation is still somewhat intact. The rigid fury that's been holding me hostage unravels slightly under his stare. My muscles unlock enough that I manage a nod before I stagger my way up the stairs.

The door to the backyard crashes into the wall when I yank it open with too much force, making Jorgie drop his phone on the concrete steps.

"Ah, fuck!" He snatches it back up, inspecting it for damage. "Asshole," he gripes.

"Let's go."

Something in my voice catches his interest because as he stands, he gives me an intent going-over. "You all right? You're a little paler than usual."

I wish I had it in me to laugh. He's been cracking jokes about my pale skin since we were five years old. But what I've done has all traces of humor locked down. Without a word, I turn on my heel and head for the front of the house.

Jorgie catches up with me out on the street. At the passenger door of his car, I rest my forearms on the roof and hang my head, needing to get a hold of myself. The jittery feeling swimming through my veins is making me nauseous.

"Scotty?"

"I'm good, Jorgie."

When I don't hear the locks disengage, I look up to find him mirroring my stance on the other side of the car, watching me with concern. How annoying that he knows me so well.

"I said I'm fine. Let's go."

He's not convinced but he nods anyway. Ignoring the twinge of pain in my hand when I grab hold of the door handle, I get in and sit stony-faced the whole way back, rejecting every attempt Jorgie makes to talk, silently stewing in satisfaction . . . or is it self-loathing? The line between the two is awfully thin with my hand throbbing in my lap and my dick weirdly semi-hard behind the zipper of my jeans. I tell myself it's the adrenaline, but mostly, I'm numb to everything except the yearning to see Ellie. It intensifies with every passing minute.

By the time Jorgie drops me off on the corner near her building, it's past midnight. I let myself in to a quiet apartment, only the light over the stove greeting me. She's gone to bed. Of course she has. It's late.

I find her curled up on her side with her palm tucked under her cheek, sleeping peacefully in the glow of the bedside lamp. For a few moments, I manage to hold myself back, to just stare down at her and wonder at how such a strong, beautiful woman ever came to be mine. She's everything I could have ever hoped for. And if I had any decency at all, I wouldn't wake her; I'm a sweaty mess with bloody knuckles, a hard-on, and a serious lack of remorse for what I've done.

I sit next to her on the edge of the bed.

She stirs and graces me with a sleepy smile. "You're here." A hand sneaks from beneath the covers to reach for my face. I lean into the warmth, my eyelids drooping at the contact. Her touch both soothes my scorched soul and sets my battered body alight.

She shifts and I open my eyes to find her much more alert and assessing. "What happened here?" she asks, brushing her finger tips along the side of my jaw.

Without thinking, I lift my hand to inspect the spot.

"Oh, Scott, what happened?" She immediately sits up to cradle my battered and swollen hand in hers. In the space between one heartbeat and the next, her sweet brown eyes snap to mine. "Oh my god, what did you do?"

"I just wanted to talk to him," I say hoarsely.

Her gaze rushes to cover every inch of me, searching for more damage. "Are you hurt?" she cries, and then her next breath is a sharp one. "Is that blood?"

My eyes drops and sure enough there's a red smear across my chest that's barely discernible against the dark blue of my hoodie. When I look up again, her distress is palpable. "Just tell me you're okay."

Sliding my uninjured hand to her nape, I pull her forehead to mine. "I am now."

Slowly, despite her concern, my lips descend onto that lush mouth of hers. She's not quite willing yet, she still wants to talk, so it takes a bit of persuasion, some nipping and teasing and sipping at her mouth before she finally relents. The kiss deepens and I sink into its comfort, letting it chip away at the raw violence of the last couple of hours.

The incredible sensation of her tongue against mine triggers a massive wave of physical and emotional need that engulfs me. I barely register that she drops the sheet and exposes her satin smooth breasts, tipped with those tightly furled, pink buds I love so much. Jesus, she was waiting for me naked.

While I feast on the sight, she unzips my hoodie and pushes it from my shoulders, carefully freeing my hands before she pulls my T-shirt over my head. Tapping my hip, she gets me on my feet and reaches for my belt. I don't help, just stand there with my arms limp at my sides, my dick as hard as stone as she tugs, unbuttons and unzips to finally let my jeans fall around my ankles. I remain motionless but for a shiver as her fingers trace the outline of my straining erection. She lowers the waistband of my boxer briefs and I feel both the cooler air and her perusal caress me.

Lying back on the bed, she holds the covers up to invite me in, every perfect line of her body on display. I need her so badly I can barely breathe. Kicking everything off, I get in beside her, reveling in the way her soft curves fit against me like a dream, especially when she coaxes me on top of her and my hips settle into the cradle of her thighs.

With the shaky fingertips of my uninjured hand, I trace her full lips. She's such a beautiful contradiction of innocence and confidence; her makeup-free face and fanned-over-the-pillow hair whisper of sweetness, while the burning sexuality from within her calls like a siren's song to my baser urges.

She lifts her head and kisses my chin where I'm guessing a bruise is forming. I follow her back down to the pillow and our lips meet in a searing kiss. Our moans mingle with our hot, questing tongues. One kiss becomes another and then another and another. After so many months together, we know each other's bodies like they're our own and we gradually wind ourselves into a more and more all-consuming state of blind, fiery ardor. Instinct begins to take over, making some very heavy demands in the form of curling hips and bending spines. Her fingers dig into my ass, pulling me in tighter against her. We both gasp, rocking into the unbearable pleasure as Nature makes it plain how this is going to go. My dick slides along her slippery core again and again, driving us mad. Greedily, my hand gropes at the back of her thigh, splaying her further open. She arches, I thrust and just like that the unthinkable happens . . . the most sublime, transcendent two seconds ever lived. A baptism of fire. I sink deep into her, skin-to-skin, nothing between us, and the unmuted feel of her flesh yielding to my invasion shocks me to my very core.

Ellie inhales sharply, but I barely hear it over the desperate sound of my, "Oh, ffuuuuuck," that flawlessly mirrors the raw, throbbing, torturous ecstasy of the moment. Time stands still. I pant hard into her shoulder, trying to keep my head, but the low, throaty moan that falls from her mouth is like the devil himself whispering in my ear.

Every muscle in my body reverberates with a pounding drumbeat of want, which only thumps more stridently as Ellie starts to squirm. I'm a single thread away from snapping. "Tell me what to do," I beg gutturally, but already, I feel my hips coiling into her, burrowing myself deeper.

"Please, Scott," she breathes.

# Chapter Thirteen

## Ellie

Despite knowing how torn Scott is, I can't not plead with him. My body and mind are delirious with the incredible feel of him inside of me, bare. And it's all magnified by the sweetest of torturous noises that he's unaware of making in my ear.

His dick kicks inside of me and I shudder. We both know there's no reason for him not to surrender to this; I'm on birth control, we're clean, we're monogamous. The only thing holding him back is fear. He takes hold of my chin roughly and pulls back just enough to see me. An electric charge surges between us, which must convince him, because he shifts back and then plunges himself back into me. It's so good I barely manage to catch the look of sheer bliss on his face before his head drops and I lose myself in the quest for my orgasm. His deep, powerful thrusts have me well on my way to completion when the unexpected thought of being filled with his come bears down on me like a freight train. My head lolls to the side as the rush starts deep within, and then languidly rolls over me until it crests in the most glorious of fashions, leaving me insensible to everything except the rhythmic straining of my pussy around his wide girth.

He ends up slumped atop me, his weight as comforting as his panted breaths at my shoulder. I nuzzle his neck, feeling nothing but contentment that one of the last barriers between us has been removed – literally.

With his next breath comes a noise of disbelief . . . or maybe it's distress. I trail my nails up his back and into the short hair at his neck, lightly scraping until he relaxes against me once again.

"I couldn't let it stand," he announces quietly. It takes a second to piece together that he's not referring to the condom but to the incident at Lolita's. From the evidence, I'm guessing that the *I just wanted to talk to him* became less of a cerebral endeavor and more of a physical one tonight. I should probably object or disapprove . . . but disapproval isn't even close to what I'm feeling right now.

"Without Rosa . . . or you," he continues, his voice cracking. He swallows hard before he can go on. "I couldn't let it stand."

"I know," I whisper.

"I want out, El."

My fingertips in his hair stall out. "What?"

He lifts his head and I'm hit by the swirling emotions in his eyes. "I want out. I'm done. I want to take you and girls and go."

"Go?" Surprise sets my pulse to racing. "Go where?"

"Anywhere."

If I wasn't so taken aback, I'd protest when he gently pulls out of me and settles at my side. I clench my thighs together to stop come from leaking out. It's been *years* since I've felt that sensation and it adds to the unreality as he arranges the blankets more fully over us.

With his head propped up on his hand, he looks down at me. "I want to start over. Somewhere that I don't know anyone who owns a gun, somewhere I don't have to see my mother on a regular basis, and most of all somewhere all four of you will be under one roof."

I blink, my thudding heart feeling like it's about to burst.

He pushes the hair back from my face before he leans in to kiss the corner of my mouth. "I need you with me." His hand settles at my throat, his callused thumb stroking my jaw possessively. "Every time I leave this bed, I lose a piece of myself. It's getting to the point that soon there'll be nothing left." His fingers slide down between my breasts, over my stomach to the apex of my clenched thighs. He doesn't tell me to give him access, his gaze just holds mine until its unyielding intensity has a bloom of heat spreading from my chest up my neck to my cheeks and I slowly unlock my thighs for him. His fingers skate through our combined release. "Especially now, El." He pushes aside the covers and gets to his knees. I don't even complain about the cold air as he settles between my legs, lifting and then splaying them wide. "Look at that," he says reverently. "I can't believe I broke my biggest rule and I have zero regrets."

I watch it all play out over his face, the wonder, the lust, the ownership. When the seeping feeling of more come sliding free has me tightening my muscles, he grunts softly and reaches for my center again. His bloodied knuckles contrast sharply with the gentle feel of his thumb against my clit.

"Scott, I —"

"Ssshhh," he hushes, dipping his thumb into his come before returning to my clit to stroke me in lazy circles. "This is mine." He uses his other hand to part my slick folds, to fondle and caress. "And if I want to watch you come," he insinuates two fingers at my opening and starts pushing forward, "I will."

I groan as his fingers slip in deep. Under his watchful eye, with an infuriating amount of patience, he very deliberately brings me off. By the end, I'm completely wrung out and in my slightly stupefied state, I accidentally squeeze his injured hand. He winces and I'm reminded that he needs medical attention.

"Come on," I tell him, trying to push off my exhaustion. "Let's get in the shower."

He doesn't argue, just follows me into the bathroom where I start the water in the shower and then take his hand in mine. "Can you move it?"

Flexing his fingers gingerly, he nods. "It's fine." The gruffness in his voice has me pulling his hand to my mouth to kiss the space above his knuckles. "And the other guy?"

Irritably, he pulls the shower curtain farther back and gestures for me to get in. "What about him?"

He lets me warm up under the water first, but once we've switched places, I ask him again. "Is that Daniel guy okay?"

Wiping the water from his face, he shoots me a look that's part glare, part concern. "The more important question, El, is if you're okay."

"Me?" Though I'm almost certain of my answer, with the sound of the water falling around us, I take my time to consider his words. "I think so. The more I think about it, the more I realize he had no intention of actually using the gun. He just wanted us to listen."

"That doesn't make it okay."

"I didn't say it did. I'm saying it makes me feel better to find a sliver of sanity in a haystack of madness."

He studies me closely as if checking for any sign that I'm brushing off the seriousness of what happened. He must not find anything because his expression morphs into something much softer before he nods. "Okay. If it starts to get to you, will you tell me?"

How I love this man. "I will," I say, tipping up on my toes to kiss him. "But that doesn't mean you're getting out of telling me what happened tonight."

The corners of his mouth turn down. "Doesn't matter what happened. It's over and done with."

He can't be serious, can he? He comes to me hurt and clearly upset, talking about life altering changes, but expects to keep an important part of the catalyst to himself? I cross my arms and wait.

With barely contained frustration, he huffs out, "I . . . I just . . . roughed him up a bit. Alejandro didn't let me get carried away or anything."

Our eyes meet, and I can feel the dominance in him flare again. He's daring me to make a fuss, to question his judgment or maybe his right to do what he feels is necessary to protect me and the girls. Or is he thinking I'd object to Alejandro's involvement?

I nod. "Okay. Thank you for telling me."

He squints at me with suspicion.

With a flicker of amusement, I reach for his injured hand again. "Were you expecting me to scold you?" I ask, gently cleaning the blood away with soap. He grimaces slightly, but doesn't otherwise acknowledge the pain. After a thorough inspection, I tell him, "I'm guessing you'll live to see an–"

"Thank you," he interrupts in a whisper.

My eyebrows lift in question.

"For not . . . scolding me. I know it wasn't the right thing to do, but . . ." He swallows hard and when he can't find the right words, he averts his gaze, his hand falling to his side.

"Hey," I say softly, waiting for him to return his attention to me.

"I couldn't not do it," he tells me passionately, both defiance and entreaty flashing across his face. "Does that make sense?"

"It does, Scott," I reassure him. "And I think I'm flattered that you care enough –"

"Care enough?" he echoes, glowering at me. "El, I *love* you." He pauses as if to let that sink in, as if I've been underestimating the true depths of his feelings all this time. "You're everything to me. Without you, I . . ." He shakes his head, not wanting to contemplate the idea. "I want you with me always. I want you to marry me."

I feel my lips part and my heart beat stutter.

His hands cup my face, and instead of the quick retraction I'm fully expecting, he plows forward. "I want it to be official. I want the whole world to know how much I love you, that I'd do anything to keep you safe. Tell me that you'll marry me, El."

"Are you serious?" I whisper, stunned. I search his expression for any indication he's teasing me. I might not have ever allowed myself to openly contemplate romantic, girly daydreams about a future with Scott McCarthy, but they've never been far from the surface. And to have something like that become real in one breath only to be taken away in the next would surely put a very big dent in my heart. "Do you mean it?"

"Every word." Leaning in to place a gentle kiss on my mouth, he looks so confident. Like he doesn't have a single doubt that I'm the one. "What do you say? Will you be my wife?"

A clichéd, involuntary gasp pops out of me. "Your wife," I repeat as goosebumps appear on my arms. "You'd be my husband."

He laughs. "That's generally how it works."

How is he not more shaken up by this? How is he taking this all in stride, like he asks women to marry him every other day?

"You going to leave me hanging here, sweetness? I know I don't have a ring for you, but –"

"What? God, Scott. I don't need a ring. I just need you. And, yes, of course I'll be your wife." A frisson of delight travels down my spine, a sensation that only grows when his smiling mouth comes for mine. And it's a kiss to end all kisses, so full of joy and wonder, and our inevitable desire for each other. In between the kissing, we fumble with the soap and use the shower as an excuse to re-explore every inch of each other.

"Are we crazy?" he asks me as he helps me out of the shower. "Is eight months enough time to know?"

Grabbing a towel, I start drying his chest. "I've always known," I say with teasing arrogance, making my way around to his back.

"Please," he says and I love that I know he's rolling his eyes.

"It's true. Ever since you threatened to take me to Applebee's."

His laughter rings like music in my ears. "I thought you were a huge pain in the ass," he claims. "With your bright smile and your annoying optimism, you were like a bad rash I couldn't shake."

"Shut up," I scoff good-naturedly, pinching his delectable, naked ass.

He reaches back and pulls me to stand in front of him, a grin firmly in place. "The truth is I couldn't get enough of you. I still can't, and I don't see that ever –"

I catch the rest of his words with my mouth, letting them stopper up this euphoric happiness that's bubbling inside of me.

Once we're dry and back under the covers, I lie in his arms unable to sleep. In my mind, I can't stop gamboling through meadows, chasing butterflies and basking in a warm, afternoon sun.

"Scott?" I whisper in the darkened room.

"Hmmm?" He tightens his hold on me reflexively and I snuggle further into his hold.

"When you said you want to start over, did you mean that you want to . . . what?" I'm embarrassed to admit that I'm having cotton candy visions of playing house and mother hen.

"I mean that I want to start our 'boring' life together."

"Really? But don't we already have our boring life?"

"I want a place of our own, Opal. I want to sleep in a real bed with you beside me every night."

I sigh. "That sounds like heaven. But what about the girls?"

"What about them?"

"Umm . . . isn't that a lot of upheaval for them? And what about your grandmother? And your other sisters?" My heart sinks; the thing about cotton candy is that it has very little substance. It's pretty, yet fragile, and I should have enjoyed it longer before I began unspinning it.

This time he's the one who sighs. "My grandmother is too old to be taking care of three little girls full time. She should be able to enjoy being a grandmother instead of having to be a parent." He runs his fingertips down my arm before he takes hold of my hand and brings it to his lips to kiss my palm. "But that would mean you'd have to step up and become much more hands on with them."

Emotion forms a knot at the base of my throat.

"You can't be *Nice Ellie* anymore," he says, "the one who agrees with everything they say and do. You'll have to become more of a mother than a friend. Are you okay with that?"

A sense of unreality blankets me, but I push my words out through my constricted throat. "What if I mess it all up? They're so young and impressionable."

"You think I don't know that? I'm constantly worried I'm not saying or doing the right thing. It might even be selfish to want your help with that."

The happiness flaring in my chest at his words does nothing to dispel my reservations. Raising kids is way beyond the pale of anything I've ever taken on.

"I think," he says softly when I remain quiet, "that you're exactly what they need in their lives. I have every confidence in you."

"I'm glad someone does."

He nuzzles my hair. "You'll do great. It's mostly common sense."

"If you say so."

"I do say so. And anyway, if I were you, I'd be more concerned that the upheaval wouldn't only be for girls, but for us too. We'll have to sacrifice a big chunk of our privacy."

"Yeah, but we'd be gaining so much more." A family, I think with wonder . . . I'd have a family . . . which leads me back to . . . "But what about your other sisters?"

He takes his time in answering. "They're old enough to take care of themselves," he finally says. "Desiree is going to be nineteen soon and Mari sixteen."

"No, Scott. If you move out, how are they going to support themselves . . . financially?"

I feel him shrug. "My mom is just going to have to step up. I think after everything, she owes me this and it's not like they have a mortgage to pay or anything. Obviously I'm not going to abandon them without a backward glance, but I'm sure between the four of them, they can figure it out how to feed themselves and keep the bills paid."

I turn this over in my head for a long while

"You don't approve?" he asks quietly. "You think I *am* abandoning them?"

"No, of course not. I'm just thinking about how much you've changed since I met you."

"I haven't changed, El, I've been at the end of my rope for a long time. Only now, I have a lot more motivation. You're at the center of everything I want to work towards."

"On the same side of the divide?"

He hums with what can only be contentment. "Exactly. On the same side of the divide."

I wake warm and happy the next morning. Stretching out my muscles, I feel a hand languidly slide over my hip and . . . I inhale sharply, my eyes snapping open.

"Scott! You didn't go home."

His chest expands with a deep breath. "I know," he says, not sounding nearly as concerned as he should. It may have something to do with the way he's gently rocking his hard length against my naked ass.

I fumble on the nightstand for my phone. It's 6:40. The sun isn't in the sky yet, but he definitely shouldn't still be here. "What about your grandmother?" I whisper, trying to keep my wits about me as he kisses the side of my neck.

A noise of disgust rolls from the back of his throat. "Never what I want to hear when I'm seducing you."

With a soft giggle, I pull away to flip the switch on the bedside lamp. Squinting against the light, I hold the covers to my chest as I turn to face him. "Shouldn't you be rushing out the door?"

The arm that he's draped across his eyes shifts up so I can see more of his handsome face. "I texted Desiree."

"Okay, but don't you have to work today?"

"The site's not far," he says lazily. "I'll make it."

As I try to make sense of his laidback attitude, I track his arm as it slides behind his head, leaving his chest on display. Biting my lip, I tug the covers farther down his body. "I could get used to waking up to this."

He grins. "That's good, because soon you'll have to."

"Huh?" My head cocks with the question, still muddled with sleep. "Have to what?"

"Wake up to me," he says smugly, reaching forward. "Every." He tugs on the blanket. "Single." It slips from my grip. "Morning." And he fixes his attention on my bare breasts. "In the *very* near future."

He reaches out to gently cup the underside, but I take hold of his wrist to stop him. "How soon are we talking?"

Thwarted, he pushes his lips together in mild disgruntlement. "I don't know. I was thinking the girls should finish out the school year where they are . . . so, summer."

*Summer?* My thoughts start racing and then funnel themselves down into the only logical, yet shocking conclusion I can come up with. "You want to get married before summer?" I gasp. It's mid-October now, leaving less than a year.

"What?" He shakes his head as if to clear it, and then starts to chuckle, a drawn-out, low sound. "Did you just imply we can't live together until we're married?"

First, I blink at him in surprise, then, I crack up. "Maybe some caffeine first?" If I move my ass, there'll be enough time to talk before we have to leave for the day. "I'm going to take a quick shower." I slide off the bed and grab the hanger with the work clothes I set aside last night. "Can you make some coffee, please?"

"Opal?"

I turn from the doorway. "Yeah?"

He gestures to his midsection and the tented covers. "I was seducing you. Remember?"

I laugh. "You'll just have to wait until tonight."

"Oh, sure," I hear him call as I'm shutting the bathroom door. "One mention of the word *marriage* and it's already started."

The outlandishly pleased grin on my face stays in place for the duration of my shower. And when I breeze my way into the kitchen and find Scott sitting at the island with his phone and a cup of coffee, the grin kicks up a notch into beaming territory.

"What's with you?" He turns on the stool as I approach to make room for me between his legs.

"Oh, nothing. Just that the man of my dreams asked me to marry him last night."

"Oh, yeah? And you're not disappointed that he proposed on the fly without ring?"

The Here and Now

Distracted by his slightly swollen hand, I take it in mine and examine his knuckles. "Does it hurt?"

Flexing the hand, he grunts noncommittally, dismissing my concern. As if to prove he's fine, he slides his hands to my waist and squeezes. "You didn't answer my question, Opal."

I lift my arms to his neck. "Which question was that again?" I ask slyly. "The one about being disappointed because there's no ring?" I let him squirm for a moment before the exuberance that's building behind my mock seriousness shines through. "Not at all," I say brightly. "But I do have a million questions."

His relief is reflected in the playful tone of his reply. "Not sure we've got time for a million."

Whacking him gently on the arm, I retreat to the coffee maker to fill my travel mug.

"Fine," he huffs, pretending to be annoyed. "Hit me with the top five before we go."

I tap my lips with my index finger as if I didn't lie awake half the night organizing my thoughts. "So the uh . . . wedding," I let my mouth hang open in a parody of shock and surprise, making him smile, "what kind of timeline are we talking?"

"Totally up to you."

I pause halfway to the fridge, feeling my nose wrinkle with distaste. I turn to send him a look that says, *you're going to have to do better than that.*

"Okay, how does within the next two years sound?"

"Are you asking me? Or telling me?" I get the milk out to pour a generous splash into my mug.

"I'm asking you, sweetness. My only requirement is the size. The smaller the better." His face screws up as if not liking how that came out. "Sorry. It's not too late to go with the millionaire instead. What was his name? Pierre? Porter?"

I give him a wry twist of my lips. "Peter?"

"Yeah, that guy. I'm sure he's got the cash to throw you a monstrous wedding."

Reaching forward, I pluck his coffee cup off the counter and sniff its contents. "Are you drinking? You know there isn't a single alternate reality in existence where I'd choose anyone over your poor ass."

His laugh is punctuated by the clunk of his mug as I set it down and go back to gathering my stuff for work. "I'll be perfectly happy with any wedding as long as I'm marrying you," I say, throwing a granola bar into my purse before it hits me again that – *holy crap* – we're getting married. "Oh, Scott, the girls are going to be so adorable in their matching dresses!" But then, just as quickly, my thoughts turn to something I hadn't considered. "Oh, God, do you think they'll insist on pink?" I head for the bathroom to grab my makeup bag and come back chuckling. "Can you imagine three little Pepto Bismol blobs going down the aisle? Maybe we can compromise with pale pink?"

Looking up at him expectantly, I'm surprised to find his expression slightly appalled. "What? Are you going to veto the pink altogether? I think we should let them have some say, don't you? They'll be so disappointed otherwise."

"No, it's not that. I just realized that keeping it small is going to be next to impossible. My grandmother alone will want to invite the entire neighborhood."

I watch him rub his palms over the dismay on his face and questions begin to lodge themselves in my throat. I don't get a chance to start asking them because he goes on.

"I don't want to be one of those idiots who spends a fortune on a one-day event."

"Oh, well, we don't have to spend a fortune. I guess we could go to Vegas . . . if you want." Suddenly, I'm mourning the loss of the tacky, neon-pink dresses. "Or there's always city hall."

He makes a tsking sound. "I'm going to go out on a limb and say your lack of enthusiasm for those options means they're off the table."

"I . . . no, I . . ." Okay, he's got me stumped. *I don't need a big wedding, do I?*

Watching me closely, he says, "I just don't think it's a good idea to spend even a portion of our down payment like that."

I stare at him blankly. *Say what?* "Down payment?" I squeak. "We have a down payment? You mean like for a house?"

"Yeah, I figure by summer you'll have been at your job for almost a year so we'll be able to qualify for something decent with our combined incomes."

"Combined incomes?" I repeat with horror. "You've actually thought about this?"

With raised eyebrows, he says, "Of course I have. Well, the combined incomes part is fairly new, but I've been saving for a long time now. Camping out in the living room didn't faze me when I was younger, but it's really lost its lustre over the years."

I lick my lips nervously. "But Scott, I don't have a single penny saved."

He grins. *Why is he grinning at a moment like this?* "Well, don't think you're getting out of paying the mortgage with me."

I have no idea what to say to that. None whatsoever.

"Come on," he says with a galling chuckle as he gets to his feet. "Forget about it for now. We're going to be late. You still need to run me home."

Forget about it? Forget about all these grown-up endeavors Scott's had years to think about? Ones I'm entirely unqualified to participate in? Mortgages and child rearing, no less? I'm about as likely to *forget about it* as I am to forget my own name.

I realize I've been stuck in my head when Scott plunks my dress flats down in front of me and I see he's already got his own shoes on his feet.

"Sorry," he says, giving my shoulder a reassuring squeeze as he moves past me to put the milk carton back in the fridge. "I didn't mean to freak you out."

Slipping my shoes on, I watch him place my travel mug and my purse together at the end of the island.

"You need anything else?" He scans the kitchen/living area before he grabs my coat from where it's draped over the back of one of the stools and helps me into it. "You got your phone?"

Nodding absently, I grab my coffee and my purse and follow him out. As we make our way through the hall and out the front door of the building into the cool morning air, he keeps his hand at the small of my back. Its weight is comforting, suggesting that even if I start drowning, he'll be there to help me find my feet again.

At my car, we pause and as soon as my gaze locks with his, I feel better. His dark eyes tell me everything I need to know, namely that everything will be fine.

"You okay?" he asks.

I give him a rueful nod. "Just a minor freak-out. Nothing serious."

His lips tip up at the corners, simultaneously melting my heart and drawing my attention to his unshaven jaw. Hell yes, I want to see that every morning! And I'll work toward that privilege day and night if I have to.

# Chapter Fourteen

## Scott

**M**y hand aches for days, but I have no regrets. How could I? My encounter with Daniel Patterson has made everything clear to me.

Over the next weeks, Ellie and I have these surreal talks about moving in together, marriage, and finances. I say surreal because I can barely believe we're going to take a run at this. My excitement dims considerably when we start looking at real estate and I realize how much prices have gone up since I first checked a few years ago. I shouldn't be surprised. I do pay the property tax on my grandmother's house after all. Since I want out of East Palo Alto altogether, I guess it didn't occur to me that its outrageous assessed value would be reflected in other areas of Northern California as well.

Ellie's not daunted at all – by any of it. Now that the initial shock of my grand scheme has worn off, she couldn't be more excited, even when we draw up a joint budget and cut way back on our main expense of eating out. She says as long as she's not forced to subsist on Ramen noodles, she's good. Actually, more and more, she eats dinner with us at home. It's worked out well; Ellie spends more time with me and the girls and we've asked my grandmother to teach us how to cook. Once we're house-poor – if we can even get a mortgage – there won't be any more takeout at all . . . or dinner waiting on the table when we get home from work. And since my work schedule is constant and Ellie's isn't, it appears the cooking will fall to me.

Which is why I'm doing more than just chopping onions for my grandmother on Thanksgiving this year. Since my birthday generally falls near or even on Thanksgiving, the two celebrations have been melded into a single event over the years. I get to choose what we eat and I always choose my favorite dish, *pozole*. Ergo, I need to know how to make it for future reference. I can see why my grandmother doesn't make it very often though. It's a bit of a pain in the ass.

With dinner almost complete and Ellie gone to check up on the girls, now is my chance to speak to my grandmother. I've been waiting all afternoon to get a moment alone with her, but now I'm unexpectedly hesitant to make use of it.

"Tell me what's troubling you, mijo. I can hear you thinking from here."

My low chuckle withers into a nervous exhalation; she knows me so well. I hope that what I have to say won't wound her, but I can't in all conscience postpone it any longer. It takes a few more moments, but I finally start with, "So you know how thankful I am to you for raising us all." I steal a peek from where I'm slicing limes to get a sense of her reaction.

"*¿Agradecido?*" she echoes, not stopping her chopping of the lettuce into thin strips, but I notice the way her head tilts with question.

"*Sí, agradecido.* Without you, I can't imagine how the six of us would have survived," I say, referring to myself, my three sisters, Rosa and Daniela. "You've always been here for us. And I never want you to think I'm not grateful."

She sends me an askance sideways glance across the few feet of counter space that separates us. "What's going on, mijo? Have you turned sentimental at the ripe old age of twenty-three?"

Despite my nerves, I laugh. I've always loved the laid back relationship I share with her. "No, not sentimental, Abuela, just, um . . . older?" I go back to the limes in front of me to avoid witnessing her reaction to my next words. "Ellie and I . . ." I pause. "I was thinking maybe . . . I just don't want to hurt your feelings . . . when I tell you that Ellie and I were thinking of getting our own place."

In my peripheral vision, the knife in her hand doesn't so much as falter. "Yes, well, I've figured that was coming."

Surprised, I look up at her. "And you're not . . . upset that I'm going to move the girls?"

Her small frame visibly relaxes. "You're going to take them, then?"

A mixture of horror and disbelief floods my system. "You thought I would leave them?"

"No," she says carefully. "No, not really, but I thought there was a chance you would only take Rosa. She is, after all, your only true responsibility."

Deliberately, I put down the knife and prop my hip on the counter as something sounding a lot like disgruntlement edges its way out of my throat.

"Do not lecture me, mijo," she warns. "I've seen a lot in my nearly seventy-three years and you deciding to split up the girls wouldn't come close to touching on the worst of it."

The fact that I'm not at the *very* bottom of her barrel doesn't make me feel any better, but she doesn't give me a chance to grumble about her lack of faith in me.

"But I'm thrilled that you've made the decision to keep them together."

"There was no decision to make. How could you think otherwise?"

"Well," she says, a sad smile directed at the cutting board, "I wasn't there for my own children, so it would be hypocritical of me to judge you,"

"What?" I stammer, my head pulling back in surprise. "What does that mean?"

Her knife stills and she gives me her full attention. "When your grandfather died, your mother was ten years old, Javier was eight." She shuffles over to the sink to wash her hands. "That's such a vulnerable age."

I watch her dry her hands before she faces me.

"I chose to work day and night to keep this house instead of being present in their lives. It's the worst mistake I've ever made."

*Mistake?* Shock reverberates through me, but she holds up a hand to stop my denials.

"Yes, I know that having the house mortgage-free is a blessing – now. But my children needed a mother thirty years ago. The price of leaving them to raise themselves was enormous. Javier is dead by gang violence and Lilia fell into alcohol and drugs."

Gut churning, I stammer, "Abuela, you can't know that wouldn't have happened anyway."

"I do," she says with a serenity that grates against my nerves. "You turned out all right. As did Desiree and Mari. Like you said, I was always here for you."

"No. Come on." I shake my head. "By that logic, Jorgie should be a doctor or something. His mother stayed home to raise her kids, giving them all the time and attention in the world. And look what happened there."

She purses her thin lips and I can only imagine what she's marshalling in her mind to refute my claim, but I head her off. "I think you're oversimplifying things. Yes, your influence played a big role in my life, Abuela. But so did my mother's."

Taken aback, she falters before turning to the huge *pozole* pot on the stove to give it a stir.

"I never wanted to be like her," I explain. "I refused to let Rosa grow up feeling even a fraction of the distrust and embarrassment that I did. Abuela, you worked hard, you set an example for your kids. If they didn't follow it, that's on them. You don't get to claim responsibility for their mistakes. They are, or were, who they chose to be."

She laughs softly. "Oh, mijo, we'll see how you feel about that statement in ten years."

"But you can see what I'm getting at, right?" I insist.

"Yes, fine. You may have a point. But we were talking about you and *la güera* starting a life together." She takes a breath, then announces, "We'll sell the house."

I don't even blink. I knew this was coming. My grandmother has an incredibly generous spirit and she's mentioned the idea casually a few times over the years. "That's so kind of you, Abuela, but we can't sell the house."

"Yes, we'll sell it and I'll buy a small apartment. You can use the rest of the money for a home of your own."

"We both know that's not possible."

She scoffs. "Why not? Lilia tries to convince me to sell the house at least four or five times a year so she can get her hands on the money."

I have to unclench my jaw before I can force out a dark, "What? Why didn't you tell me?"

"To avoid this," she says wryly, waving a hand in my direction. "No sense in her upsetting the both of us."

Reining in my rising temper at my mother's gall, I manage to stay on topic. "Well, whatever reason you gave *her* for not selling the house, stands. Where would Mari and Desiree go? For that matter, where would *she* go?" I shake my head. "No, El and I are capable of doing this on our own . . . I hope."

"But I want to help," she protests.

I grin at her before going back to finish with the limes. "That's good because we're going to need a lot of that."

"Oh, mijo, come here." She puts her spindly little arms around me and squeezes tight. "I'm so proud of you."

I wrap my own arms around her. "I haven't done anything yet."

"That's not true. You've met every challenge you've been presented with. And rest assured, I'll do everything I can to help you and –"

"Ugh," sounds from the doorway as Desiree walks in. "Abuelita, I've told you that encouraging Scotty only gives him more of a hero complex. It's not healthy."

I laugh as I let my grandmother go. "Nice of you to show up, Des."

She gives me an ironic quirk of her brows before greeting our grandmother with a kiss to her cheek. "I'd never miss *pozole*. It smells amazing."

"I made it this year," I brag, overstating the truth by a mile.

"Are you serious?" She's impressed for about two seconds. "If I end up with food poisoning, I'll kick your ass."

"Mija," our grandmother despairs, giving a long-suffering sigh. But I don't care, I'm happy to see my sister. Our paths don't cross as often anymore now that she's working full-time and taking night classes at the community college. And I know she's been staying with her boyfriend here and there.

Desiree grins back at me. "I guess I should be nice to you since it's your birthday."

"I guess you should."

Our grandmother tires of us quickly. "Desiree, please set the table. Scotty, please go gather all the girls."

Dinner is everything I could ever want; the food is incredible and I'm surrounded by the women I love so much, all of whom tease me about getting old. At least they do until Daniela casually asks Ellie how old she is, and then all the teasing shifts to my girl. Seems I've never mentioned how much of a cradle robber she is. She takes it all with good humor, adding another check to the column of reasons why she's the only woman for me.

When the kitchen is cleaned up a bit, Ellie and the girls disappear and then return carrying a homemade cake. Mari hits the lights and all twenty-three candles on the cake glow as everyone serenades me, first with a verse of *Las Mañanitas,* and then with Happy Birthday.

"Make a wish!" the girls exclaim in unison. I flick my gaze up to Ellie's and let the shining brilliance I find there envelop me before blowing out the candles.

As I'm cutting the cake, Ellie leans in and whispers, "I barely convinced them that you wouldn't love pink frosting."

Laughing, I steal a quick kiss. "Is this where you guys disappeared to this morning? To make this for me?"

She nods. "Amelia helped us, so it should be edible. I got some good pictures of them in their aprons that I'll show you later."

I have to swallow back some emotion. "Thanks, Opal," I murmur only for her.

Turns out I don't have fake any of my enthusiasm for their work. The chocolate cake with blue, buttercream frosting is more than edible. And of course, it tastes all the better because they made it for me.

"Abuela," whispers Carmen from beside her. "Is it time?"

"Time for what?" I ask, butting in.

"I think it is," Abuela confirms without acknowledging me.

The girls giggle and rush from the table. They come back holding a decently-sized box wrapped in shiny paper between them. It has what appears to be a decorated list of names taped down the side.

"I thought," I say, directing a meaningful look to my grandmother and Ellie. "That we agreed to no presents this year."

"It wasn't my idea," Ellie says, moving my cake plate away so the girls can put the box in front of me.

When I narrow my eyes at my grandmother, she's completely unaffected. "When you get it open, you'll see that it isn't really a gift at all."

"Open it!" Daniela cajoles.

Carefully ripping around the list that says *Con mucho amor de Ellie, Carmen, Rosa, Daniela, Mari, Desiree, and Abuela*, I stare at the revealed box in confusion. "It's a pot?"

"I told you," Abuela says with a chuckle. "Not a gift. It's so you and *la güera* can make *pozole* for me on my birthday."

I frown at her. "But —"

"Abuela says you never know when you'll need your own *pozole* pot," Rosa explains.

I throw a questioning glance at Ellie that says, *Did you tell her we were moving out?* But she shakes her head.

"Don't you like it?" Daniela asks, concerned.

"Actually, I love it," I say, fighting emotion *again* as I get to my feet and go around the table to dole out kisses and thank you's, wondering how my abuela could have possibly known.

When Mari and Desiree start clearing the table, I get everyone's attention with, "Hang on. There's one more thing." Reaching up on top of the fridge, I pull down a small, wrapped box I have stashed there. I re-take my seat beside Ellie and place it in front of her, ignoring the way my heart starts to nervously clatter behind my ribs.

"What's this?" Ellie asks with innocence, not yet grasping what's going on.

"I got you something for my birthday."

Understanding flares in her expression. "What did you do?" she whispers.

"Open it." I nudge the box closer to her.

"How come Ellie gets a present on your birthday, Papá?" Rosa asks.

"You'll see," I say, not taking my eyes off of Ellie's which are now filling with tears.

"But you said —"

"It's not that," I reassure her. "This is just until we're on our feet."

With trembling fingers, she unwraps the silver paper so slowly that I almost want to take it from her and do it myself. Once she gets to the velvet box underneath, Desiree gasps and lets loose a hushed, "No way."

"It's not that," I repeat, now worried that Ellie's going to be disappointed.

"It better not be *that*," Ellie says gravely. "Because we decided together." She cracks open the box and her gaze flashes to mine.

"I wanna see!" Daniela exclaims, coming around the table, while Carmen and Rosa strain their necks to see. "It's a ring!"

I don't know who calls it out, because I'm focused on Ellie, trying to gauge her reaction.

"Oh, Scott," she says on a shaky exhale, turning to hide her face in my neck. I barely hear her with all the surprise and delight that's erupted around us.

I pull her close and kiss the top of her head. "Does that mean you like it?"

"Of course I like it. I *love* it," she says tearfully, the words brushing my collarbone.

Urging her to sit up, I take the ring from the box and slide it onto her ring finger. She holds it up to the light to get a better look at the white gold filigree engagement band. Giving me a watery smile that's so full of love, she kisses me on the cheek. "I love it so much."

With pride, I lift my head and announce what everyone has already figured out. "Ellie and I are getting married."

Another round of happy exclamations fills the air, this time with hugs and kisses and even a few tears on the part of my grandmother.

"Is Ellie coming to live with us?" Daniela asks excitedly.

"No, *chaparra*," I laugh, pulling her in for another hug. "We're going to move to a new house."

"We are?" Her eyes widen as if such an outrageous idea has never occurred to her.

"We are. But not for a while yet. You guys need to finish the school year first."

"But what about Abuela?" Rosa asks from Ellie's lap.

"Abuela's still going to live here," I say. "But we'll visit her all the time."

Rosa looks unsure, but Daniela is excited and moves on to what she considers pertinent information. "Will I have my own room?"

"Probably not."

"Awww. Can we get a dog?"

"What?" I shake my head. "That's a lot of responsibility."

"A cat then?" she negotiates. "Cats take care of themselves."

I'm about to tell her *no* when I notice Ellie appears more than a little interested in the idea. "We'll see," I hedge. "Maybe a goldfish."

Daniela makes a noise of complete scorn. "A goldfish? I'd rather have no pet."

"That can be arranged," I tell her drolly.

I swear I watch her calculate her next words, but never could I have predicted them. "Can I call Ellie *Mom*?" I don't know if she asks for the shock value or if she really means it seriously, but I don't let it faze me. She may only be eight years old, but she already tests my resolve on a very regular basis.

"You'll have to ask her."

Her face lights up. "Ellie?" We both turn to her, actually everyone in the kitchen turns to her. "Can I call you Mom?"

Like a deer caught in the headlights, she's frozen one second, then the next, her lips pull into one of her mega-watt, signature smiles. "If that's what you want, I'd be honored."

"Me too?" Rosa squawks from Ellie's lap, turning to face her. "Me too, right Ellie?"

"Of course. You guys can call me anything you'd like."

"Can I try the ring on?" Daniela asks, pulling the spotlight back to herself.

The *not on your life* that's about to come out of my mouth is pre-empted by Ellie's, "Of course you can." Inside, I cringe, sensing this is our future; me being a hard-ass, Ellie being accommodating. Hopefully we'll balance each other out in the end.

"When's the wedding?" Mari asks as I watch Ellie supervise Daniela and Rosa's turns with the ring that only fits on their thumbs.

"We haven't decided yet," I tell her. "It's more of just an idea right now."

"An idea?" Desiree says doubtfully. "I'd say a ring means it's way more than just an idea."

The slight edge to my sister's tone has me eyeing her warily, but Ellie distracts me by getting to her feet. Placing Rosa in her vacated chair, she whispers, "Be right back."

As soon as she's left the room, my sisters come at me with some very thorny questions about how I see things playing out once I'm no longer living here. Their alarm tells me I probably shouldn't have sprung this on them like I did. These aren't only big changes for the girls, but for all of us.

Under their onslaught, it takes me a while to register that Ellie hasn't come back yet and that none of the girls are in the kitchen with us.

# Chapter Fifteen

## Ellie

I only make it halfway down the hall before I have to stop and stare at it.

There wasn't supposed to be an engagement ring – with or without a diamond. We agreed. Not only that, it's his birthday, not mine. And isn't it just like him to ignore his own moratorium on expenditures? Except as I study the delicate braided coils that make up the white gold band, there's not a single outraged bone in my body. In fact, even if I'm suspicious he was partly motivated to buy the ring to satisfy his possessive streak, I couldn't be happier.

The muffled sound of movement coming from the girls' bedroom reminds me that I didn't come down here to admire my new ring in private. The door is partially open, but I tap lightly.

"Carmen? Are you okay?"

Her only answer is a quiet sniffle, which sends a frisson of worry up my spine. *Is she crying?* I noticed her reaction when Scott mentioned the move, but I wasn't expecting this.

Nudging the door farther open, I find Carmen lying on the bottom bunk, facing the wall. I perch on the mattress and touch her shoulder gently. "What's wrong, honey?"

I get another sniffle in response.

"Is it because we're moving?"

Her next breath comes out as an actual sob, taking me completely by surprise. Yes, Scott and I knew this would be a lot of change for the girls, but I don't think either of us thought it would be upsetting enough to bring on tears.

"Would you rather talk to . . ." It's always so hard when I'm addressing Carmen, because Scott isn't her *Papá* and he isn't her *Tío*, he's just Scotty, a name that I've never once heard her use. "Would you rather talk to Scott?"

Under my touch, she turns and then buries her head in my lap, crying openly now. "Oh, honey, what is it?" I ask, curling my arms around her. "Are you unhappy that we're getting married?" Her small chest heaves with another mournful exhale. "Tell me what's wrong so I can fix it."

"I don't think you can fix this, Ellie," she says, peering up at me through her tears. More worry inundates me.

"Tell me. Maybe we can work something out."

She places her head on my thigh again and in a small voice says, "It's just, what if Mamá Lilia makes me stay here?"

"What?" The hand that's stroking her hair stills. "Why would she do that?"

"She's always reminding me that Scotty's not my dad."

Foreboding rises in my chest. This is the first I've ever heard of this.

"And she says that soon my real dad is coming home and that we're going to be a family again," she says, her voice filled with misery.

Internally, I balk. *Her real dad? The one that's in prison?*

"It's true," I hear from behind me.

I turn to find Daniela in the doorway with Rosa peeking around her shoulder, both of them looking solemn. As I beckon them in, Carmen sits up and wipes her tears away, probably so she's not taken for a baby. Daniela gets on the bed beside her and Rosa comes to lean against me. I loop my arms around her waist.

"You're sure that Mamá Lilia said your real dad's coming home?" I ask cautiously

All three girls nod before Daniela, very primly, informs me, "She said we weren't supposed to say anything to anyone, that it was a surprise." Her demeanor tells me she thinks the whole thing is garbage and I fight a twinge of amusement. If this is true, it's serious.

"So Scott doesn't know?"

"No," Carmen says passionately. "And now he's going to leave me here."

"Hey," I say. "No one is going anywhere without you. Ever. Okay?"

"Really?"

"Really."

"And Ellie can be your mom too," Daniela says. "Right, Ellie?"

"I . . ." Shit, I'm not sure what to say. Even when Rosa asked me earlier, it occurred to me that she already has a mother, and I don't want to cause friction within the family. But . . . "I'm fine with whatever you guys want to call me." I consider it for a moment. "Rosa, sometimes you call your mother *Mamá* in Spanish and sometimes *Mom* in English. Maybe you can stick to one name for her and you guys can use the other one for me?"

"Mom in English for Ellie," Daniela calls, giving Rosa a meaningful glance, like she'd better get on board or there'd be trouble.

Rosa's face blooms with happiness and Carmen seems to shed some of her melancholy. "Okay then, but it will always be your decision, and you can change your mind at any time, all right?" They all nod in a rare consensus. "But no matter what, I'll always be here for you guys. Even if Scott and I are upset with each other, you can always talk to me."

Rosa turns to see me better. "But you're getting married," she says, making it sound like Scott and I are now cemented forever in happiness. And I suppose to her that's what it *does* mean. She takes my hand in hers and we all study the way the ring shines in the light.

"Isn't there supposed to be a diamond?" Daniela asks with all seriousness.

"Usually. But we decided not to spend money on an expensive ring. We'd like to buy a home for all of us first."

"But how come we can't stay here?" Rosa asks.

"There's not enough rooms for everyone," Carmen tells her gently.

"Ellie can have our room," Daniela exclaims with sudden inspiration. "And we can set up a tent in the living room."

Rosa hums with excitement, then squirms out of my grip. "I'm going to tell Papá."

Carmen gives me a resigned look and I almost laugh. Next month she'll be nine. Combined with the maturity that's knitted into her very DNA, the year or two she has on Daniela and Rosa sometimes seems more like a decade.

Daniela doesn't notice as she launches into how she envisions the setup of their new sleeping arrangement, with her taking the prime spot closest to the TV. While she's going on, I pull Carmen into a hug.

"I love you, Ellie," she whispers.

"Oh, I love you too. Don't you worry about anything, okay?"

"What's going on?" Scott asks as Rosa tugs him into the room.

"Tío, we're moving to the living room! That way Ellie can live here with us."

"Yeah, um, Rosa told me," he says, coming to sit on the lower bunk with me. "But there's not enough room for all of us here."

"But it'll be so much fun!" Rosa exclaims, climbing up with the other girls.

"I'm sorry, *Calabacita*. It's just not possible. What brought this . . . plan on?"

Carmen fixes me with a panicked expression, but before I can say or do anything, Daniela sums up the situation in a very concise nutshell. "Mamá Lilia won't let Carmen go with us and Ellie says we can't leave her here."

"Pardon?" Scott's entire body stiffens. "Mamá Lilia said that?"

Carmen shrinks down against my shoulder, but Daniela nods happily, still certain her life is about to become one long camping trip.

"When was this?"

"In the summer."

"The summer?" he repeats, his voice starting to sound like crushed gravel. I place my hand on his thigh in warning and he takes a deep breath before he asks his next question. "Why would she say that?"

"Because she says my dad is coming home soon," Carmen says, her face crumpling back into tears.

"*¿Tu papá?*" Scott echoes, his disbelief palpable.

Carmen nods. "He's going to get a job or something." She switches to English, "Like payroll."

"Parole?"

*"Sí, eso."*

I watch as emotions rise on Scott's face, shock leading the way, followed closely by anger, fear, suspicion, and defiance.

"Does it mean he's coming to live here?" Carmen asks.

"No," Scott says emphatically, pushing to his feet. "It doesn't. You never have to worry about that." He pauses in the doorway. "I'll be right back."

Five seconds later, voices from the kitchen start to gain in volume, the loudest of which is Mari who's obviously dismayed at the possibility of her father's return.

"I shouldn't have said anything," Carmen whispers, her lower lip wobbling.

"No," I tell her firmly. "You did the right thing. It's never okay for an adult to ask you to keep a secret."

"Never?" Rosa asks, frowning.

"Never. Unless we're talking birthday presents."

"What about Christmas presents?" Daniela asks in alarm, probably because Christmas is coming up soon.

"You're right," I say, loving her literal mind. "Presents of all kinds are good secrets. But other than that, if an adult asks you to keep a secret, I want you to tell someone. Like your abuela, or Scott, or me, or Desiree, okay?"

They mull this over as we listen to the indistinct ebb and flow of the conversation coming from the kitchen.

Daniela is serious when she says, "Anne Marie told me that her brother has a secret girlfriend."

"Oh? How old is Anne Marie's brother?"

"Seventeen."

"But *he* didn't ask you to keep the secret, right?"

"Anne Marie's brother?" she squeaks in horror, pulling a face. "I've never met him, but Anne Marie says he's a meanie. He doesn't let her play on his Xbox and he . . ." Daniela gives us a long list of Anne Marie's brother's faults, which Rosa and Carmen add to as she goes. I gather it's an on-going discussion between them and I'm pleased to be included. Plus, getting them used to sharing things now will probably pay off later when they're teenagers.

A few minutes later, Scott comes back, asking if we want to watch a movie, false cheer barely masking his grim countenance.

"*Frozen?*" Carmen asks, perking up.

"You bet."

The girls cheer and jump off the bed to make a bee-line for the front room.

Gathering some courage, I ask, "So what'd you find out?"

"Nothing. No one's heard a word about it."

"You think the girls have it wrong?"

"I sure hope so. I tried my mom's cell but she's not picking up."

It's late by the time the movie's over. Desiree has long since left with her boyfriend and Mari has retreated to her bedroom. Scott is putting the girls to bed and his grandmother and I are in the kitchen, where she's filling a Tupperware container for me with leftovers when I hear the front door open. I know it can only be one person: Lilia.

Scott's mother and I have only crossed paths a few times over the months. Her attitude toward me can be summed up as aloof at best, and cold at worst. I've always been extra polite, but nothing I say or do seems to crack the woman's hard exterior. Scott's vague explanations for her attitude haven't been very comforting. In the beginning, I was worried that my presence was keeping her away from Sunday night dinners, but Scott set me straight, saying she'd rarely attended before I came along and he wasn't broken up about it if she was now avoiding them on purpose. What else could I do but take my cues from him and push it to the back of my mind?

"We need to talk, Mamá," I hear Scott say in English from the living room.

"What are you still doing here? Why aren't you out with Ms. Wonder Bread?"

My brows pull together. *Ms. Wonder Bread? What does that mean?* But my pondering will have to wait because Scott's only interested in what he heard from the girls earlier. "When were you going to tell me that Robbie's up for parole?"

At first we don't hear an answer, so Scott's grandmother and I both drift closer to the doorway, sharing a bit of a guilty look.

"Why would I tell you?" Lilia asks, sounding bored. "He's not your father."

"So it's true?" Scott says, sounding skeptical and horrified in equal measure. "What were you planning to do? Just show up with him one day?"

"This is his home too."

Scott laughs, a short, cruel sound I've never heard from him. "You're out of your mind. I'm not a fifteen-year-old boy anymore, Ma. Robbie will never set foot inside this house again."

"You don't get to make that decision!"

"You're right. I don't. But I can't imagine why you'd think Abuela would agree. Or were you just going to ignore her wishes like you did after Javier died?"

"Robbie is my *husband*," she says, like that should clear everything up.

Beside me, Scott's grandmother shakes her head sadly, looking a little unsteady on her feet. As quietly as I can, I pull a chair from the kitchen table and move it the short distance to our spot near the doorway so she can sit down. It seems our shameful eavesdropping may take a while.

"You have no right to tell me how to live my life, Scotty."

"True. And if you want to ride off into the sunset with Satan himself, I won't stop you. But Robbie's not coming here."

"Fine," she says almost petulantly. "But I'm taking Mari and Carmen with me."

"What?" Scott demands, clearly baffled. "Why?"

"Why?" she cries. "They're my daughters!"

"Is that right? Tell me, what's the name of Carmen's teacher this year?"

After a stony silence, Lilia says, "That's not important."

"You don't think a judge would find it curious that you can't name your own child's teacher?"

"A judge?" she spits. "You wouldn't dare."

"You're damn right I would."

And even as he says it, I realize we'll have to have some kind of official custody agreement in place before we move.

"I can't believe you're threatening me."

"Well, I can't believe you'd let Robbie back into this house! What did you think, that I'd sit back with a bucket of popcorn and watch while he knocks you around? While he pushes Mari or yells at Carmen?"

Lilia's disgust reaches us. "Don't exaggerate. He never . . . he wouldn't . . ."

"Ma, let's keep this real, all right? He was always abusive and I seriously doubt prison has made him see the error of his ways. Now, I don't want it to come to lawyers and judges, but I'll do whatever's necessary to keep my sisters safe."

"God, do you ever listen to yourself?" Lilia says, her voice laced with contempt. "You've always been such a smug bastard. Always so holier-than-thou."

"Yeah, thanks to you."

"What?" she sputters.

"You heard me. You forced me to become who I am. Someone had to be the parent while you were off living your booze-soaked existence."

"I love how you're always conveniently forgetting *your* sins, Scotty. As if fathering a child at fifteen is perfectly acceptable."

Scott sighs tiredly. "I haven't forgotten a single thing, Ma. And I'm not interested in re-hashing any of our past, all right? I just need to know what's going on with Robbie."

Lilia, too, sounds weary with her next words. "Why are you so against my dream of living as a family?"

*Huh?* Scott also seems to struggle with the shift, because it takes a moment for him to respond. "You *do* have a family, Ma. You just never wanted to be a part of it. You have four kids and we're all right here."

"You know what I mean. First your father wanted nothing to do with us, and then Desiree's father left too. I have a chance now with Robbie."

There's a pause, and then, "Pardon me?" Scott's voice is so cutting that I look to his grandmother for clarification, but she seems to be at a loss as well. "I think this is the first time you've ever slipped up."

"What?" Lilia says, sounding as confused as I feel.

"How do you know my father wanted nothing to do with us?" he asks in a smooth, measured tone. "I thought he didn't know I existed. Isn't that what you've always claimed?"

*Ohhhh.*

The silence from the living room is deafening and I can just imagine Scott's hard expression, daring his mother to deny her blunder. The tension has me chewing on my thumb nail while I study a spot near the wall where the linoleum is curling up.

After long moments, she says, "You don't sound very surprised."

"No," he says dully. "Secrets have a way of coming out sooner or later, don't they? Even if it takes twenty-three years."

"How did you . . ?"

"Completely by chance. Turns out you haven't been honest with me from the beginning."

"That was for your own protection."

"Actually, Ma, I'll give you that one. He's definitely not father material. But the thirty-five grand you stole from this family? I can't let that go."

In the ensuing hush, the ticking of the clock on the kitchen wall seems to grow louder and louder.

"I didn't steal it," Lilia finally says, her tone firm. "I went looking for it. If I hadn't, there'd have been no money at all."

Scott's abrupt, humorless laugh makes me jump. "Really? That's what you're going with?"

"I did what I had to, Scotty."

"You had to rob your son of his last year of childhood?"

"Don't be such a martyr."

"You don't even feel guilty, do you? You think you had every right to force Abuela and me to scrounge up whatever we could to stay afloat. You don't regret it at all."

"No, I don't! I needed that money for more important things."

"What could be more important than your family?" Scott thunders.

"Robbie could have gone to jail for life. *Life,* Scotty!"

Scott makes a sound more suitable to a dying animal than a person before he says, "You're unbelievable. Why you'd choose that lowlife over your own kids, I'll never understand. But I'd say it's pretty ironic that your choices made me into a man who won't hesitate to sue you for custody and reimbursement of that money."

There's a dramatic pause then the sound of the front door being wrenched open.

"Ma," Scott calls loudly. "When is he getting out?"

But there's only the slamming of the door.

# Chapter Sixteen

## Scott

I've never understood my mother. As a young child, I yearned for her attention, but she was just as likely to look at me with loathing as she was with love. Not only did she forever run hot and cold, but she was in and out of my life constantly. Whenever she had a new boyfriend or fell off the wagon, she would either leave me behind with Abuela, or occasionally, she would take me with her when it suited her needs. So many of my early memories of her are characterized by that insecurity and confusion.

Curiously, my life became far more stable when Desiree was born because for a long stretch, I didn't see my mother at all. I was four years old when she left and I barely recognized her when she showed up on our doorstep two years later with my baby sister in her arms.

From there, I did my best to make sense of her baffling mood swings and erratic behavior. In turns, I downplayed her cutting comments, avoided the embarrassment she caused me with my friends, or deflected her attention away from Desiree who was much too young to cope with it all.

I was seven when Roberto, or Robbie, came along. Early on, I knew he was trouble. He and my mother would have raging, drunken arguments that would occasionally degenerate into physical violence. I did everything I could to keep myself and Desiree out of his way. The first time he told my mother he never wanted to see her again, relief like I'd never known came over me. That was until my mother begged him to stay and my relief became bewilderment. So many times over the years I watched her make choice after choice that made no sense to me. If some kids mimic their parents' behavior and follow in their footsteps, I wasn't one of them. By eight or nine, I started filing it all under headings like *how not to act, what not to do, how not to let people treat me.*

By ten, I'd lost all interest in her. To me, everything she touched was toxic and I dismissed her as irrelevant to my survival. She always hated that, and I admit I took satisfaction in knowing I could inflict on her even a fraction of the distress she'd caused me over the years.

So I'm willing to take partial responsibility for the animosity that exists between us today. But this thing about the money . . . I'm not sure I'll ever get past it. And now her decision not to mention Robbie's pending parole? That just blows my mind. But none of it changes the fact that I need a plan for when that mean bastard is getting out. I follow her out the front door.

I'm expecting to have to chase her down the driveway, but when I get outside, she's sitting on the top step, lighting a cigarette. Since no one remembered to turn the porch light on this evening, the end glows cherry red in the dark as she takes a drag.

Taking a seat with my back to the railing post, I face her, but she doesn't look at me.

After a minute of silence, she says, "It wasn't supposed to be like this. No girl dreams of a life filled with one disappointment after another."

I fight the urge to roll my eyes. She's entitled to her feelings after all, no matter how fatalistic they are.

"I'm forty-one years old and I've been in love with a man who probably doesn't love me back for more than fifteen years, half of those he's spent in prison. I have a grown son who hates me and two teenage daughters who disregard me."

"Ma, I don't hate you."

She doesn't respond to that though, just takes another drag and stares out into the empty street. I occurs to me that her problems are self-made . . . an idea that strikes me as familiar. Didn't Ellie tell me once that I did that? Created my own problems? The idea slinks through my brain until my mom's voice calls me back to the present.

"So you met your father?"

"Not really. I got introduced to him, that's all." A dog barks in the distance as I watch the TV in the front room across the street create shadows that ebb and flow.

"Every year you look more and more like him."

"Is that why you treated me like you did when I was a kid?"

That gets her attention. Instead of dismissing my words like I'm expecting, she says, "That's not why, no." Averting her gaze, she takes another drag. "If you want the truth, I despised how your father made me feel like such trash."

"But that had nothing to do with me. God, I was a kid, Ma."

"Well, so was I. Did you know he accused me of getting pregnant on purpose?" She shakes her head angrily. "We didn't even discuss protection. Protection didn't even occur to either of us until after all was said and done . . . but it was *my* fault?"

I can hear the rising indignation mixed with sadness in her voice.

"Then, he tried to claim he wasn't the father. But when I agreed to any test he wanted, he still wasn't happy. I should have known it was a lost cause, but I couldn't face it alone. I was eighteen and scared, you know? Then I found out he was thirty years old and already had a wife and kid at home."

I feel bad for her, I do, but something about her attitude rubs me the wrong way. "I understand that you got a raw deal. But what about now?"

"What about it?"

"If you want things to change, then change them."

In the light thrown by the streetlamp, her silhouette sags dramatically, as if she's finally succumbed to the weight of the world. I watch her finish her cigarette in silence, not much closer to understanding her than I was earlier.

"Listen," I say, when it seems like she's preparing to leave. "I need to tell you that Ellie and I are getting married."

Her head swivels toward me. "You can't be serious."

"I am. And I'm taking Carmen with us."

"Taking her? You're moving out?" She's truly shocked. "You can't do that. You'll never be able to swing two households."

"You're right, I won't. That means everyone here will have to pull their weight."

I have no clue what's going through her mind as she studies me, but she finally gets to her feet and heads down the stairs.

"Where are you going?"

She blows out a heavy breath. "I'll stay with Alonso for a couple days."

"Alonso?" *Alonso her boyfriend?* "I thought Robbie was getting out."

Hesitating at the base of the steps, she turns part way. "His parole was denied."

*For. Fuck's. Sake.* With inhuman effort, I keep my every accusatory thought bottled up inside of me. I take a deep breath, then say, "I don't want to separate the girls, Ma. It's the right thing to do."

After a moment, she nods faintly and whispers, "I know," before she gets in her car and leaves.

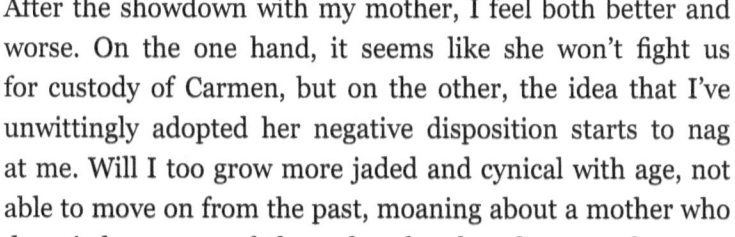

After the showdown with my mother, I feel both better and worse. On the one hand, it seems like she won't fight us for custody of Carmen, but on the other, the idea that I've unwittingly adopted her negative disposition starts to nag at me. Will I too grow more jaded and cynical with age, not able to move on from the past, moaning about a mother who doesn't love me, a father who abandoned me, and an ex-girlfriend who has a drug problem?

The possibility really unnerves me and when I ask Ellie for her opinion, she's skeptical but she doesn't dismiss it out of hand. In the end, she tries to lighten the mood by saying she can definitely see me as the old man on his porch, yelling at the neighborhood kids. She laughs her butt off, while I find it . . . less amusing.

It's with this in mind that I finally agree to meet with my grandfather and my half-brothers the week before Christmas.

If I want to make peace with the past, this seems like the most obvious place to start.

We're already parked in the restaurant's lot, having decided to forgo the valet parking when I tell Ellie for the fifth time today, "I don't think I can go through with this."

She's patient with me, like she has been not only today but all week long. "We don't have to, but I think you should get it over with. If you cancel, it'll only be harder the next time."

"What if it's awkward?"

"There's no what if, Scott. It will be awkward, at least to start."

"Opal, your pep talks suck, you know that?"

She smiles. "Come on, let's go. We're already here. And it's only lunch. I'll be right beside you the whole time."

As we get out, I mutter, "You make it sound like it's my first day of kindergarten or something."

Taking her hand, we make our way to the front of the restaurant. It's some ritzy place that I hope they haven't chosen because it will intimidate me. Of course, the location doesn't matter, I'll still feel like some poor-relation exhibit at the zoo.

On the other side of the heavy front door is a very sedate and deserted waiting area. The host looks us up and down but doesn't seem to find anything amiss as Ellie announces us. Thankfully, Ellie made me wear my dress clothes. I just wish my stomach weren't so tied up in knots over this.

The host leads us deep into the restaurant, which is all dark wood and private booths. When he turns left down a somewhat dimly lit hallway at the back, clearly expecting us to follow, Ellie whispers, "If this was a mob movie, I'd be getting nervous about now."

A flicker of a smile pulls at my lips. Leave it to Ellie to distract me when I'm feeling like I really am marching toward some kind of tragic end. When the guy starts up a set of narrow stairs, we look at each other and try not to laugh aloud.

Finally the host knocks on a door before opening it. "Your guests, Mr. McCarthy."

"Yes, thank you."

As we go in, three men rise and I'm immediately hit with a rush of relief that none of them is my father. Yes, I was assured he wouldn't be here, but there are never any guarantees in life.

We're in some kind of private dining room. The long, rectangular window along the back wall appears to mirror the placement and size of the table that could probably seat at least twenty people. Only one end of the table is set though.

My grandfather approaches. Dressed in his usual formal, three-piece suit, he's all smiles as he greets Ellie warmly. "Ms. Summers. How nice to see you again."

"Please, call me Ellie," she says, allowing him to help her off with her jacket, which he hangs on a coat rack next to the door. "Thank you."

While this is going on, my attention is all for my brothers. My eyes are first drawn to the older one, because he's blond like me . . . except he's not looking back at me, but at my girl in her charcoal grey dress. A second later he notices my hard glare and immediately looks sheepish.

"Scott." The sound of my name breaks the spell and I find my grandfather holding out his hand to me. I shake it. "I want to thank you again for agreeing to come."

"Uh, yeah, no problem." He's shorter than Ellie in her heels, with the same lined face and thick head of mostly-white hair that I remember. At least it appears I won't go bald in my old age.

"This is my younger grandson, Shane," he says, gesturing to the guy standing beside him.

"Hey, so good to meet you, man," Shane says, his smile blazing as he pumps my hand with too much enthusiasm. His over-long messy brown hair makes it look like he just rolled out of bed and he's wearing a baggy black hoodie with CU emblazoned in big gold letters inside the outline of a buffalo, trackpants . . . and shower sandals with socks. Apparently, he has zero concern for appearances.

"Same," I say, unable to resist his infectious cheerfulness.

"And this is my older grandson, Eric."

Compared to his brother, the one who was checking Ellie out is physically much more like me. We're about the same height and build, though his hair is blonder and his complexion is definitely fairer. He's dressed in khakis and a black Polo shirt. As we shake, I relax a fraction because the repentant apology in his expression strikes me as genuine.

"Hey," I say and he lifts his chin. It's clear that he's not as keen on this meeting as his brother. I definitely respect his wariness more than the younger one's effusiveness, probably because it matches my own.

And speaking of the younger one, he's already chatting Ellie up like he's known her for years. Though there's nothing untoward going on, I still curl a hand around Ellie's hip possessively.

"Come, let's sit," my grandfather says politely, leading us toward the enormous table. My brothers go around to the far side as I pull out the chair next to the head of the table for Ellie. The bright, untroubled smile of thanks that she gives me, further settles my nerves.

"So Grandad says you've got a kid," Shane says, like he doesn't quite believe the information he's been given. "How old is she?" He runs his hand through his already messy hair, making the front part stand up on end.

"Uh, she's seven."

The curiosity on Shane's face refashions itself into confusion. "Wait, how old are you?"

I won't be cowed or embarrassed, so I answer him directly. "I'm twenty-three."

It takes less than a second for his confusion to become wry amusement. "Oops."

Without glancing around the table, I can sense that everyone else is appalled, but I can't think of a better way to describe getting a girl pregnant at fifteen. "Yeah," I say on a bit of a laugh. "Oops."

"You got a picture?" he says without missing a beat before he turns to his brother. "We're uncles, you believe that shit?"

A huff of exasperation from *Grandad* and a soft giggle from Ellie combine to set the last of my nerves free as I get my phone out and pull up Rosa's school picture from a couple months ago.

After a quick study, Shane passes the phone to Eric. "Cute kid. She's not yours though, right?" He looks at Ellie.

My grandfather almost spills the water in his glass on its way to his mouth. "Really, Shane!"

"What? It's a perfectly valid question."

"It's fine," Ellie says. "No, she's not my daughter. But I treat her like one." Then to change the subject, Ellie gestures at his sweatshirt. "Is that where you go to school? The University of Colorado?"

Shane brightens. "Yeah, I'm a freshman. They," he jerks his thumb at his brother and grandfather, "hate it that I'm there more to be on the ski team than anything else. Are you in school still?"

"No, I finally graduated last spring."

"Oh, yeah? Where'd you go?"

"Stanford."

He turns to me. "Wow, smart *and* beautiful. You scored big time."

I can't stop a smile, my like for this kid increasing by the minute. "I did."

"Did you go to Stanford, too? Is that where you met?"

I half choke/half laugh. "No," I say like that's the most laughable thing I've ever heard, because it is. "I only got my GED last year."

Eric finally adds to the conversation with a shocked, "You were allowed to drop out?"

"Allowed? No, man. I had to work."

In comical unison both brothers' heads tilt to the same angle as if in thought. "What do you mean, like . . ." Shane can't seem to conceive of a reason for having to work.

"Like I had to work to live." They continue to stare at me blankly. "As in . . . if I didn't work, we'd starve."

"Dude," Shane says with a deep furrow between his brows. "Grandad said you live at home."

"Yeah," I say slowly, realizing that the old man only gave them a rough sketch of my life and left out all the gory details. Maybe that's why they've been mostly cool with this meeting. But I refuse to sugar coat anything. Better to know from the start if they're judgmental assholes. "And there were a lot of bills to pay and mouths to feed. There still are."

"But where were your parents?"

"Uhhh . . ." I'm almost tempted to ask if that's a joke, but Shane – and Eric for that matter – seems sincere in his bewilderment. "Well, the one we share wasn't anywhere and my mom isn't always the most reliable. Not that she could have kept us afloat on her own anyway."

"I see," Shane says, but his creased brow remains, telling me he probably doesn't *see* much. I brace myself for his next question, but it turns out to be a harmless one. "So you have brothers and sisters?"

"Yeah." I smile. "Well, I have sisters. Three of them – all younger of course."

"I always wanted a sister, but all I had was this guy." Shane elbows his brother, but Eric's expression doesn't lighten as he asks in a very serious tone of voice, "Why do you say *of course?* Why is it obvious they're younger?"

"Oh, just that my mom was pretty young when I was born."

Shane's sudden laugh of delight diverts everyone's focus. "Hold up. Your mom had you when she was young. And you had your daughter when you were young. Did you learn nothing from history?"

Okay, call me crazy, but I really like him. "Apparently not," I say glibly.

Our grandfather, seeming to grow impatient with Shane's questions takes over the conversation, steering it into safer territory. He asks about my job, and then I ask about his company, which, if I understand correctly, is some kind of mega-conglomerate that's made up of a million little companies.

Shane, who grows steadily more fidgety with the uninteresting topics, tries to get back in on the conversation as soon as there's a lull. "So tell me about –"

He's interrupted by Eric, who, in contrast to his brother, has been glowering throughout the *uninteresting* exchange. "Hang on for a sec. I want to know how young we're talking."

He's addressing me, but I'm not sure what he's talking about. "Pardon?"

"How young was your mom when you were born?"

"Uh, eighteen. Why?"

"Let me get this straight," Eric says, looking from me to his grandfather and back. "My father got a teenager pregnant around the time I was born, and then abandoned her and the kid to a life of poverty?"

My brain wars with wanting to agree with the abandonment and to argue the finer points of 'poverty'. "Nah, come on. It's not like I went hungry."

"Well, then," Eric says, his tone shaded with sarcasm. "That makes it okay."

Shane turns to his brother. "Kind of proves me right for siding with Mom in the divorce, doesn't it?"

"Shut up, Shane. This isn't about you." My older brother almost appears sullen when he turns to me. "Do you know what my father," he pauses, then amends to, "our father's net worth was last year, Scott?"

I shrug, while trying not to frown. "No idea."

"Three hundred and thirty five million."

My stomach clenches at such an inconceivable number. "Hey, listen, that's got nothing to do with me."

"What?" Eric scoffs. "Why aren't you pissed? I'd be fucking irate if I were you."

"Who says I'm not pissed?" I bite back. "But I'm not pissed for myself. I'm pissed that my sperm donor ducked out on my mom."

"Scott –" my grandfather starts, but I'm upset now.

"She never really got over it. So yeah, I am pissed. But I didn't come here to be reminded of that, and I'm not interested in your pity or your outrage on my behalf." I focus on Eric who's still wearing a sulky grimace. "So I'd appreciate it if you'd wipe that stupid look off your face."

Across from me, Shane chuffs with surprise and then starts to laugh, followed by Ellie, who tries but fails to not fall victim to the same. I look between them in exasperation, but then Eric cracks a reluctant grin and the tension really begins to dissipate.

"Let's order some food," my grandfather suggests.

After that the talk turns to less sensitive topics like Shane's current girlfriend, Eric's MBA program, and Ellie's work at the Settlement Project. And it's fine, enjoyable even . . . now that I don't feel under attack. A few times I find myself staring at my new family members, especially Eric since we really do look like brothers. My mind catches on his individual features that remind me of mine, like his eyebrows, his nose, and the shape of his face. It's very surreal.

After we've finished eating, the news that Ellie and I are planning to get married comes up.

"That's wonderful news," my grandfather exclaims. "You have my most heart-felt congratulations."

"Thank you," Ellie enthuses. "I'm very excited."

"I'll expect my invitation in the mail," Shane proclaims in his now familiar, good-humored manner.

I hear a withering noise seep from my throat, one that Ellie feels compelled to explain. "My *wonderful fiancé* is already at the end of his rope with how many people his grandmother wants to invite."

"I have one word for you, Scott," Eric says, taking a drink from his glass, trying to suppress a smile. "Vegas."

"I tried," I say, only half-joking. "But my *wonderful fiancée* doesn't like the idea."

"Well," Shane drolls. "That's what trust funds are for, right Grandad?"

I frown as silence falls over the table. It takes a second for my affable little brother to pick up on it, but when he registers the awkwardness, he doesn't back away, he pushes forward. "Scott got his trust fund, didn't he?" Though it's phrased as a question, he doesn't consider the possibility of its inexistence. He turns to me directly. "The five mill isn't enough to set you up for life, am I right? It's just enough to make you want to work for more. He's a smart old dog, our Grandad."

A split second later, I bark out a scornful, incredulous sound that echoes in the room. "Well, on that note, we're going to take off." Placing my napkin on my plate, I get to my feet and start to pull Ellie's chair out for her all the while shaking my head.

"What?" Shane asks, nonplussed. "He's over twenty-one."

"Oh, Shane," my grandfather says wearily. "I haven't broached the subject with him yet, but yes, of course he has a trust fund."

"What?" I say with utter derision. "No." I go for Ellie's coat and return to find them all staring at me. "No," I say again as I help her into it. "Absolutely not." Denials are backing up in my throat faster than I can get them out. I'm choking on them.

"Of course, you're right." The old man rises from his seat. "And I apologize. I never meant for this to catch you unawares." He immediately launches into his goodbyes to Ellie, thanking her, congratulating her, charming her. All I want to do is make a break for the door. Five million dollars my ass. These people cannot be serious.

Shane comes around the table and draws me into a hug. "Welcome to the family." My annoyance just makes him laugh. "Don't worry. I'll grow on you. I'm a bit of an acquired taste."

While my grandfather bids me goodbye I barely heed his words as I watch Eric hug my girl. He's lucky he doesn't let his hand go anywhere near her ass or I'd have had to rip his arm off.

"Relax," Eric says quietly as he pulls me in for a brotherly slap on the back. "She's incredible, but there's plenty of fish, right?" My half-growled response only makes his smirk deepen.

"I'll be in contact, Scott," is my grandfather's parting shot.

# Chapter Seventeen

## Ellie

The bitter tang of Scott's silent outrage hangs in the air of the truck on the ride home. It advises me to keep quiet; I know he prefers to stew before he vents and rushing him will only make it worse.

Arriving at my apartment, he heads for the bathroom, closing the door harder than necessary. While I slowly get my coat off and climb onto a kitchen stool with my phone to wait for the eruption that's surely coming, I listen to the loud bang of the toilet seat and the rush of the water as the faucet is yanked on and then off

Appearing in the kitchen, he props his hip against the island, arms crossed over his chest. Every line of his posture vibrates with hostility. "Well?"

I set my phone down. "Well what?"

"I'm still waiting for all those unsolicited opinions you claim to have."

"I'm reserving judgment until I hear what you have to say."

"Me? I think you know how I feel. I mean, what the fuck?" The volume of his voice starts rising. "Five million dollars?

That's insane! What are they trying to do? Buy my loyalty?" He shoves off the counter and starts pacing. "I knew it was a mistake to get involved with them. I bet they figured I'd jump all over their money like a fucking monkey."

He turns to me expectantly when I remain quiet. "Opal?" But he must see my opinion in my expression. "Oh, no. No. You're not going convince me to change my mind on this."

"Why are you assuming that the money has some nefarious purpose?"

"How can it not? I bet they're embarrassed that I'm using their last name."

"Scott," I say with a hint of mockery. "That's absurd. Your last name is your birthright. And I bet they see the money that way too."

He scoffs. "Nobody gives away something for nothing, and I can't even imagine what they're expecting for that kind of money."

"Well, they've already missed out on your first-born child, so I think you might be safe."

His lips press into an angry line. "Are you seriously making fun of me right now?"

"I'm sorry. But I think you're overreacting." He opens his mouth to argue with me, but I keep going. "Let me talk for a second. Five million dollars to Richard McCarthy is pocket change, Scott. The grant he pledged to the Settlement Project is probably worth five times that over the next ten years. And that's only one of many charities that he contributes to."

He gives me a scornful look that tells me I'm doing nothing to convince him.

"Okay," I say, "I'll put it in perspective for you. You think my parents are rich, right? They have a big house in Palo Alto, a vacation place in Palm Springs, they drive nice cars. But my dad still needs to work, Scott. Your grandfather does not . . . that number Eric gave you for your father doesn't even begin to apply to him. In fact, I bet your grandfather couldn't spend all his money if he tried."

"But that's not the point," he says, his frustration with my failure to toe the line growing. "It doesn't change the fact that I didn't *earn* that money, El."

"Would you turn down a winning lottery ticket?"

His hands land on his hips as he stops his pacing to glare at me. "Don't split hairs with me. You know what I mean."

I do know, but that doesn't mean I agree with him. Growing up, I knew plenty of kids who had trust funds. They're not meant to be burdens . . . though I'm glad I never had one. How much more damage could I have done to myself at twenty-one if I'd had a bunch of money to burn through? I shiver at the thought.

I decide to take one more stab at making him see a bit of reason. "You do know the government sees it as income, right? They'll want their fair share. And with what's left, you could send all the girls to college, Mari and Desiree, included. Even you if you wanted to go."

His handsome features pinch, like I've got some nerve, hitting below the belt like that. I don't let it put me off. If he wants a biddable wife who agrees with everything he says, he'll have to find someone else.

"And Shane's right," I go on. "It's not enough to set us up for life. We'd both still have to work. It would only be enough to take the edge off all the financial pain that's bound to come up over the years."

Cursing under his breath, he takes a few steps before he turns back. "I won't let you talk me into this."

"All right, I won't say another word about it." I slide off my stool to stand in front of him, running my fingers along the buttons of his dress shirt. "Anyway, we shouldn't let what happened at the end taint how well the rest of the meeting went."

He just grunts softly as if agreeing with me in actual words would mean he'd have to accept the money.

"I liked your brothers."

Grudgingly, he nods. "They weren't total assholes . . . as long as the older one keeps his hands off your ass."

"What?" I laugh. "What are you talking about?"

"I didn't like the way he was checking you out."

Though I'm internally rolling my eyes, I hum my agreement. "It's understandable though. You guys do look a lot alike and all that shared DNA means he's probably attracted to me."

His eyes narrow dangerously before a snort of laughter bubbles out of me. "You made that way too easy, Scott. Don't you know by now that you're the only man I'll ever want?"

As Christmas approaches, Scott and I talk about the newest members of his family a few times, but never about the trust-fund bombshell. I understand his reaction, I do. To Scott, money comes from working hard, not from an accident of birth, especially not one that involves being born the illicit offspring of a despicable man. And I respect him for sticking to his principles.

My only clue that he hasn't come through the meeting unscathed comes when, with only two days to go, he has a spur of the moment desire to buy the girls bikes for Christmas. My first instinct is to tell him that the plan hardly fits in with the austerity measures we've imposed on ourselves, but then I realize it probably has more to do with his need to reaffirm our ability to provide for the kids without any outside help. Not that kids *need* bikes, but I get where he's coming from.

Turns out I'm so glad we go through with it.

My first Christmas with the girls dawns extremely bright and early. Even though they try to keep their delighted screeches muffled behind their small hands, I'm still jarred awake.

"Tío?" I hear Daniela whisper shout. "Are you guys awake? Santa came!"

"He did?" Scott mumbles from beside me.

I stayed the night in order to be here for this. We haven't slept much, but not for the usual reasons. After coming back from Midnight Mass and putting the girls to bed, we were up most of the night talking softly by the light of the Christmas tree. It's going down as one of my favorite nights ever.

Sleepily, I ask, "Are you sure? I didn't hear him."

"Look, Ellie! I mean, Mom," Rosa whispers just as loudly as Daniela, her voice quaking with excitement. "Santa did come!"

Sitting up, I blink and then focus on them, standing by the tree, checking out the three identical pink bicycles. The shocked looks on their faces are priceless.

"This one has your name on it, Rosa," Carmen says reverently, noticing the small license plate on the back of the bike.

"This one's mine," Daniela calls, which has Carmen moving to the far side to check her name. When she looks up, she's absolutely beaming. I could totally get used to this parenthood stuff.

"No, come on, Daniela," Scott says blearily, hauling himself up to rest his back against the sofa. "You can't ride it in the house."

"Can we go out now?"

"It's still dark, *chaparra*."

I grab my phone off the coffee table. It's 6:17.

"How about we open the rest of the presents and after breakfast we'll try them out," he says as I get myself half-way vertical next to him. "Why don't you guys go and wake everyone up?"

They don't need to be told twice. It takes some time before the mobilization is complete though. Tía Mari is particularly uncooperative until the smell of brewing coffee convinces her to pull herself out of bed. Almost all the presents are for the kids, but their excitement, the glow of the lights, and the excellent company make for a wonderful morning. If this is a reflection of my future life, I doubt a happier woman could be found on the planet.

By the time all is said and done – the presents opened, the waffles and bacon eaten, and the adults showered – the girls are bouncing off the walls with wanting to get outside.

But like all children with their first bicycles, they're forced to smile for a million pictures on the sidewalk first. Then, finally, under a partly cloudy sky, on the deserted street, with pink helmets firmly in place, we get underway. We have varying levels of success. Carmen, who's paired with Scott, gets the hang of things first, and soon she's making hesitant trips up and down the street by herself, a toothy grin firmly in place. Daniela seems to have no sense of balance whatsoever and it's not long before she's in tears because I fail to catch the back of her seat before she goes down. It breaks my heart the way she clings to me, sobs wracking her body.

Scott jogs up. Pushing the hair away from Daniela's tear-stained face, he smiles at her. "You're okay," he assures her, then noticing the misery on my face, he adds, "You're okay, too, Mom."

Daniela sniffles as she pulls back to look at me. "I scraped my knee."

Passing her over into Scott's arms, I inspect her knee. "I think it's pretty minor, honey."

"I put a hole in my leggings," she says desolately.

"Don't worry," Scott says, placing her feet on the ground. "We'll get you a new pair, okay?"

"Car!" Desiree yells, and we watch as Carmen moves to the side of the street and stops.

"Hey, my sister's here," I say, feeling better now that Daniela has stopped crying. "I bet she's got something for you guys."

Immediately, Daniela perks up. "Really?"

"Really. Let's go."

During the summer, we got together with my sister a few times. The girls adore her and vice versa. Today, Sophie is dressed down in a pair of skinny jeans, a hoodie, and sneakers, which is unusual for her. Usually she's done up to the nines like our mother taught us.

"Merry Christmas!" Sophie exclaims, holding out her arms for me to hug her.

"You too!"

She moves on to hug the girls. She even has one for Scott, with whom she's come to a mostly friendly ceasefire.

I introduce her to Scott's sisters and then she opens the rear gate of my father's SUV.

"I got you guys a present," she announces, revealing a huge, wrapped box that elicits gasps and exclamations of surprise. "Maybe your dad can carry it to the house for us?"

Scott gives her an exasperated look that borders on being a scowl as he pulls it out and maneuvers it up to the porch. The girls follow closely behind.

"Soph, what did you do?" I ask in a low voice. "When I said to get them ponies. I meant My Little Ponies, not an actual horse."

She shrugs, her sleek blond ponytail swinging with the movement. "Dad let me use his credit card. I wasn't going to squander the opportunity on ten dollar ponies, now was I?"

"Can we open it now?" Rosa asks as we approach the porch where they're gathered around the box.

"You bet," Sophie says happily.

Together, the girls tear into the paper and squeals of excitement fill the cool morning air. "It's a Barbie house!" Rosa shrieks.

Sophie gets right in there with them, going over the features and whipping them up into even more of a frenzy. Scott turns a flat look my way and grumbles, "Where the hell are we going to put that?"

I give his shoulder a good-natured shove. "I don't think our lack of space was part of her decision making process."

Sophie starts to unseal the box, but Scott calls a halt. "Let's ride the bikes for a bit longer, then we'll take it in and open it."

Daniela and Rosa both start protesting.

"So we don't lose any pieces."

His logic convinces them . . . barely. They're already getting tired, I can tell. They haven't slept much more than we have.

Sophie and I sit on the steps, watching Scott and his sisters continue to help the girls learn to ride. Rosa, much to Daniela's chagrin, seems to be getting into the swing of things.

"You look happy," Sophie says out of the blue, pulling my attention away from the street.

"I am happy," I tell her truthfully, giving her a smile. "Actually," I pull my glove off my left hand, "I have something to show you."

My sister gapes. "Holy shit. Did you get married?"

"No," I chide. "I'd never get married without telling you. It's just an engagement band."

"Just?" she says, wonder and surprise mingling, her bright blue eyes shining in the natural light. "I thought you guys were still in the talking about it stage."

"We are. We still haven't set any kind of date."

"You know Mom's going to have a bird, right?"

"Why do you think we haven't said anything yet?"

Daniela comes up. "Mom, I'm tired."

"Are you? You want to sit here with us for a few minutes?" I pull her down onto my lap and hug her close. Over her head, I notice that Sophie's eyes are as round as dinner plates.

"Mom?" she mouths silently. "I know," I mouth back.

Daniela sits up. "Is that Jorgie?"

Sure enough, Jorgie and Scott approach, their heads together, laughing about something. They're followed by Mari, Desiree and the girls.

"Hey, Jorgie," I say. "Merry Christmas." Like Scott and Sophie, Jorgie and I have come to an understanding. We'll never be the best of friends, but we're plenty civil when we're in the same room.

"You too." He leans in to kiss my cheek. "Who's this?" he asks, looking my sister up and down like she's a prize piece of steak he's about to sink his teeth into.

"That," Scott says, "is my sister-in-law and she's completely off-limits to you and every person you know."

Sophie tsks. "I'm Sophie," she says, extending her hand for Jorgie to shake. He kisses it instead.

*"Jorge Alberto a su servicio,"* he says in exaggerated Spanish, making Scott burst out laughing. Jorgie throws him a dirty look.

"You're *way* out of your league, *cabrón*," Scott informs him.

"Can't blame a guy for trying," he says with a shrug. Then as if the whole exchange never took place, he changes the subject. "Okay, where are your kids? The ones you're always talking about?"

"We're right here, Jorgie," Daniela says loudly like he's being silly.

"Nah, you guys are way too big. I'm looking for kids about this size," he says, holding his hand flat at about knee-level.

The girls break out into giggles and Jorgie smiles wide. "All right, fine. I know who you are and I've got something for you. Come here and line up. Hands out, eyes closed."

When the girls are in place, he pulls out his wallet and proceeds to place a fifty-dollar bill on each palm.

"Christ," Scott mutters, but the girls are highly impressed.

*"Gracias,"* they all chirp as they eagerly compare the bills to make sure they all got the same. When Scott starts to round up the money for safekeeping, there's a bit of grumbling until Daniela notices someone else coming up the walk.

"Tío Alejandro!" she calls, squeezing through the crowd gathered in front of the steps.

Alejandro crouches down to greet her, but they're too far away for me to hear what's being said. Everyone gravitates that way to say hello.

Sophie and I watch Alejandro hand Daniela one of three big gift bags he's carrying. "Who's that?" she asks and something in her voice has me turning to her.

"Alejandro. Scott's uncle's best friend."

"Scott has an uncle?"

"Not anymore. Daniela's parents were killed soon after she was born."

"Oh, right. So this Alejandro guy . . ."

*Is she fishing for information?* "He's Daniela's godfather."

"Hmmm," she hums absently, not taking her eyes off the man. I look him over for myself, taking in his almost-black hair that's longer on top than on the sides, his full beard and his dark, piercing eyes. He stands now and I notice he's a few inches shorter than Scott, but most men are. He's wearing jeans and a black, long-sleeved Henley T-shirt that molds nicely to his shoulders and mostly covers his tattoos, except for a curl of black that's just visible on the right side of his neck . . . and it clicks.

"Sophie!" I laugh, bumping my shoulder to hers. "You have a boyfriend."

Her ponytail swings as she turns a startled expression on me. "What?" And then she giggles. "Don't be silly, Els." Then, with barely a pause, she gets to her feet and offers me a hand up. "Come on, we should go over there. I don't want to be rude."

If my sister weren't the most level-headed woman I know, I might worry about the gleam in her eye.

Later on that evening, after a full day of people coming and going, Scott comes to sit next to me at the picnic table in the back yard. He places a mug of his Abuela's *ponche* in front of me. "Thanks," I say, wrapping my fingers around the warm cup.

The girls are already in bed and though I'm tired, I'm not looking forward to getting in my car and driving home. As if reading my mind, he says, "I don't want you to go."

I smile sadly at him. "Me neither."

With a sigh, he leans in and kisses my temple. "I guess if we took my grandfather's money, we could start looking for a house right away."

"I guess we could," I answer neutrally, slowly rotating the cup between my palms.

The sound of traffic in the distance fills the space between us until he says, "The girls could have their own rooms."

"They could."

"And there'd still be enough left over for college funds."

"And for things like braces," I add.

"And a new roof for this house," he says, sounding resigned.

The night's noises engulf us again as he blows on his own cup of *ponche*. Before it makes it to his lips though, he puts it back on the table with a clunk. "Am I crazy for not wanting to take the money? For wishing we could do everything on our own?"

"No, not at all."

"I just feel like all the years that I've been pinching pennies would be for nothing. It took me so long to save that money."

"Well, it's not like we're going to make a bonfire with it here in the back yard, Scott. You could use it for something you want, like a new truck."

He blows out a breath laced with amusement. "That's a low blow, Opal. You know how much I'd love that."

"And it's practical. The girls aren't going to fit in the one you have for much longer."

He groans. "Do you have to be so logical about this?"

Resting my head on his shoulder, I let the love I feel for him suffuse me from head to toe. "Well, I have to maintain my reputation as Sister Opal, the Wise. It's one of the reasons you love me."

He lowers his head to rest on mine. "Yes, it is," he says and I can hear the smile in his voice. "One of too many to count."

# Epilogue

## Scott - Seven years later

Seemingly engrossed in the stormy weather, Ellie stares out into our back yard. The rain-streaked glass of the patio door and the grey sky beyond serve to frame her profile from head to toe as she absently strokes the ear of our black lab cross, Lucy.

Lucy's tail gives a few happy thumps against the carpet, announcing my presence before she comes to say hello. Ellie turns and I watch a gentle spark ignite in her tired eyes and bring a touch of color to her slightly-off pallor. After all these years, she's still happy to see me. "You're home early," she says, her palm circling her belly as she smiles.

After a few cursory pats for the dog, I cross the room, my gaze roving over my beautiful wife, trying to assess everything from her state of mind to her level of exhaustion.

"Stop that," she says softly, amusement tinging her tone. "I'm pregnant, not dying."

Leaning in, I nuzzle her neck and inhale her scent before I finally kiss her sweet lips. "You're supposed to be resting," I accuse, but there's no heat to my words as my hands slide down to rest on her very pregnant belly. "How are you feeling today, Mrs. McCarthy?"

She waves the question away with a casual hand as if to say *it is what it is*. My poor Ellie has had a rough pregnancy, plagued for the duration by morning sickness and insomnia.

I change tack. "How's my son feeling today?" Just saying the words has me grinning from ear-to-ear like a fool. I can't believe our baby is a boy. After living my entire life surrounded by women – because even the dog is female – I was one hundred percent certain we would have a girl. I was happy and so very excited at the prospect until the doctor threw me for a loop by announcing it was a boy. My stunned reaction of *'Are you sure?'* had made Ellie laugh.

"He's restless," she says, guiding my hand higher to feel what can only be a heel jabbing at his mother's abdomen. It evokes the same emotions in me that it always does; wonder and concern. I spent so little time with Lolita when she was pregnant, so everything is new and awe-inspiring this time around. And a bit stressful. I feel irrationally guilty for even suggesting the idea of having a baby in the first place. Ellie and I had been content with the girls until I opened my big mouth.

"He's not the only one who's restless," I say, giving her a pointed look. "A little birdie tells me you haven't been following the doctor's orders."

"A little birdie named Carmen?" she asks with a touch of exasperation.

"Maybe. But I got texts from Daniela and Rosa, too. They all worry about you. You know that."

Ellie's always been able to maintain a positive relationship with the girls, probably because she's not into boundary setting or rule enforcement. Ellie and I hit a few rough patches in the first few years; I didn't like always having to be the bad guy while she thought I needed to chill out more. Eventually we found our groove. Since all three of our girls are still in one piece, living at home, working toward college and not pregnant as far as I know, I'm going to say our groove has been successful.

Their three personalities all developed along the lines that were pretty much set from birth. Carmen, who'll be sixteen in a few weeks, continues to be the most reasonable. Daniela has managed to push every button I have and then some. She's even tried Ellie's patience a time or two. And my sweet little Rosa, who's now fourteen, falls in somewhere between her two sisters. In my honest opinion, I think she's been observing everyone for so long that she now knows exactly what does and doesn't work to get her own way. I have the feeling my battles with my daughter haven't even started yet.

Ellie grimaces slightly, pulling me from my thoughts. "Why don't we sit down?" I suggest, sliding my arm around her back.

"I'm just uncomfortable," she says in protest, though she lets me guide her to the loveseat where she's got a nest of sorts set up. Now that she's supposed to be on bedrest, she spends most of her time here in the rec room which is currently decorated to the gills for Christmas. With its many windows and view of the yard, it's her favorite room in the house.

We took my grandfather's money. Of course we did. Though we didn't go crazy and buy a mansion, we didn't hold back either; each kid has her own bedroom, there's a pool, and it's in a great neighborhood. And best of all, we've been happy here.

Settling into her spot, she sighs, though it sounds more like with resignation than relief. With only ten days left, I don't know which of us is more eager for the baby's arrival.

The Here and Now

I sit beside her, carefully pulling the throw blanket over us both and she lays her head on my shoulder. "I hear your mother made an appearance earlier," I say.

She gives a hum laced with amusement. "It was fine. She means well."

I snort. "I'm surprised she deigned to drive the fifty minutes out here, let alone step foot in the house." Ellie's mom never liked where or how we chose to live, our middling existence far below her hopes for her daughter. Though I'll admit to developing a deeper appreciation for her perspective every time I meet one of Daniela's boyfriends.

Ellie shrugs, conceding the point. "I appreciate her effort. She says she just came to drop off the Christmas presents, but I think she's secretly excited about the baby. She's not as appalled about becoming a grandmother as she'd like us to believe."

"You'd think she'd be used to it by now." It's not like ours will be her first official grandchild. Matt's got a couple of kids now.

Ellie laughs softly to herself. "We'll see how you feel, old man, when one of the girls gives us a grandchild and you're called *Abuelo* for the first time."

"Hold your tongue, woman," I mock-scold, though I can't help but shake my head at the *old man* moniker she and the girls have been using since my thirtieth birthday two weeks ago. The hilarity, it seems, is going to have a long shelf-life. "You and I both know how babies are made and our kids will *never* do that. Hence, no grandchildren."

The fact that Ellie handled the initial 'sex talk' with the girls and every single follow up discussion that's happened over the years is something I'll be eternally grateful for. I think

I almost fainted when Ellie told me about some of their more recent questions. Ever since, for my mental sanity, I've done my best to pretend that they're sexless creatures who'll be forever single.

"You're like an ostrich with its head in the sand."

"You make that sound like a bad thing."

Trying to keep her laugh gentle and easy, she says, "You never did tell me who explained sex to you."

"Please, I learned about sex the proper way, from TV, Jorgie, and later porn."

Laughing outright now, she says, "Sounds healthy. And how is Jorgie?"

"Still basking in the glory of his new career as a car salesman as far as I know." My best friend finally got himself together a couple of years ago and realized his easy-going personality is perfect for selling shit. He works at a Hyundai dealership now.

Again, Ellie's features twist faintly with discomfort. "Oh, sweetness," I breathe. "I think we should cancel this thing tonight."

She shakes her head. "No, I don't want the girls to be disappointed."

We're celebrating Christmas tonight, two weeks early, before the baby comes. But in my opinion, too many people were invited. "The girls will understand."

"I want to do this, especially because all I'll have to do is sit here. Your grandmother is already cooking up a storm in the kitchen." She shifts her position slightly. "And Amelia will be here to help soon. Is your mom still not coming?"

"No, they're still in Tulsa." My mom finally got rid of Robbie, who got out a couple of years ago. She got re-married last month to a mostly decent guy. Even though I'll never have a great relationship with her, we've remained mostly amicable since she never did fight us for custody of Carmen. "What about Sophie?"

A scowl that has nothing to do with the baby comes over Ellie's lovely features. "No, she and Alejandro aren't coming."

Failing miserably to keep my face neutral, I give in to the urge to smile. Ellie has never quite adjusted to the idea of her baby sister and Alejandro shacking up together and she responds to my amusement by needling me with her own ammunition. "And how about Desiree and Shane?"

The smile falls from my face. Shane, that little bastard, seduced my sister and I have no plans to forgive him anytime soon. It's horrendous; my half-brother and my half-sister together. I don't care if they don't share a single drop of DNA. It's gross. "Yeah, unfortunately, they're coming with my grandfather later."

Ellie's giggle draws my attention. "When are you going to admit that Shane never stood a chance against her?" she asks.

"Never."

"My big baby," she coos, leaning in to kiss me. "And Lolita?"

"Yeah, she, Anton, and the baby are coming."

Ellie gives a little nod of satisfaction. She's backed Lolita tirelessly over the years, convincing me again and again that I have no right to restrict her access to Rosa. She's been clean for years now and Rosa dotes on her one-year-old sister, Elizabeth.

"I swear," I say, "our life would make a great telenovela, wouldn't it?"

The bright smile spreading across her face is interrupted by a grunt that has her curling in on herself.

"What is it?" I ask in a hushed voice.

When she manages to pry her eyes open, she says, "I think your son has decided he's had enough of this waiting around."

Blankly, I cock my head. Then it hits me. "As in right now?" I half-squawk.

"Yeah, as in right now."

In the early morning hours, our son, Michael Diego McCarthy is born. Mother and baby are doing well . . . and a new chapter begins.

# Other Books

Not So Far Away (A Worlds Collide Duet, #1)
The Here and Now (A Worlds Collide Duet, #2)

TBA - Alejandro and Sophie (A Worlds Collide Duet, #3)
(Coming in 2021)
TBA - Alejandro and Sophie (A Worlds Collide Duet, #4)

TBA - Shane and Desiree (A Worlds Collide Duet, #5)
(Coming in 2022)
TBA - Shane and Desiree (A Worlds Collide Duet, #6)

His Lucky Penny (The Penny Books, #1)
Pennies for Wishes (The Penny Books, #2)
Find a Penny (The Penny Books, #3)
Pennies from Heaven (The Penny Books, #4)

Written as Lisa Lynn Meyer
A Touch of Silence

www.ingramcontent.com/pod-product-compliance
Lightning Source LLC
Chambersburg PA
CBHW031342020726
47499CB00005B/1370